THE CHILD I LONG FOR

CAROLINE FINNERTY

B
Boldwood

First published in Great Britain in 2024 by Boldwood Books Ltd.

Copyright © Caroline Finnerty, 2024

Cover Design by Head Design Ltd

Cover Photography: Shutterstock

A CIP catalogue record for this book is available from the British Library.

Paperback ISBN 978-1-80549-760-8

Large Print ISBN 978-1-80549-756-1

Hardback ISBN 978-1-80549-755-4

Ebook ISBN 978-1-80549-753-0

Kindle ISBN 978-1-80549-754-7

Audio CD ISBN 978-1-80549-761-5

MP3 CD ISBN 978-1-80549-758-5

Digital audio download ISBN 978-1-80549-752-3

Boldwood Books Ltd
23 Bowerdean Street
London SW6 3TN
www.boldwoodbooks.com

For my beautiful daughter, Bea

PART I

for funerals. Karen was sitting on the pew beside her, doing her best to keep her three children under control but, as the Mass wore on, they were starting to grow restless. She had two little girls named Keeva and Cara and a pudgy-cheeked baby boy named Seán. Keeva was seven while Cara was almost five. They were all beautiful children; the two girls were dressed in matching navy dresses and their amber-coloured hair was tied back with gros-grain bows. Karen was bouncing Seán on her knee; his cheeks were flaming red. 'He's teething,' Karen had explained earlier with a sigh. Yesterday had been the first time that Emily had met her nieces and nephew. Having not been home for almost ten years, she had only ever seen them on FaceTime up until now.

'Would either of you like to say a few words?' the priest asked from the altar, startling Emily from her thoughts. Karen was looking pointedly at her and Emily felt her body tense.

'I-I can't...' she whispered, feeling panicked as her sister's eyes bored into her.

Karen hissed, 'But we told Father Flynn that we'd do a eulogy.'

'But I thought you were going to do it...' Emily trailed off.

'Why did you assume I would be the one to do it?' Karen retorted before nodding pointedly towards the baby that she was jiggling on her lap. 'Besides, Seán is going to scream blue murder if I leave him to go up there...'

'I mean, I guess I could...' Emily offered half-heartedly, feeling her heart start to thud wildly inside her ribcage at the prospect of walking up onto that altar in front of the packed congregation.

'It's okay, I'll do it!' Karen snapped after a sigh laden with impatience. She brusquely handed the baby over to her husband, Dave, and Emily tucked her knees to the side to allow her sister to squeeze out past her. Immediately, Seán began to cry just as his mother had predicted. As the baby howled, Karen made her way up onto the altar and Dave bounced him on his knee in a bid to keep him quiet. Emily felt terrible for leaving it to Karen to give the eulogy but she hadn't spoken in public in such a long time that she was afraid she would freeze if she stood up there. There was a time once in her life when she could have stood up there with ease. She had regularly spoken to hundreds of people in a room without giving it a second thought, but these days the very idea overwhelmed her. Besides, she knew she'd never be able to keep the tears at bay up there with the entire eyes of Ballyrath church looking up at her.

Things had been tense between Karen and herself ever since Emily had arrived back in Dublin the day before. Emily knew there were a lot of old wounds still festering between them, and now their mother's sudden death had come like a scalpel, sharp and swift, and reopened them. Silence fell on the church as Karen stood behind the lectern and adjusted the microphone. A screech of feedback reverberated around the vast space and then Karen began to speak.

Emily watched her sister, her athletic frame dressed in a simple black shift dress and her auburn hair tied back in an elegant chignon. Karen looked just like their mother whereas Emily had inherited her father's looks. As she listened to her sister speak, Emily felt a wave of emotion rise within her as Karen brought to mind their mother. Things she had forgotten, like how she had been so particular about their table manners when they were children and had insisted on the girls wearing matching clothes right up until their teenage years, which Karen had loved but Emily, as the older sister, had detested. But as Karen talked about her mother's life more recently, it felt to Emily as though she was talking about a stranger. Why hadn't Emily known that her mother volunteered at the local resource centre that catered for disadvantaged families or that she had recently taken up playing bridge? Or that her team had won a golf tournament just three weeks ago? She usually spoke with her mother once a week but they were always fleeting conversations due to the time difference – she would be waking up and her mother would be going to bed. A wave of shame consumed her. Why hadn't she asked her more questions about what she was up to in her life? Taken more of an interest?

The congregation began applauding as Karen finished her eulogy and returned to her seat.

'You did great,' she whispered to her younger sister as she sat down beside her and took Seán onto her lap again.

Karen pinched her lips together in a tight smile and, once again, guilt whacked Emily.

When the Mass came to an end, the coffin was hoisted onto the shoulders of the pall-bearers and the sisters followed behind it as they made their way outside to the churchyard where heavy rain was teeming from the sky. They did their best to dodge the puddles as they trudged along the path that led to the cemetery next door.

As they reached the plot where their mother was to be buried, the smell of freshly dug earth hung sickly-sweet on the damp air. The undertakers had laid the bouquets and wreaths brought by sympathisers on top of the mounds of sticky clay. She noticed one that said *Nanny Pat* spelled out in white roses. Karen must have organised that from her children, she thought. She looked around at the people gathered there, crowding beneath umbrellas. She saw aunts and uncles and cousins she hadn't seen in years but there were so many more people she didn't recognise. Her mother had been active in the community and now Emily realised how well thought of she was, how many people knew and respected her.

Her mother's coffin was lowered into the ground and then the priest blessed it with holy water before he began a decade of the rosary. Emily recited the familiar words, which had been imprinted on her brain since childhood.

When the priest had finished, a steady line of mourners began to crowd around her sister. Emily watched as they shook Karen's hand and mumbled well-worn platitudes: *Sorry for your troubles. So sorry for your loss. She's in a better place now, Lord rest her.* In her time away, Emily had forgotten the rituals of Irish funerals. How people liked to shake hands with the mourners and offer their condolences face to face. Emily watched as they squeezed her sister's hand and hugged her tightly but when they reached her, it was like they had forgotten she existed. It felt as though Karen was the chief mourner and Emily merely a minor side character.

'Oh, Emily, it's yourself,' they would say when they noticed her. 'I didn't know you were back.' Or, 'I didn't recognise you after all these years away.'

She accepted their condolences, feeling like a fraud. She realised with searing shame that she felt like an interloper at her own mother's funeral.

Eventually, the crowd filtered away until it was just themselves left.

'Emily, will you give the priest some cash, please?' Karen asked.

Emily was shocked. 'We have to pay him?'

'No,' Karen sighed. 'It's just what people do... to say thanks.'

'But I didn't bring any money with me... I only have my bank card.'

Karen exhaled heavily yet again and shifted the baby up on her hip. She rooted in her crossbody bag and removed her wallet. She opened it and pressed a fifty-euro note into Emily's hand. 'I've no idea what the going rate is for tipping priests but hopefully he'll be okay with that,' she muttered.

'Thanks,' Emily mumbled, feeling more than useless as she accepted the money. How did Karen think of all this stuff? It would never occur to her to give money to the priest at a funeral but

'Daddy?' she asked in a sing-song voice. 'Why is that woman being mean to you?'

Daddy: the word seared an imprint on her heart. *This was his child. Rob had a daughter now.*

'Come on now, love,' he coaxed. 'We have to go.'

The child looked up at him in confusion and Emily couldn't help but admire her; her hair fell in soft golden waves around her shoulders and she had the most arresting blue eyes. Just like his. She watched as he clasped the little girl's hand inside his own as they began to walk away.

Just as her breathing began to recover, she felt someone tap her on the arm and she turned around to see a diminutive, silver-haired woman standing alongside her. 'Ah, Emily, there you are. I'm so sorry for your loss.' She stretched out her arm and began pumping Emily's hand. She was similar in age to her mother. Emily vaguely recognised her but couldn't remember her name or what the connection was. 'It must have been terrible getting that news all the way over in New Zealand and you on your own like that...' she began.

Emily nodded and went through the motions as she had done so many times over the last few days. Her head was spinning with everything that had taken place, burying her mother and then coming face to face with Rob and his daughter. 'Thank you, I appreciate it,' Emily mumbled.

'It's Mrs Mannion,' she prompted, obviously noticing that Emily didn't know who she was. 'I play – well I guess it's *played* now – golf with your mother, although you might not remember, with you being away for so long... At least Patricia always had Karen close by; she was very good to her.'

'Ah yes, Mrs Mannion, of course I remember you.'

'Thank God it wasn't dragged out,' she continued. 'There's a lot to be said for that. My Fintan was sick for three years before he died. Your mother probably didn't even know what was happening to her; please God it was all over before she even realised it. When my time comes, that's the way I want to go too. It must have been tough though all the same; you didn't even get the chance to say goodbye... You just never know, do you? We all take life for granted but none of us know what the future has in store for us.' She tutted and shook her head.

'Yes, I suppose so...' Emily was finding cold comfort in Mrs Mannion's words. Ever since she had got the call from Karen to say that she had found their mother unconscious on her bedroom floor, she had been tormented by thoughts of her final moments. Had she felt unwell? Had she known she was dying? Had she tried to get help but wasn't able?

'Excuse me, Mrs Mannion. I have to go,' she said, releasing Mrs Mannion's hand. She needed to be away from this woman and her clumsy words.

3

THREE DAYS EARLIER

Emily lay in Jonny's springy double bed, with its geometric-patterned duvet cover and matching pillowcases, their skin clammy with sweat. She was just about able to make out the contours of his face in the dawn light that was breaking behind the curtain.

Emily and Jonny had a thing, if you could even call it that. He was a chef at the restaurant where they both worked. Sometimes, the staff would stay back for a few drinks after closing and they usually ended up going home together. As she looked around the small room at his built-in wardrobes where he hung clothes on the corners of the doors so they didn't close properly, she felt him stiffen beside her. His breath stilled and she knew there was something he wanted to say.

'Emily?' he began eventually.

'Yeah?'

'You know my brother's getting married next month,' he went on and she could hear the nerves playing with his voice.

'Uh-huh.' She nodded. He had mentioned it to her before.

Several times. She knew he had been dropping hints at her but she had deliberately pretended not to pick up on them.

'Well... erm... I was wondering if you might come with me? As my plus-one.'

'Oh, Jonny, I don't really think... I wouldn't really know anyone... Sure you'd have more fun without me...'

He propped himself up on one elbow and turned to look at her face-on. The tan on his bare chest was accentuated against the pale bed linen. He owed his dark skin to his Tongan mother. 'Please, Emily,' he begged. 'I'd like you to come. I'd like you to meet my family. They're really nice, I promise.' He smiled at her. A smile that said so much. A smile she wished she could take for herself, to be her smile whenever she opened her eyes in the morning. But there was something stopping her from reaching out to it. She knew that that feeling could be hers to keep if she wanted it but there was something stubbornly insistent within her that wouldn't allow it.

'I don't think it would be my scene. I'm sorry, J.'

'Come on, Em, we've been like this for months now. Don't you think it's time we... eh... made things more serious between us?'

Emily felt herself freeze. 'How do you mean?' she asked, buying herself time.

'Well, I'd like us to officially become a couple. I hate running around behind people's backs in work or acting like there's nothing going on between us. I'd like it all out in the open. I guess what I'm saying is that I want you to be my girlfriend. Sorry, I know I sound like a corny teenager...' He laughed awkwardly. 'But I'm serious, Emily; I want us to be a proper couple.'

A lock of his black curly hair fell in front of his eyes. She reached out and brushed it back off his face. 'Come on, Jonny, we both know it would never work,' she said softly. 'It's just a bit of fun.'

'Maybe to you it is, but not to me,' he retorted. 'I don't get you.' He shook his head in frustration. 'Why won't you let me in?' he asked. 'I don't know what happened to you in the past – whether it was a bad break-up or what – but I wish you'd give me a chance to prove to you that I'm serious about us.' He lowered his voice. 'I would never hurt you, Emily.'

'I'm sorry, J, it's not you. I just can't...' Sometimes, she would catch him looking at her across the pass in the restaurant like she was a puzzle he just couldn't figure out. She hadn't told him anything about what had happened before. He would often ask her questions about her life in Ireland. He would ask her about her upbringing and her family or what had made her decide to move to Auckland and she would fob him off with a story about how she had wanted a change of scenery and then divert the conversation on to another topic like some gossip from the restaurant or a new movie that she wanted to see in the cinema.

He flopped back down on the bed and exhaled heavily. 'Do you know something? I've wanted to say it for a while now but the timing never seemed right but what the hell, now is as good a time as any... I think I'm falling in love with you, Emily,' he said.

Emily's heart sank. Did he think this confession of his love was going to change how she felt about him? Perhaps he hoped that by being candid with his feelings, she would feel safer about opening up to him, but instead it had the opposite effect: it made her want to run. She had told him before that she wasn't ready to get into something serious and yet he always seemed optimistic that perhaps, in the future, she would change her mind, the longer they were together. 'No, you don't—'

'I do. I love being with you. I love this – having you lying beside me. I love *you*.'

She stayed silent.

'Aren't you going to say it back to me?' he challenged.

As she continued to remain mute, she could feel his body tense with frustration as he balled the duvet with his fist.

'I'm sorry, Jonny, but I can't change how I feel...' she said eventually.

He exhaled heavily and rolled over, turning his back towards her. She pulled back the covers and got out of bed.

'Where are you going?' he asked, turning around again. 'Why don't you just stay the night? It's nearly morning anyway.'

'I need to get back to my own place,' Emily said, moving around the room and gathering up her clothes. She proceeded into the bathroom and dressed herself. She returned after a couple of minutes, wearing the same black trousers and a long-sleeved black shirt that she had worn to work the previous evening. She sat on the edge of his bed and tied the laces on her trainers.

'I just don't get you,' he repeated furiously. 'You've never once spent a full night here! You know if you like having your own things around, you could leave some stuff here?'

'We've been through this...' she said as she picked up her bag. She leant over the bed to give him a kiss but he sulkily dodged her face. He had never been like that with her before. 'Jonny, please, don't be like this—' she begged.

'What is it that you want, Emily?' he demanded.

'What do you mean?'

He shook his head. 'Maybe you could explain it because I just can't understand it. Why won't you allow yourself to be happy? Do you want me to treat you badly, is that what you want? Would you like me then? Because if that's what you want, it's not going to happen. Call me old-fashioned but I wasn't raised that way.'

'I'm sorry, J.' Her voice was a whisper. 'I'm sorry I can't be the person that you want me to be.'

Emily walked out of his bedroom and headed down the narrow hallway, squeezing past his bike, where the black rubber handles

She stopped at traffic lights and took a moment to catch her breath and wipe the sweat from her forehead before the lights went green and she continued on again. She headed down by the waterfront where motorboats and yachts bobbed in the harbour, their moorings whipping in the gentle breeze. She saw traffic was already building on Harbour Bridge. She looped around towards home, the stench of urine rising off the street as she let herself into her building. After she showered, she fixed herself some breakfast. She pottered around for a while and, soon, it was time for work.

She entered the restaurant kitchen later that day, feeling the heat hit her like a wall. The chefs had started work several hours ago and, already, beads of sweat laced their brows as they concentrated on their work. Between the hot summer weather outside and the warmth in the kitchen, the place was like a furnace no matter how high the air conditioning was cranked up.

'Hi everyone,' Emily greeted as she breathed in the heady aromas of that evening's service.

'Hey,' they chorused without raising their heads. She looked over to where Jonny was expertly chopping asparagus. He raised his head and gave her a half-smile and she felt her heart twist. She had been feeling bad about how she had left his place that morning. Jonny was a good guy; it was just a pity she couldn't give him what he wanted from their relationship.

'Emily?' he said, following her out to the back of the kitchen where she went to hang up her coat. He glanced behind himself to make sure no one was listening to them. 'Look, I'm sorry about this morning,' he began sheepishly. 'I shouldn't have been like that. I was just frustrated... I wish you would give us a chance, that's all...'

'I'm sorry too, Jonny,' she said sadly. How she wished she could be the person he wanted her to be.

They noticed Henry the head chef watching them as he tenderised steak.

Jonny cocked his head back towards the kitchen. 'I'd better get cracking. We've sixty-four covers booked in for tonight. It's going to be a busy one.'

Emily nodded as she took her notepad and pen out of her shirt pocket, before heading out front of house to begin taking orders from customers who had started to arrive for dinner. Before she knew it, she was run off her feet, her brain in a chaotic tangle as it tried to remember extra requests that customers liked to throw at her as she passed their table: *Can we get some ketchup, please? Can you tell the chef to put the sauce on the side? Could you bring more wine? Could I order an extra side of the chargrilled broccoli?* She knew she and Jonny would both go about their jobs and continue on as if nothing had happened, not out of any lingering awkwardness but because this was the way it always went with them. He would probably bring it up again in a few months. She would give him the same response, and so the cycle would continue.

A while later, she was standing at a table, twisting a corkscrew into a bottle of wine, when Barry the manager came over and said there was a phone call for her. Emily was surprised because nobody ever called her at work; they always phoned her on her mobile. She finished opening the wine, waited while the woman who had ordered it sampled it, going through the routine of swirling and sniffing, eventually taking a sip and nodding her approval. Then finally, when she had filled all the glasses for the rest of the table, she headed behind the bar area and lifted the phone.

'Hello?' she said.

'I've been calling your phone,' she heard her sister Karen's voice launch straight in without even a greeting.

'Karen?' she asked, feeling a chill spread down along her body and the hairs on her arms stand to attention. Why was her sister calling her on this phone? 'What is it? What's wrong?'

'It's Mum. We think she's had a stroke.'

The words were buzzing in her ears. 'Oh God, is she okay?'

'You need to get home.'

'Is she okay?' Emily repeated, hearing a tremble in her voice.

'I'm sorry...' Karen dissolved into tears. 'Just come home.'

Emily replaced the phone on the receiver and wandered back out to the restaurant in a daze. One of the tables she had been serving were glaring in her direction; they wanted her attention.

'I-I'm sorry,' she said, quickly hurrying over to them on autopilot before she remembered that she had to get home. Then she turned away from the table and ran back of house to find Barry in the kitchen. She explained that there was an emergency and she needed to get back to Ireland.

'Emily? Are you okay?' Jonny asked, placing down the knife he was using to chop and coming over to her. 'You look like you've seen a ghost.'

She shook her head, unable to form the words. 'It's my mum,' she blurted. 'They think she's had a stroke. I need to get home—'

'I'll go with you,' he said quickly.

'I mean to Ireland.'

'I can help you get your stuff packed up. Come on, let's go.'

She nodded, grateful to have him help her when her brain was in a spin. Jonny ran and got her coat and bag from the staff area and then the two of them hurried out of the restaurant. On the street outside, he walked onto the road and flagged a taxi. They went back to her flat and she scrambled around, trying to pack a few things and grab her passport.

'I've a taxi waiting downstairs,' Jonny announced as she came out to the living room a few minutes later, carrying a small suitcase containing her belongings.

'Thank you,' she said, feeling a huge surge of gratitude for him.

'Let's go.' He lifted her case and they headed down in the lift wordlessly together. On the street, he opened the rear door of the taxi, she climbed in and he followed after her. The city lights streaked neon past the window as they drove towards the airport. Eventually, they pulled up outside the terminal building.

'I'd better go,' she said, climbing out.

Jonny followed after her and stood on the pavement beside her. 'You know, I could go with you...' He hesitated. 'I mean, only if you wanted...'

'I don't think—'

'Not like that,' he added quickly. 'I mean just as a friend... to keep you company...'

'Thanks, J, I'll be okay. But thank you for being with me tonight.'

He nodded. 'Take care of yourself, all right? Let me know how she's doing when you get there. I'll be thinking of you.'

'I will and thank you. For everything.'

He pulled her into a hug and she breathed in his manly scent, combined with a faint trace of the aftershave he always wore and food smells from the restaurant. She released him and he got back into the taxi, while she headed inside the building.

Eventually, she managed to get on a flight to Dubai which would then connect to London and on to Dublin. As she sat in her seat on the plane, images of her poor mother lying on the floor or surrounded by bleeping machines in a hospital bed assaulted her. Karen's words had sounded serious. She prayed that her mum would hold on.

She must have eventually fallen asleep because she was startled awake somewhere over the Indian Ocean by a nightmare where her mother was calling out for her daughters and they had stood there, ignoring her.

She called Karen as soon as she landed in Dubai and from London too, hoping for an update, but Karen said she still hadn't

walked down the hallway, she realised she was waiting to hear her mother's sing-song voice calling out to her: 'I'm in here, Emily. Sit yourself down there and I'll stick the kettle on.' She noticed that her mother's bottle-green woollen overcoat was still hanging on the hallstand as if waiting for her to come downstairs and slip it on. It felt like walking into a stranger's house; it wasn't home without her mother here waiting for her.

Guilt choked her as she thought about how it was almost a decade since she had left. Every year, her mum would ask, her voice laden with hope, if she might be coming home for Christmas this year? Emily always disappointed her with some feeble excuse about having to work because it was the restaurant's busiest time of year or not being able to afford the cost of flights. She knew now she would regret it forever. Her mum had been in her seventies; she should have visited her. Emily should have known she wouldn't always be around and to cherish the time with her more. The truth was that although she missed her family, she just hadn't been able to face coming back to Ireland. It was easier to keep postponing the visit and fob her mother off with various excuses and a promise that she'd definitely come home to see her the following year. Emily desperately wished she could see her mother one more time. She would apologise for everything; she would hug her and tell her that she loved her. She would listen to her stories and updates about what was happening in their village without getting impatient. She would tell her that she was sorry and how much she meant to her, but now she was gone and it was too late.

Emily entered the living room which had been done up since she was last home. She remembered her mother talking about that; something about there being a delay with the furniture shop delivering the new sofa, after she had donated her old one to the St Vincent de Paul and how she had asked the manager of the shop if he expected her to sit on the floor while she waited? Emily hadn't paid much attention to her mother's banal updates but she wished she had. She hadn't realised it at the time but they had made her feel connected to home and now she knew that no one was going to do that for her. No one was going to check in with her, or just sense when something was wrong. Karen was busy with her children and her dad had left when they were young. Like a lot of families in those days, their father had gone to England for work in the eighties because of the high levels of unemployment in Ireland. He had been working on a building site in Coventry but he had met someone else over there and told her mother by letter that he wasn't coming home. They had never divorced; Emily wasn't sure why but perhaps it was something to do with the fact that divorce was only legalised in Ireland in 1995 and, by that stage, neither of her parents had the energy to reopen old wounds. They knew that her father had a new family now and neither she nor Karen had a relationship with him any more.

After her father had left, the three women had banded together. They had been so tight in those days. 'Us Gallagher girls have to stick together,' her mother would always say. So how had they all drifted apart? As she had watched her sister accepting condolences earlier, it was obvious that Karen and her mother had retained that same closeness that she had walked away from. Despite her absence for the last nine years, her mother had always been at the end of the phone when she needed her. Patricia had been the one constant in her life and, without her, she felt so lost and at sea.

She looked up at the collage of photographs that her mother had displayed proudly on the wall above the sideboard. There were school photos, as well as communion and confirmation photographs of both girls. Her dad had still been in Emily's communion photo, he hadn't left at that stage, but he was gone by the time her confirmation had rolled around. She stood up and

moved closer to a photo of her taken at her graduation from
university. She was wearing a black cloak and mortar board,
holding a scroll with her marketing degree inked in Latin. She had
had caramel highlights in her sandy-coloured hair and her skin
was bronzed after spending the summer previous working in Ios.
She looked so different to what she looked like now: young and
carefree. There were professional black-and-white portraits taken
of each of Karen's three children as newborn babies and beside it
was a wedding photo of Karen and Dave taken at their reception. It
was only then that she noticed that her own wedding photo that
had once hung here too had been taken down.

Emily sank down onto the sofa. She was so weary but she knew
she'd never sleep if she went to bed, and even if she did, she was
afraid of the fresh pain she would face when she woke up again
and remembered that her mother was gone. It felt as though she
had been upended by a wave that kept battering her, and every
time she tried to get her footing, it would wipe her out once more.
Seeing Rob earlier hadn't helped. She still couldn't work out why
he had come. And with that beautiful child in tow; was he trying to
get a dig in? Rub her face in it? Show her what she could have had?
Bumping into him had brought her right back to that awful time in
her life, stirring up so many emotions that she battled with daily to
keep buried. Regret, pain, anger and so many more feelings all
swirled around in her stomach in a seedy mix. Since she had come
back home, it felt as though she was standing on a bed of quick-
sand and if she didn't move fast, she would sink beneath it. The
sooner she got back to her life in Auckland, the better.

6

When she woke the next morning, Emily's head was thumping and her brain felt muzzy. Jet lag and grief had entwined in a heady mix and ensured she had spent most of the night awake. As the light changed from the inky black of night, to cool purple dawn, she had lain in bed looking around the walls of her childhood bedroom feeling bereft. Her mother had kept her room exactly as it was; her old clothes still hung in the wardrobe and her calendar still displayed the same month and year that she had moved out of home.

She dragged herself out of bed and headed for the shower. She dressed and felt slightly more human afterwards. As she walked down the landing, she paused outside her mother's bedroom door. She placed her hand on the pine timber and traced the knots in the wood, deliberating whether she should go into the room or not. She decided she wasn't ready yet to face it, so instead, she continued along the landing and went downstairs. She filled the kettle to make a coffee. Children's artwork decorated the fridge and Emily guessed they had been done by her nieces. Her mother had clearly been a very proud grandmother.

She thought about Karen and wondered how she was doing today. Was she suspended in a fog of grief too? Emily realised that she needed to make amends with her sister; things were strained between them and Emily knew it was her fault. It frightened her to think that Karen was the only family she now had left in the world. She needed something to tether to in the midst of this squall. She decided to call around to see her younger sister and attempt to set things right between them again.

She returned upstairs and found an old puffa jacket that she had worn in college still hanging in her wardrobe. She hadn't even thought to pack a coat as she had been scrambling around her apartment in Auckland putting clothes into a case. She put it on and was surprised to find it still fit. Despite its dated style, she was glad of its warmth.

She left her mother's house and walked the short distance down Seaview Road to her sister's house. The rain from the previous day had finally stopped and the sun had managed to push through the cloud with a skirt of sunbeams. Unlike Emily, Karen had stayed in Ballyrath and she and her husband Dave had bought one of the larger houses on the same road as where their mother lived. As she came up the driveway, Emily noticed subtle changes in the façade of the house since she had last been there; the white PVC windows had been replaced with modern charcoal-coloured frames that complemented the red-brick exterior. A heart-shaped wreath fashioned from wicker hung on the front door to welcome people. A scooter lay abandoned on its side in the middle of the driveway and small pink wellies were lined up inside the porch. Karen had got married and become a mother. She had bought a four-bed semi-detached house with a large garden. She had ticked all the boxes you were supposed to tick: house, marriage, kids. It was like Karen had taken over Emily's role in the family and become the sensible, organised sister and Emily had got stuck in time somewhere. In fact, she wasn't even stuck; that would imply that she had stayed the same. Emily had actually gone backwards in life. She lived alone, she didn't have a child, she no longer owned a home, her job wasn't well paid, she didn't even own a car. Compared to her younger sister, Emily's achievements in life were paltry.

She pressed the bell and waited.

'Emily...' Karen said when she opened the door to her, clearly taken aback to see her there. 'I wasn't expecting you... Come in.'

Emily followed her down the hallway which she noticed her sister had had panelled and painted in a soft shade of dove grey. They entered the kitchen which had been extended since the last time she had been here to make a large open-plan living area where watery morning sunlight flooded in through glass sliders, overlooking the garden.

'The place looks great,' Emily said, looking around the room. 'You've had a lot of work done since I was last here.'

'I forgot you wouldn't have seen it. We got it done two years ago now; we needed more space with the kids. Sit down.' She gestured towards the leather-clad chairs tucked in beneath the island. 'Dave has taken them out on a walk to give me five minutes of peace so I was just going to make a coffee; would you like one?'

'I'd love one, thanks.' Even though it was her second coffee of the morning, she needed all the caffeine she could get.

Emily pulled out a chair and sat down at the island that was covered with the detritus of children. There were cereal boxes and toys. A pair of pyjamas hung over the back of a chair. There was porridge cemented onto the tray of the high chair beside her and pieces of mushed-up toast. 'Sorry, I still haven't tidied up after breakfast,' Karen said, nodding towards the mess.

She began lifting half-eaten bowls of cereal and draining them into the sink before putting them in the dishwasher.

'The house is like a tip. I can't seem to focus on anything. Normally, by this time of the day, I'd have the kids up and out the door, the washing machine would be on, the dishwasher loaded up, the kitchen would be tidy and I'd be upstairs at my desk getting stuck into work but I feel like I'm going around in circles for the last few days,' she said as she made a pot of coffee and plonked it down in the middle of the island with two mugs. She poured out the coffee and didn't automatically wipe up a drip that spilled onto the quartz surface, which startled Emily because her sister had always been a perfectionist just like their mother had been. Karen didn't offer any milk and Emily didn't want to disturb her by asking for it so she just drank it black.

'Don't worry about any of that. How are you doing?'

'I don't think it's really hit me yet.' Her voice wobbled. 'I still can't believe she's actually gone... It doesn't seem real.'

'Me neither. It feels strange being back in the house and she isn't there waiting for me.'

Karen nodded and sighed. 'I guess we'll eventually have to think about sorting out her things and what we are going to do with the house but I can't face that yet.' Her hands fiddled with the gold chain around her neck.

Emily nodded and placed a hand over her sister's on the countertop. 'One day at a time, yeah?' She felt Karen's hand stiffen beneath hers. She removed it from below Emily's and clasped her mug. 'People said some lovely things about Mum yesterday, didn't they?' Emily tried again. 'Obviously, she was our mum and we loved her but I don't think I realised how well thought of she was outside of our family. It felt good to hear it.'

'So many people loved her,' Karen said wistfully. 'Did you meet

Rob at the graveyard?' She was looking directly at her and Emily knew she was baiting her, goading her for a reaction.

Emily shifted in her seat and fingered the swirling pattern on the mug. 'I wasn't expecting to see him there,' she retorted.

'You know he and Mum always got on well,' Karen said in a tone that implied she'd have known that if she ever bothered to visit. 'They kept in touch, you know, after everything...'

Emily stared at her sister in disbelief, blindsided by this revelation. The pain hit her afresh. How lost she had been back then. How broken. 'Sh-she never told me...' was all she could manage in response.

'Well, do you blame her?' Karen snapped back before falling silent. 'We see a lot of him. His little girl, Molly, is best pals with Cara; they're in school together.'

Was Karen doing this on purpose, Emily wondered. Rubbing salt in a wound that had only recently closed over but hadn't healed fully. Didn't she realise how long it had taken to build herself back up after what had happened back then? She had been left raw and broken. It had taken her a long time to get to where she was today, hoisting each heavy brick up single-handedly and she was a lot stronger now but with that inner strength came self-awareness of how easy it would be to fall apart once more. She knew how fragile she still was and how quickly things could unravel if you didn't protect yourself.

'So, how long do you think you'll stay for?' Karen asked, changing the subject.

Now that the conversation was back on safer ground, Emily found herself relaxing once more and sat back in her chair. 'I'm not really sure. A week, maybe. I didn't book a return flight because I didn't know how long I'd be here for. My boss told me to take as long as I needed.' When she had received the call from Karen to say their mother had taken ill, she had really believed she would get better. She had only booked a one-way ticket. In her head, she had planned to stay on for a few weeks to take care of Patricia while she recovered. She hadn't expected to arrive home and have to bury her. Emily wasn't needed here now, but the thought of leaving her mother's house empty seemed unbearable to her. Like she would be abandoning her all over again.

'Still working in the restaurant then?' Emily wasn't sure if she was imagining it but she was sure she could detect a note of disapproval in her sister's voice.

Emily nodded. 'I'm part of the furniture now.'

'Do you like it? I have to admit, I can't picture you as a waitress.'

'It's all right; it pays the bills...'

They both fell quiet and Emily could almost see Karen's thought process in the air in front of her. She knew that Karen was thinking about the glittering career she used to have and how much she had fallen from those dizzy heights. It was like she had been an entirely different person back then. And in many ways, she had been. The old her was unrecognisable even to herself. Sometimes, she thought about the life she used to have in disbelief; how had it all gone so wrong?

'Why did you do it, Emily?' Karen said after a beat.

'Do what?'

'Leave like that without saying goodbye to any of us. Mum was heartbroken.' Her voice wavered as she became overcome with emotion.

'I'm sorry. I wasn't thinking straight after everything that happened. I didn't do it on purpose... I just wanted to escape my pain and I thought that was the best way.'

'I know what you went through was awful but it still doesn't excuse what you did to Mum. There was nobody stopping you from coming home to visit. In spite of everything, you know Mum would have welcomed you back with open arms.' Her voice choked.

'It was difficult, you know. Facing up to everything... and then the longer time went on, the harder it became...' Emily trailed off.

Karen shook her head. 'You can't just run away from your problems. You're an adult and that means you have to face up to them, no matter how unpalatable. Every year, Mum hoped you'd come home and then eventually, she gave up hoping. You crushed her. At her seventieth birthday party a few years ago, she seemed really deflated. She kept looking around the function room at all her guests but she just couldn't get into the party spirit. I couldn't figure out what was upsetting her and eventually, when we went home that night, she admitted that she had hoped you'd turn up and surprise her. Apparently, she had seen it on some TV show where a long-lost child walked in and surprised their parents and somehow, she had got it into her head that you might do the same. So of course then she was disappointed when you didn't come.'

Emily's heart twisted as the grief and pain of her mother's loss rose up inside her like a spectre. 'Oh, Karen, I'm sorry. I feel awful. I didn't realise she felt like that... I thought you were all too busy getting on with your lives over here to be thinking about me.'

'How could you think like that? Of course we missed you!' Karen retorted.

'I missed you both too,' Emily admitted. 'More than you'll ever know.'

'Well, if you missed us as much as you claim to, wouldn't you have at least spared us a visit in the last *nine* years?' Karen snapped as her voice climbed higher with each word that left her mouth. 'The three of us were so close until you left. We weren't just a mum and her two daughters; we were best friends, Emily!'

'We're both hurting here.' Emily tried to reason with her sister, to get her to calm down. 'I wish I could do things differently but I don't get to go back and change the past. Believe me, I would if I could.'

'When you left, a little part of Mum died too. She never really recovered from it. She blamed herself; she always felt she should have done more to help you. The worst part of it all was that for her, it was exactly like when Dad walked out on us; you reopened all that old pain again for her. Dad broke her heart, Em, and then when she managed to piece herself back together again, you shattered it to smithereens.'

Guilt pressed right down on Emily's solar plexus, pressing the air from her lungs until she couldn't breathe. Why hadn't she thought of it like that before? Karen was right: of course her sudden departure would have caused her mother pain and allowed all those old hurts to resurface.

'Karen, stop!' Emily cried, covering her ears with her palms in a bid to block out her sister's horrible words and accusations. 'That's just cruel.'

'I'm sorry, Emily, but it's the truth,' Karen said bitterly. 'You're just like Dad: running away when times get tough, instead of dealing with your problems!'

Emily's hands flew to her mouth in a gasp as her sister's words sliced her apart. How could she say that? Comparing Emily to their father was the very worst insult Karen could throw at her and she knew it. Emily of all people knew that grief did funny things to people, made them say or do things they wouldn't ordinarily, but she was upset too and it wasn't fair for Karen to lash out at her like this. Karen was deliberately trying to push her buttons. Although Emily knew there was more than a grain of truth in what her sister was saying, she wasn't able to hear it now.

Karen's contorted face was frozen in the air as Emily jumped up from the table and ran towards the door. She needed to get away from her sister. She hurried outside into the chilly air and only then did she realise that she had left her coat behind her. She couldn't go back for it so she continued on until she had left Seaview Road and headed down towards the promenade. Rowdy seagulls squawked and cawed and in the distance she saw the big wheel of the fun fair slowly circling. She had spent so much of her youth hanging around that place. It was a rite of passage for all teenagers growing up in Ballyrath. She walked quickly, putting as much distance as she could between her and her sister's awful words. She was assaulted by another image of her mother in her final moments, lying alone on her bedroom floor, her dying regret being that she had never got to see her eldest daughter again. The worst part was that Emily knew there was some truth in Karen's words. Although nobody would ever understand just how tough the last few years had been on her, even she knew there was no excuse for not coming home to visit her mother. It was selfish to live in exile from her family and problems, cocooning herself inside a bubble, but she just hadn't felt able to face it. How she longed now for her simple life in New Zealand. She would book her return ticket as soon as she went home tonight. Karen would probably never speak to her again but too many painful memories lurked around every corner here.

She hurried along the path with her head down as babies were pushed in buggies, couples strolled hand in hand and children whizzed past on scooters. She nearly tripped over a lead belonging to a Jack Russell because she wasn't watching where she was going.

'Sorry,' she mumbled to the owner as she moved around them.

In the distance, a cargo ship lumbered across the Irish Sea. Soon, she had reached the end of the promenade and turned to come back facing into a bitter headwind. The wind sliced through her and she dug her hands deep into the pockets of her jeans, wishing she hadn't forgotten her coat. The door to her old life had been pushed open, a door that she had firmly shut a long time ago.

All the old pain and hurt flooded in and it felt like it had only happened yesterday. She had managed to wrestle it, beat it down and force it inside a box, but first Karen's words and then meeting Rob with Molly at the funeral had pulled back the lid and she realised that pain was still as wild and unwieldy and ferocious a beast as ever.

PART II

7

ELEVEN YEARS EARLIER

Butterflies careered about her stomach as Emily looked around her. The large function room was full with circular tables seated with advertising executives just like her, their gazes fixed upon the stage, all hoping they might be the one to go home with the award for 'Marketing Campaign of the Year'. E Creative, the advertising agency that she had founded, was nominated for their campaign with Global Beauty, an online skincare retailer. Her company was only young but Emily had worked hard and after only three years in business, E Creative had already established itself as one of Ireland's top advertising agencies and were sitting amongst the heavyweights of the industry.

'And the nominees are: E Creative with their campaign for Global Beauty, Kevin Byrne Marketing for Santana, Go Viral for Heaven's Gold Healthfood Store and Pender-Bradley for Bettervalu Supermarket...' the host began. He paused to open the envelope and pulled out a square piece of gold-foiled cardboard. Emily held her breath and looked around the table at the anxious faces of her team seated beside her. They wanted this just as much as she did;

they all worked so hard and it would be brilliant for their efforts to be recognised.

'And the winner is...' A drum roll was played over the speaker. 'E Creative!'

Blood rushed to her head. They had won! She couldn't believe it. Instantly, she felt Rob's strong arms wrap around her. 'Well done, you, I always knew you would win.'

Her colleagues rushed over then and they hugged her too.

'Go on – go up there get your award,' Cliona, her second in command, encouraged. 'You deserve this.'

Emily picked up the end of her gown so she didn't trip on the way up the steps and made her way towards the stage. The whole room clapped as she walked over to the host and he handed her a microphone.

'Congratulations, Emily. Not bad for a company that has been in business for less than five years. How does it feel?'

'Amazing!' Emily cried into the microphone. 'Especially when the standard was so high and I was up against some truly outstanding campaigns. This is testament to the hard work of my brilliant team in E Creative. I would like to thank them all from the bottom of my heart. They get stuck in no matter what I throw at them and are never afraid to run with my concepts.' Just then, she spotted Rob in the crowd; he was standing out of his seat, cheering her on. His face beaming with pride. He was always her biggest champion. He loved her so wholly that it made her love him even more. 'I also have to thank my lovely husband, Rob, who puts up with me and doesn't mind me waking him up in the middle of the night to listen to my crazy ideas.'

The audience rewarded her with a laugh.

'I really couldn't do it without him,' she continued. She meant every word of what she was saying. People said these things all the time without really meaning it but she did.

She had met Rob through work. Back then, she had been working as a business development executive for an advertising agency. Her company could see the digital revolution was on the horizon as marketing shifted from print towards online advertising and they had spotted an opportunity to guide businesses through the transition. Emily spent her days going around to companies and pitching for their business to help them navigate the new territory of digital advertising. She had just finished giving a presentation to the management at the insurance company that Rob worked for. It hadn't been one of her better pitches. The audience had been resistant to the idea that the landscape was changing and had been hostile towards her picking holes in everything she said, dismissing her research. People had begun filtering out of the room, muttering about 'newfangled trends', and as she began to pack up her belongings, a man had come up alongside her. The first thing she had noticed about him was that he was about the same age as herself and he was tall, she guessed at least six foot one. He wore a white open-necked shirt and had his hands stuffed casually in his pockets. He had struck her as someone who was very laid-back and easy-going.

'Great talk. I liked what you said up there,' he said as she wound up her laptop cable. 'The world of advertising is going to change completely.'

'Thank you. I think you were the only one.'

He leaned in conspiratorially and raised his brows towards a group of men who were deep in conversation across the room. 'This lot wouldn't be the most progressive. I'm not sure everyone believes in the digital revolution. I reckon you've sent a few scurrying back beneath their rocks.' He changed his voice and mimicked an older gentleman in a tweed suit who had stood up from the audience and said, 'Excuse me, but who on earth is going to read a newspaper on a computer?' He had spluttered:

'Reading a broadsheet is a part of our daily culture. I'm around a long time, and I've seen many things hyped as the next big thing, only for them to come and go. I think you'll find it is a fad, young lady.' He had stuck his thumbs behind the elastic of his braces, plumped out his chest and shared a triumphant look around the room with his counterparts. Emily had been humiliated.

'I'm used to it.' She laughed and splayed her hands to the side. 'I guess every revolution has its flat-earthers.'

She went to lift her laptop bag and a box of brochures that she had brought along to advertise her company's services, not one of which had been taken by the audience.

'Here let me give you a hand with those.' He made to pick up the box. 'Where are you parked?' he asked.

'I'm down in the basement,' she said as they began walking out of the room.

They made their way into the lift and pressed the button to take them down.

'I'm Rob, by the way,' he said as they descended through the building. 'I'd shake your hand but your box is kind of heavy.'

'I'm Emily.'

When the lift juddered to a stop, the doors opened and they emerged into the underground car park. Rob followed her over to her black Audi sports car.

'This is me,' she said.

'Nice wheels,' he remarked with an appreciative whistle as he walked around and inspected the car.

'Thank you.' She fumbled in her bag for her keys.

'So where are you off to next?' he asked as he placed the box down on the concrete floor.

'I've still got three more pitches to do today.' She opened the boot. 'Let's hope they go a little better than that one.' She exhaled heavily as she cleared space for him, then he lifted the box and put it into her boot.

'Bit of a badminton fan then?' He nodded towards her racquet.

'Not really...' She hastily pushed it aside, feeling embarrassed. 'I did it for a few weeks until I realised my strengths lie in other areas.'

'Oh yeah?'

'Well, I like to run,' she admitted. 'I'm training for a half-marathon at the moment, actually.'

He pouted. 'Aw, that's a pity.'

'Why?' she asked, not following him.

'Well, I was going to ask if you wanted to go out for a drink sometime, but with all that training, you probably can't...' he teased.

'You were going to ask me to go for a drink?' she repeated, wondering if she had heard him right or was misinterpreting what he was saying.

'Yeah.' He was grinning at her. 'I know it probably seems a bit forward but nothing ventured, nothing gained, right?' He cocked his head to the side and smiled, showing white, evenly spaced teeth.

She opened the door of the car and climbed in, then pulled it closed after her and pressed the button to lower the window. 'Maybe,' she replied, non-committal, still unsure what to make of him and whether he was being serious or not.

'So can I have your number?' he asked.

She called it out and he keyed it into his phone. 'I'll see if I can fit you into my training plan,' she said before closing up her window and reversing out of the space. She was fully sure that she would never hear from him again but Rob had called her the next day and they had gone out for a drink the following weekend. They had hit it off straight away. Her first impression of him had been right: he was very chilled but he also had a solidity and depth about him that told her that he wasn't like a lot of the guys she had met recently on the dating scene who weren't after anything too serious. His calm, relaxed manner was the perfect antidote to her stressed and anxious personality type. They spent all their free time together and she found herself telling him things she usually kept private; she opened up to him about her dad and how he had left them. She had brought him home to meet her mum and Karen pretty soon after and he had brought her to Cork to meet his family. They had moved in with one another next before buying their first home together, a tiny red-bricked ex-corporation terraced house in Ringsend. They had married soon after and then Emily had set up E Creative that same year. When she had been thinking about starting her own agency, she had been full of doubts about walking away from her steady job with its pension plan and sick-pay scheme, but it was Rob who had finally convinced her to take the risk. 'So what if you fail?' he had said as she had given him a list of reasons why she shouldn't go it alone. 'What's the worst that can happen? Okay, your pride might be dented, you'll lose some money or you might just be really successful but you won't find out unless you try.' He was her counterbalance, always able to flip over her negatives. Whenever something went wrong or she had a decision to make, he always knew the right thing to say or do. No matter what happened, he was able to steady the ship and keep her on course. Just knowing he was by her side made her feel invincible and she knew the success of her company was in a large part down to him and his unwavering belief in her.

She lifted the trophy and raised it in his direction. 'Rob, this is for you. I love you.'

8

Emily went back down to the table and her colleagues buzzed around her. Rob uncorked a bottle of champagne and golden nectar bubbled over the rim of the glass and flowed down along the neck of the bottle, soaking into the white linen tablecloth.

They spent the rest of night celebrating and dancing along with the band and eventually, when the music ended and the lights came on, they went home together in a taxi. Emily sat back against the leather upholstery clutching her award, utterly exhausted but basking in the glow of her win. The combination of champagne bubbles and the exhilaration of the win had made her light-headed. She let her head fall back against the headrest, still in disbelief at how the evening had gone. She didn't think she had ever been so happy. Sheer hard graft had got her to where she was now and it had finally paid off.

She thought of all those years she had spent as a lowly assistant working in agencies, making the tea and coffee for meetings and answering the phones. How many times had she walked into companies like Rob's and given pitches, only to be sneered at and left feeling belittled? She had worked her way up gradually, climbing the rungs into more senior positions before taking a leap of faith and setting up her own agency and now look at what she had achieved. Winning this award was validation at last. She felt like she had journeyed to the top of a mountain and had finally reached the pinnacle of success. She knew it would change everything. The company that she had founded was making the heavy players in the advertising industry sit up and take notice. Their services would be in demand; E Creative would have companies coming to them now for a change. And the very best bit was that she had her soulmate by her side throughout it all. She looked across at her husband and felt her heart swell with love for him. How had she got so lucky? Rob was loving and supportive. They had their dream home. Sometimes, she had to pinch herself that this really was her life.

He leaned across the seat and draped an arm around her shoulder as if reading her thoughts. 'My wife, the big advertising ninja,' he said proudly. 'You know, you were so sexy up on that stage. I couldn't stop thinking, that's my wife up there and I'm the lucky guy who gets to take her home tonight.'

She snuggled in closer to him, her head slotting into the curve of his neck. 'I meant what I said, you know; I couldn't do what I do without you pushing me on.'

The taxi eventually pulled up outside their home on the sycamore-lined Groveton Road. They'd recently sold the terraced house in Ringsend and bought this three-bedroomed Victorian red-brick, which with the help of an architectural design team they had renovated into her dream home the year previously. Their remodel had even been featured in one of the lifestyle supplements that came with the Sunday papers.

Rob put his key in the lock and opened the door. They stepped inside onto their parquet flooring, the moody navy-blue hue of their hallway soothing in the night. He took her into his arms and kicked out his leg to shut the door closed behind them.

'I can't believe I get to sleep with Emily Kavanagh,' he said, taking her into his arms and nuzzling delicately at her neck. Tiny bolts of electricity danced down her spine.

She cupped his face between her two hands and kissed him passionately before pulling back breathlessly. 'I've been thinking—'

'Doesn't that mind of yours ever switch off?' he muttered as he caressed the tender skin along her collarbone.

'This isn't about work...'

'Oh yeah?' he asked, intrigued. He pushed her hair back from her face and kissed her forehead.

'I think maybe we should start trying for a baby.'

He pulled back and held her at arm's length, his face shocked. 'Are you serious?'

She bit down on her bottom lip and nodded nervously. They had discussed it before and she knew he was keen to start a family but the timing had never been right. She had set up E Creative just after they got married and she had been building up her business since then.

'Well, it's just now with your award... won't you be busier than ever?'

'I'm thirty-four; I'm not getting any younger. I spent a long time getting my career established but winning this award tonight means, for the first time, clients will be approaching us. I think the timing is right.' The award would mean a more certain future for her agency and, for the first time ever, she felt she might have the financial security to be able to take some time out to have a baby without worrying that they would lose clients.

His face lit up with childlike excitement. 'Really? You know how much I've always wanted to be a dad,' he said giddily.

She looked at him, feeling her heart pulsing with love. If the way he treated her was anything to go on, he would be a great dad: the best of the best. He balanced her out and made her a better version of herself. He was relaxed when she was uptight. He was funny where she was serious, he could see the silver lining when she just saw storm clouds. She was a better person by being with him and now she wanted to share that love with a baby.

'Let's do it.'

'Well then, in that case...' He took her by the hand and led her up the stairs.

'Right now?' she giggled, following him up the steps.

'No time like the present!' He raised his brows cartoonishly. 'Let's go make a baby.'

9

Emily took the stick in her hands, willing the result to be what she wanted it to be, but resigning herself to the fact that it most likely was not. She spent a good part of every month squashing down the seeds of hope that sprung up like weeds no matter how hard she tried not to let them take over. Wasn't it said that the definition of insanity was doing the same thing over and over again but expecting a different result? Well, in that case she was clearly insane because each month they tried to have a baby and it didn't happen.

As the weeks went by, the more her hopes and dreams were being snatched away from her. Every time she thought about the baby she yearned for, she felt a familiar tightness in her chest. The urges were getting stronger. The need to connect with something outside of herself felt more powerful than ever. She was feeling a longing that was like nothing she had ever experienced before. It felt like an insatiable hunger growing inside her, a hunger that wouldn't rest. Her body ached for a baby.

She thought back to how naïve she had been on that November evening almost a year and a half ago. She had assumed, like everything else in her life, that once she was ready to have a baby, it would just happen. When Emily had been in school and she wanted to do well in an exam, she would study hard and achieve the desired result. When she wanted to run the Dublin Marathon, she had followed a strict training plan and achieved it. When they had been renovating the house, she had done her research, chosen the best tradespeople and had achieved a beautiful home. It was the same in her job: when she put the hard work in, she saw success. Stupidly, she had thought she could apply the same formula to having a baby. She had come off her pill, taken her prenatal vitamins and folic acid. She had cut down on alcohol and upped her intake of fruit and vegetables to help her body prepare to carry a baby. And then they had waited. And waited. Now she looked back on that naïvely optimistic woman with pity. How silly she had been to think that because *she* was ready, her body would cooperate. Month after month, she waited for a second line to materialise and, when it never did, she felt like a complete failure; why couldn't she do the one thing a woman was supposed to do? Something that women all around the world did every day? Sometimes, without even planning it. Why wasn't she able to get pregnant when every other woman seemed to conceive with ease? Her friend Jodie had just announced her second pregnancy in the space of eighteen months, so what was wrong with her?

Rob had suggested several months back that maybe they should seek some help. 'Maybe we should just go and get some tests done or something?' he had said. But admitting they had a problem almost felt like some sort of personal failure. And Emily never failed. She had always been able to control the things in her life by controlling her input – you put in the work and you reaped the rewards – but this was the first time in her life where it wasn't going the way she expected. And she knew as much as she was heartbroken, it was worse seeing the pain etched on Rob's face as he tried to put on a brave face for her sake every month, telling her, 'Don't worry, love, next month will be our month, just you wait and see, Em.' He didn't blame her or think she was some kind of pathetic failure. She almost wished he would; his kindness made it unbearable. Coming downstairs from the bathroom to tell him every month that the test was negative was nearly worse than dealing with her own disappointment.

Rob had wanted to be a dad ever since she had known him and she suspected he had been the same when he was child. He had younger twin brothers whom he took an almost fatherly approach to. When Emily had first met Rob, the twins had been in college and he had helped them out whenever they were short for their rent and made sure they got their assignments in on time or didn't forget it was their mum's birthday. Both of his brothers still lived in Cork where they had grown up – they were married now and had children of their own – and Emily was keenly aware that they had overtaken their older brother in the game of life. Rob was the grown-up that would play with his nieces and nephews at parties, throwing them up into the air and swinging them around. Children would clamber at his feet, crying 'Again, Uncle Rob, swing me again!' but Emily knew he was growing tired of being the 'fun uncle'; he wanted that same unconditional love for himself. She herself had never felt very maternal – she wasn't one of those people who cooed over newborn babies – but recently, something had changed inside her. She had taken to peeping in at tiny babies blanketed in prams, feeling an empty aching in her heart. She couldn't help it. She would see a baby in a supermarket queue and it could quite literally take her breath away. She wanted it so badly; she wanted to be the person who saw that faint second line appear on a pregnancy test. She wanted to be the one to rush down the stairs to tell her husband that finally it had happened for them.

She wanted to feel the fluttery first kicks. She wanted to be the one to suffer the aches and pains that only pregnant women knew about and, when the time came, she wanted to be the one to deliver her baby into the world. When would she get the chance to push her pram and have strangers stop her in the supermarket queue to peer in over the hood to admire her bundle? She had been to so many baby showers and although she was always happy for her friends, she couldn't help but wonder when it would be her turn. It was like she had boarded a train but, instead of arriving at the destination, she had to stop at everyone else's stop first. Meanwhile, her own languished further and further in the distance.

For the most part, people didn't pry; as her business flourished, everyone assumed she wanted to concentrate on her career and, once upon a time, that might have been true, but not any more. The buzz of winning a new client or bagging an award had lost its satisfaction; it was like her yearning for a baby had left a gaping hole in her heart that couldn't be filled.

She turned the pregnancy test over in her hands, feeling that now familiar clench in her stomach. *Please, please, please,* she begged, *please let it be our turn.* She saw the sugar-pink of the control line and in the panel beside it, instead of a blank space like there usually was, the faintest hint of a pink line was visible. It was so faint that she wasn't sure if it was the reflection from the line beside it. She brought it over to the window, keeping her eyes fixed on that second line in case it should disappear again if she dared to look away. She felt a tiny seed of joy begin to unfurl inside her. Was this real? Might she be pregnant, at last? Holding the stick carefully, she left the bathroom and went downstairs. She took the steps two at a time and hurried into the kitchen where Rob was sitting at the table, reading the Sunday papers. Without saying a word, she carefully placed the stick down before him on top of one of the papers.

'What's this?' he asked, lowering the newspaper he had been holding out in front of him.

'Have a look and tell me you see it too.'

She studied his face for a reaction as he recognised what it was. He took it up in his hands and examined it carefully. She hardly dared to breathe; she hoped this wasn't a figment of her imagination. She had heard of women doing this, when they were so desperate to get pregnant that they started imagining lines where there were none.

'Well, what do you think?' she prompted nervously after he had been silent for too long.

She watched his face light up and she knew that he saw it too.

He grinned up at her. 'I think this means we're pregnant.' He put the test down, stood up and took her into his arms. She felt great heaving sobs of happiness, or perhaps it was relief, overcome her. *Finally.* Finally, it was their turn.

'I was starting to think it was never going to happen for us,' she admitted as tears flowed down her face. All those months, those long, tortuous months of desperate hoping and wishing, only to be crushed over and over again.

'Of course it was, these things always work out in the end. You're going to be a great mum, Emily.'

'And you'll be the best dad.' And he would be. She could picture him, gently cradling their infant in the crook of his arm with a miniature fist gripping his index finger, softly crooning as he tried to get him or her to sleep. He would teach them to dribble a football and hold their hand on the way to school. He would be an amazing father; she knew that. Already, a life was starting to plan out for their baby in her mind. Images of a future flashed before her. She looked out to the garden where May sunlight streamed in through the French doors in slanted beams, bathing her in warmth. She could see lazy, sunny days spent lying on the grass making daisy chains. She could see a child blowing dandelion clocks and running beneath the arc of water gushing from a hose as the cool droplets fell on their skin. There was a large sycamore at the end of the garden where she could imagine tying a rope swing over one of the boughs. She could see it all so clearly. She placed a hand on her slender stomach and whispered, 'What a wanted little baby you are. You are going to be so loved.'

10

Six weeks later, Emily put her bum down on her office chair and took a sip of her decaf takeaway coffee. She had stopped drinking caffeine as soon as she learnt she was pregnant.

'Morning,' Cliona sang as she stuck her head around the door.

'Hi, Clio,' Emily replied.

Cliona's face creased in concern. 'You're looking a little pale; are you okay, Em?'

Emily nodded. 'I'm just a little tired,' she explained. They still hadn't told anyone that she was pregnant. 'Let's not jinx anything,' she had said cautiously, and Rob had agreed with her to wait until after the first trimester to share their news with their families and friends. She was almost eleven weeks along now and she was lucky that everything seemed to be going well so far. She didn't have morning sickness and her energy levels seemed to be holding firm. People had warned her about the debilitating tiredness that they had experienced in the early weeks or the ever-present nausea but she didn't have any of that. She placed a hand on the waistband of her trousers and thought about the life that was growing in there. The miracle that it was. For now, it was their secret and, as she placed her hands on her stomach, she marvelled at all that was going on below the surface. She knew from her pregnancy book that at this stage the cells were dividing to form shoulders and elbows. It amazed her how the foetus knew exactly what is was supposed to do and just when it was supposed to do it. 'Thank you for being such a good baby,' she whispered whenever she lay in bed at night.

'Just reminding you that we've that meeting with the Geri Moran at twelve,' Cliona began. 'Oh, and Kevin called in sick so Jenna is looking after the Builder's Base account while he's out.' She paused. 'We... um... also had a call from Maeve Murray. She's the marketing director of Irish Alliance Bank.'

'Maeve Murray?' Emily repeated in disbelief, sure that she must have heard Cliona wrong.

'I think that's what she said her name was...' Cliona replied uncertainly as she double-checked her notepad.

'I know who she is.' Maeve Murray was one of the biggest marketing directors in the country. Of course Emily knew who she was. She had read a newspaper interview with the woman recently where she talked about her role in the bank and their marketing budget had blown her mind. She was a formidable character in the industry with a reputation for being cut-throat.

'Did she call herself? It wasn't her assistant or anything?' Emily asked.

Cliona shook her head. 'No, it was her. She wants to set up a meeting with you as soon as possible.'

'Wow.' Ever since they had won the award almost two years previously, they had been approached by bigger and bigger companies, but this was another level. *Stay calm*, she told herself. *It's only a meeting; nothing might come of it.* But Emily knew that a woman like Maeve Murray wouldn't waste time meeting her unless she was serious. 'Okay, well, schedule her in whenever suits.'

'She's suggested this evening at five?'

Emily blinked. 'This evening?' That didn't leave much time to prepare. She had once dreamed of being in this position, but it was typical that it had happened when she was finally pregnant and could do with being a little less busy. Although having a client with a budget the size of Irish Alliance Bank was the stuff of dreams, she knew they'd have to work hard to earn every penny. Companies like that demanded blood, sweat and tears for their money.

'Will I push it out to later in the week? Unfortunately, Luke is away which means I have to pick Lola up from the crèche today, so I won't be able to join you.'

Emily waved her hand. 'No, no, let's do it today.' She was long enough in the game to know how things worked; if Maeve Murray wanted to meet you at five, you met her at five. It did however mean that she was going to have to work late. Again. She had promised Rob that they would catch a bite to eat together after work but now she'd have to cancel. She already knew how he would greet the news. He'd understand though, once she explained. That was the thing with Rob; he always did. He wasn't resentful or petty. He would, however, probably start harping on at her about how hard she worked, which had become a bone of contention between them lately.

'You need to be taking it easy,' he seemed to be saying on a loop these days. 'All that stress isn't good for you or the baby.'

'I will,' she would promise. 'I just need to get these bits sorted first and things will calm down again.' Then she would grab her keys and rush out the door with a piece of toast sandwiched between her teeth. It was the same mania every morning and even she didn't believe her own lies any more. Things never calmed down. Her work never got quieter. In fact, the opposite was true; ever since they had won the award, it felt like she hadn't been able to catch a breath. She had expected an upswing in business but

nothing could have prepared her for just how in demand their
services were.

Since the night E Creative had won the award, marketing directors from some of Ireland's top brands had contacted her the very
next morning with a view to getting her team involved with their
marketing. However, because they were such big-name companies
– clients she could only have dreamt of when she had been
starting out – she felt she needed to be their main point of contact
which meant her schedule had exploded. She kept telling Rob that
once she got the clients on board, she'd pass them over to her
account managers, but that didn't seem to be happening. They all
wanted her. She knew it was a good complaint but as the months
had gone by and she wasn't getting pregnant, Rob had started to
suggest that her stressful job wasn't helping matters. Deep down,
she knew he was probably right but now that she had finally got
pregnant, he had started going on about stress not being good for
the baby. She felt she couldn't win. Of course she wanted to do
everything possible for their baby to grow and develop properly
but she also had to work. Without her job, they wouldn't be able to
afford their house with its designer interior in a sought-after part
of Dublin or the Range Rover that was parked in the driveway.

She envied Rob in many ways; although he worked hard and
was good at his job in insurance middle management, he wasn't
ambitious like she was. Rob worked nine to five and he never
thought about work as soon as he stepped foot outside the office.
He didn't feel his stomach knot every time his phone pinged in the
evenings or on weekends, just in case it was a client looking for
something. He didn't have the worry of employing twenty-two
people and the responsibility of ensuring that there was enough
work in the pipeline so that everyone could pay their mortgages.
He didn't lie awake at night worrying that he had forgotten to
respond to a client's email or that an invoice remained unpaid past

their standard business terms. He slept soundly beside her every night while she tossed and turned. She knew she had to start delegating some of her workload but it was hard when everyone turned to her for the answers. Every time she thought about the maternity leave that she would have to take in a few months' time, her tummy constricted; although she had a brilliant team, she just didn't see how the business would function without her.

She had made the mistake of sharing her worries with Rob recently as they sat in a café having brunch. 'Are you saying you don't want to take maternity leave?' he had asked in disbelief as he chewed on a piece of sourdough.

'No. Of course not,' she had replied testily, using her fork to spear a piece of avocado, 'but I just don't see how I can. I won't be able to take the full amount of time off anyway.'

'How long have we wanted this, Emily? Your job will always be there but we get one shot at this. Babies are only small for a short while. I can share it with you, but you'll still need to give yourself time off to recover from the birth.'

She knew Rob was good; he would gladly step in and would be a hands-on dad. She wanted to do it too but she felt she couldn't or her whole business might go down the tubes.

'We'll make it work,' he had reassured, placing his hand over hers and squeezing it.

She had smiled gratefully at him. 'How did I get so lucky?' She meant it. He was literally the man of her dreams, kind and caring and she still wanted to rip his clothes off because she found him insanely attractive. And now they were going to have a baby. She couldn't think of a better person to have by her side.

11

As soon as Cliona had gone back to her desk, Emily closed the Crittall glass door leading to her office and called Rob. She looked out at the broad sweep of the River Liffey cutting a line through the city and the glass office blocks of the IFSC glinting silver under the sunlight.

'Guess what?' she began breathlessly as soon as he answered.

He sighed. 'You're calling to cancel our date.'

'You know me too well,' she admitted. 'But only because something really amazing has happened.'

'Go on,' he said with mild amusement. 'George Clooney has asked you out instead?'

'Darling, I'd never ditch you for George Clooney,' she replied in mock horror. 'Maybe if it was David Beckham...'

'Okay then, so what is this amazing thing?'

'Well, remember last year when I showed you that interview with Maeve Murray from Irish Alliance Bank in the *Sunday Business Post*?'

'Am I going to get in trouble if I tell you that I don't? I barely remember what I read five minutes ago.'

'Well, anyway, she wants to meet me here. Today. At five. I actually can't believe it.'

'Good for you, you deserve it.'

'A client like that could change everything,' she went on excitedly. 'I can't even imagine what getting her business would be worth to us but with ongoing TV, press and radio campaigns, it has to be one of the biggest budgets in Ireland!'

'So what you're saying is that you're ditching me because this woman has more money than me?'

She laughed. 'If you put it like that... But, Rob, this could be the start of my business going to the next level. This could be life-changing.' Suddenly, she began to doubt herself; there were no guarantees, Maeve might just be being nosy and want to have a snoop around. 'If I get her business—' she added nervously.

'Of course you will. There is nobody better out there.' He always believed in her, even when she didn't have faith in herself. Maybe it was just his unwavering sense of loyalty towards her but she loved him for it all the same.

'So, you don't mind?'

'Of course not. Go get her, tiger.'

After she had hung up, she began researching everything she could find on the internet about Irish Alliance Bank and Maeve Murray. She brushed up on their most recent campaigns and critically analysed their strengths and weaknesses. She saw one of her rivals, Go Viral, had been retained to do their advertising for the last few years; they had been nominated alongside her at the awards ceremony last year but E Creative had beaten them. She felt goosebumps break out along her arms. She began jotting down ideas as they came to her. This was always the part of the job she loved: being creative and coming up with winning slogans and funny tag lines. Unfortunately, it was an aspect of her job that she got to do less and less now as her business had grown but she would need to handle Maeve personally.

It was twenty past five when their receptionist Paulina called to tell her that Maeve had arrived and was waiting for her in the boardroom.

Emily's heart started thumping wildly as she carried her laptop down the hall. She just hoped Maeve would be impressed. She felt completely out of her depth but she knew she'd have to fake confidence that she didn't feel if she wanted to have any chance of winning the woman over.

'Maeve,' she greeted as she walked in and stuck out her hand to shake the other woman's.

Maeve returned the handshake firmly, in a manner that told Emily she meant business.

Maeve cut straight to the chase. 'Thank you for meeting with me, Emily. I must congratulate you on your award last year. I've been keeping an eye on you and your agency since then and I like what you're doing.' She twisted the cap on a bottle of Ballygowan sparkling water that rested on the table and, as the water fizzed, she poured herself a glass.

'Thank you.' Emily took a seat opposite her.

She listened carefully as Maeve explained her reasons for requesting the meeting and took detailed notes. Maeve explained how the bank's contract with Go Viral was up for renewal at the end of the year and she wanted to make sure that they were still the best fit for the bank. To Emily, it seemed she was hinting that she wanted a fresh set of eyes working on the campaign. When it was Emily's turn to speak, she began talking her through a presentation she had prepared earlier, on what they could do for the bank and the fresh approach they would take with their campaigns. Emily highlighted what she felt was a disproportionate age profile for the bank's customers and how there was a huge opportunity to entice a younger customer base using social media. Emily knew it was a risk, albeit a calculated one, given how archaic most banks were. Irish Alliance Bank was an institution but with new players coming on stream all the time, the bank needed to move with the times and capture the younger market or they could find themselves in trouble down the road.

Maeve stayed silent long after Emily had finished speaking. She sat back against the leather chair, steepled her hands together and eyed her thoughtfully.

'I like it,' she said eventually. 'It might take a while for some of the dinosaurs on the board to agree but I've suspected for a long time now that this is the direction in which we need to be moving. We've stagnated and if we don't move with the times, we'll be left behind.'

Emily felt herself sag with relief. She had been worried that Maeve might take offence to her pointing out flaws in the bank's current marketing strategy. Thankfully, it hadn't backfired.

While Maeve spoke about what her next step would be, Emily felt a sharp stabbing in her abdomen. She gasped and instinctively placed a protective hand over her stomach.

'Are you okay?' Maeve asked, seemingly annoyed at having been interrupted.

'Yes, of course,' Emily assured her, trying her best to concentrate on what Maeve was saying to her as she was caught in the throes of an unbearable cramp that felt as though a vice was holding her at either side and pulling and twisting. She prayed it wasn't the baby. *Please, just be okay.*

Eventually, Maeve began to tidy up her belongings and Emily tried to stand to see her out but had to use the table to steady herself.

'Are you sure you're okay?' Maeve asked. 'You're looking a little off colour.'

'Yes, I'm fine.' She wanted to save face. If she told Maeve that she was pregnant, she might not want to give E Creative the business, assuming there would be an impending maternity leave. 'I'll show you out.'

She forced herself to stand upright and, even though her abdomen had seized with pain, she walked Maeve to the reception. She could feel warm liquid pooling between her legs with every step she took. She knew what this meant but she prayed she was wrong.

'Thank you, Emily, I'll be in touch.' Maeve shook her hand firmly before heading towards the lift. As soon as the woman had been swallowed by the double doors, Emily allowed herself to bend double and clutch her stomach. Everyone in the office had already gone home and she was thankful she didn't have to see anyone. She made her way over to the reception desk and grappled for the phone. She lifted the handset and dialled Rob's number.

'Can you come get me? I think I'm losing our baby...'

12

A breathless Rob arrived at her office less than ten minutes later and Emily dissolved into tears at the sight of him. 'Thank God you're here,' she cried, filled with relief that he was right there by her side. He was the one person in the world she could depend on for anything and she knew that no matter what happened, he would take care of her. She could fall apart and he would keep her together; if she fell down, he would help her back up again.

'Are you okay?' he panted. His face was ashen and she could see the concern in his eyes as she gripped his hand fiercely while her stomach clenched and cramped.

She shook her head wordlessly, feeling despair pour into her like concrete. How had she allowed herself to think that they could have a baby? She had known this was too good to be true and now good old reality was there to smack her back down again.

'Let's get you to the hospital,' he said, guiding her upright.

He helped her down to where his car was parked in the basement. Every now and then, a sob would escape her throat and he would reach across from the driver's seat and squeeze her hand.

'Let's not assume the worst; there could be a good reason for all of this.'

But she knew what was happening because women knew these things. She had gone to the bathroom while she was waiting for Rob to arrive and her worst fears had been confirmed when she saw blood. Blood wasn't good. Blood meant she was losing her baby.

The sight of the hospital building broke her. She had been counting down the weeks to her first scan but she hadn't thought that the first time she would be setting foot in the maternity hospital would be like this. It felt wrong: cruel and unfair. Like someone had pulled back a curtain to give her a glimpse of a life she could only dream about but then the curtain had fallen again.

Rob pulled up at the set-down area and silenced the engine.

'I'll go get you a wheelchair,' he said as he climbed out.

While she waited for him to return, she saw a heavily pregnant woman being assisted by her husband as she made her way into the building. She kept stopping to take deep breaths, clearly in the throes of labour. How Emily wished they could swap places; although the woman was clearly in tremendous pain, soon it would be all over and she would be holding her blanketed bundle in her arms. Emily knew that if her fears were confirmed and that she was indeed miscarrying, that even long after her body had healed, her pain would outlive the physical.

Rob was back and he helped her out of the car and gently lowered her into the waiting wheelchair. He pushed her inside the building and headed for the reception desk. He spoke to the lady seated behind the counter and as he explained the situation in concerned whispers, she directed them to the Early Pregnancy Assessment Unit. As Rob pushed her down the corridor, Emily couldn't help but notice that there were pregnant women every-where. *Of course there are*, an angry voice chided inside her head.

What did you expect? It's a maternity hospital, after all. It felt like salt in the wound.

They found the unit on the first floor and they took a seat in the waiting area.

'How are you doing?' Rob asked as he sat down beside her and reached for her hand.

The cramping had eased on the drive to the hospital and she wondered if that meant the miscarriage was complete? She nodded, unable to form the words to reply to him.

She looked around at the other couples waiting to be seen. Some were stony silent while others spoke to one another in hushed tones. One partner was pacing up and down the floor. They all looked as worried as she felt. She didn't know what circumstances had brought everyone else there that evening, whether like her they suspected a miscarriage or perhaps there was something else wrong, but the one thing they all had in common was that nobody wanted to be there.

'Emily Kavanagh?' Finally, she heard her name being called by a woman in blue scrubs. 'I'm Dr Forde.' She offered them both her hand. 'If you two want to follow me in here.'

She led them into a cubicle and listened carefully as Emily explained what had happened. She asked Emily some questions including the date of her last menstrual period, before instructing her to lie up on the bed so that she could do a scan. As the doctor spread cool gel over her abdomen, Emily held her breath. She was torn between wanting to know what exactly was happening and wanting to hold back the bad news that was coming because, right in this moment, she was still pregnant; if Dr Forde confirmed her worst fears, then that was it, the dream was over.

'I'm going to do some measurements first so just give me a few minutes,' Dr Forde explained as she turned the screen away from them.

She began clicking on the screen and dragging a series of lines across it. It seemed to be taking forever.

Eventually, Dr Forde turned back to them. 'Now then,' she began. 'If you want to look here.'

Rob reached out for her hand and she clenched it tightly as they both focused on the grainy image on the monitor beside them. Emily studied the screen, eagerly trying to interpret what she was seeing, but she couldn't work out what they were looking at. She glanced at Rob and saw he was just as confused as she was.

'It's bad news, isn't it?' Emily interrupted. She wished the doctor would just hurry up and put them out of their misery. 'We've lost our baby, haven't we?'

Dr Forde laughed. 'No, you two, I have good news, in fact.'

'You do?' Rob sat up straighter in his chair to make sure he was hearing Dr Forde properly while Emily dared not move on the bed in case it changed anything.

'Everything looks good with your baby. It's growing exactly as it should be at this stage and measuring about eleven weeks, which is in line with your dates.'

Emily could hardly believe what she was hearing so she turned to Rob to make sure she wasn't imagining it. He was grinning like a loon and she knew this was real. Warm and joyous relief spread through her.

'Would you like to listen to the heartbeat?' Dr Forde continued.

'Yes, please,' they both chorused excitedly.

She turned on the volume and soon the room was filled with what sounded like horses' hooves galloping over arid land.

'Wow,' Rob said.

'That's a good, strong heartbeat.'

Emily listened to the sweet music and was filled with immense gratitude. *Thank you, baby*; she said a silent prayer of thanks to her little bean for staying with them. She could finally dare to imagine their future with their baby in it and what it might look like, something she had been too afraid to do before.

'You'll have your dating scan at twelve weeks and then we'll be doing a detailed anomaly scan around twenty weeks but you can both relax; everything looks perfectly healthy. You've a head, two legs, two arms; all the right bits, exactly where they're supposed to be.'

Emily laughed as she used a tissue to wipe off the gel.

'Well, at least it has a head,' Rob said. 'I don't think a headless baby would look good in our family photos.'

They all laughed.

'So why did I bleed?' Emily asked, still in disbelief as she sat up on the bed. 'And I had cramping too?'

The doctor shrugged. 'Nobody knows why some women experience bleeds like this in early pregnancy but one theory is that perhaps stress plays a role. Do you have a busy lifestyle?'

Rob looked at her pointedly. '*Busy* is one way of putting it,' he muttered.

'Well... yes... my job can be stressful,' she admitted.

'Look, we can't avoid stress entirely,' Dr Forde counselled. 'It's the way of the modern world, but just do your best to alleviate it where you can. Perhaps you could consider a pregnancy yoga class and make sure you're getting a full night's sleep.'

Emily nodded, knowing she hadn't had a full night's sleep in years – the last time she had slept properly was definitely long before she set up the agency – but maybe she could try yoga. She would do anything to ensure that they weren't in this situation ever again.

'Well, thank you so much,' Rob said, shaking her hand.

Rob took Emily in his arms as soon as they were outside the hospital and happiness flooded through her.

'Can you believe it?'

'I really thought we'd lost our little bean.' She pressed herself against his solid chest, still so full of gratitude to get another chance. It was such a relief to have had the first scan and to know that all was okay and everything was growing exactly as it should be.

'Me too. He or she is already keeping us on our toes.' Rob laughed. 'This is only the start of it. Wait until we're sending them off for their first day of school or waiting to pick them up when they go out clubbing. Our worries are only just beginning.'

She laughed. 'I love you, Rob, like *really, really* love you.' It was true; she didn't think she'd ever loved him more than in this moment.

'I love you too.' He bent down and talked to her stomach. 'And you too, little bean, even though you gave us all a heart attack today! I feel I've aged about fifty years.'

She placed her hands on her abdomen. 'Never mind your dad; you're our little miracle. Thank you, little bean, for holding on.'

13

Emily's phone vibrated on her desk and when she saw the number, her heart sank. As it continued to buzz, she thought about letting it go to voicemail but she knew the woman would just persist. From experience, it was easier just to deal with her now so she lifted the phone and pressed the answer button.

'Maeve,' she greeted in a faux-cheery voice. 'What can I do for you?'

'I need you to meet with me to go through the radio ad budget. I'm not happy with a few things.'

'I'm sorry, Maeve, I can't meet you this afternoon. I have an appointment.' The day of their anatomy scan had finally arrived and Emily and Rob had been counting down to it for weeks. They had a calendar hanging on their fridge at home and were crossing off each day with a large X. They had decided to find out the sex – well, Emily had; Rob said he wanted to keep it as a surprise but Emily wanted to be organised so she had managed to persuade him to find out.

She hadn't had any further bleeding or cramping and every-thing seemed to be going the way it was supposed to. The midwives had assured her that everything looked good at her booking appointment until they had taken her blood pressure and told her it was elevated. *Of course it's elevated*, Emily had thought. *I've just had Maeve Murray on the phone demanding fifty things be done before close of business today*, but instead she smiled and said she was trying hard to reduce her stress levels.

The baby kicked loads, especially at night-time when she was lying in bed. That was their special time, she thought, both of them awake together, their shared secret with one another. The fluttery kicks had initially felt as delicate as a fairy dancing on an elastic band but they had grown stronger over the last few days. Sometimes, she would even feel their baby hiccuping, in rhythmic, even beats.

Her pregnancy book was her reading material in bed every night and she loved finding out how the baby was growing and developing. These days, it seemed as if she started every sentence with, 'Did you know...?' The other night, it was, 'Did you know our baby is now growing hair?' she had told Rob. Over the last few weeks, Emily's tummy had pushed forward and she now had the beginnings of a bump. Her jeans and work clothes were getting too tight and the time had arrived for her to wear maternity clothes. She had arranged to go shopping with her mum and Karen the following weekend. Her family had been overjoyed when she had told them the news. It was going to be her mother's first grandchild and she had already started knitting shawls and crocheting tiny cardigans. They had told Rob's family at the same time and the reaction had been overwhelmingly positive, although it had irked Emily when one of Rob's twin brothers had elbowed him in the ribs and said, 'About time.' As if they had purposely been putting off having a family.

'People don't realise they're being insensitive,' Rob had argued when she had mentioned it to him later that evening. That was

Rob all over; he always saw the best in people and never held a grudge. It was one of the qualities she loved most about him.

Rob had suggested they should go look at buggies at the weekend and she had started looking on Pinterest for ideas for their nursery. Emily had longed to be doing all of these things for so long and it was finally her turn. Finally. Now when the tiny buds of excitement began to unfurl inside her, she didn't try to push them away or suppress them like she did before, because she didn't want to get her hopes up, fearing disappointment; instead, she was allowing herself to get excited. This was really happening. They were going to be parents.

'Well, can't you reschedule whatever it is that you think is so important?' Maeve retorted and Emily's first thought was to call the hospital to see if she could change the scan time or push it back by a couple of hours. Then she thought of Rob and what she would say to him. She knew if she called him and explained the situation, although he would be disappointed he would understand, but as the thought played out in her head, she didn't want to reschedule it. She had been looking forward to this appointment for weeks now – in fact, forever if you took into account all the months she had spent yearning to be pregnant. She thought about Rob and their little bean and knew where her priorities lay.

She took a deep breath. 'No,' she said firmly, steeling herself for Maeve's reaction. 'I can't meet you today.'

Emily still hadn't told Maeve that she was pregnant, although she knew Maeve would guess soon enough whenever they met one another next in person. Emily had kept putting it off, hoping that she would have garnered Maeve's trust and proven that trusting E Creative with the bank's marketing budget had been a good move so that when Emily announced her pregnancy and informed her that she would be taking maternity leave, Maeve wouldn't be too perturbed. However, as the weeks went on, Emily

was starting to have her doubts. She was beginning to realise that
Maeve never relaxed, that she was always 'on' and expected
everyone that she interacted with to be the same. Over the last
few weeks, as Emily dealt with one demand after the next from
Maeve, she wondered if the business was even worth it. She
would just get one thing resolved when Maeve would call her
with another problem; it felt as though she was always firefight-
ing. She had tried to involve Cliona, her senior account manager,
more in the dealings with Maeve but the woman had reduced
Cliona to tears the week previous by calling her an imbecile, and
Emily knew it was unfair to ask Cliona to continue working with
her. Maeve was the most demanding client she had ever had; she
liked to throw her weight around and remind Emily of the fact
that the bank was E Creative's biggest client. Emily felt squeezed;
her other clients were falling by the wayside as the team put
more and more effort into satisfying Maeve's demands. They
were starting to get annoyed now too because the team just
didn't have the same time to put into their projects like they had
before.

Maeve liked to call Emily at random times: eleven o'clock at
night just as she was getting into bed or at seven on a Saturday
evening as they were tucking into a takeaway. Rob would raise his
brows as she took the calls. 'Just don't answer her,' he would say as
if it was a perfectly reasonable suggestion but Emily knew Maeve
would just keep calling until she eventually picked up. One night,
Emily had taken a call just as she had been massaging stretch-
mark oil across the taut skin of her bump before she went to bed.
Maeve wanted her to change something in a proposal so she had
gone back downstairs and opened up her laptop and made the
amendments that Maeve had requested and sent it off to her. It
seemed the woman never slept and she didn't want Emily to do so
either. It had been almost 1 a.m. when she had finally climbed into

bed. As she had wearily sunk down into the mattress, she had felt Rob's arm curl around her.

'You need to start saying no to her,' he had mumbled sleepily before falling back asleep again as she had lain there all night, staring at the shadows creeping across the ceiling as darkness changed to dawn. 'You need to start taking it easy,' he would say, or, 'Can't you delegate it?' He would remind her of what the doctor had told them about stress not being good for her or the baby and then she would feel even worse about the situation because the last thing she wanted was to jeopardise the pregnancy.

'I see...' Maeve replied testily. 'So, when can you fit me in then in your busy schedule?' Her tone was laced with sarcasm and Emily fought with the urge to tell Maeve where to stick her contract.

'How about first thing tomorrow?' Emily suggested.

'Fine, but you can come to me. I haven't got time to go across the city.'

'That's no problem at all, Maeve. Thank you for being so understanding,' she replied as sweetly as she could muster. She refused to be dragged into a war of words with Maeve; she was going to kill this woman with kindness.

Emily was proud of herself when she hung up the phone. She had finally done it. How many times had Rob told her that she needed to stand up for herself?

She picked up her phone from her desk and dialled his number.

'You were right.'

'Hang on a minute... has hell frozen over? I'm looking out the window and I'm pretty sure the world hasn't stopped turning and, no, I don't see pigs flying...'

She rolled her eyes. 'Very funny, Rob.'

'Well, it's not every day you tell me I was right about something. I should record this for posterity. In fact, you should put it on my headstone when I die: "Here lies Rob Kavanagh. His wife once told him he was right about something."'

'Hahaha. You're bloody hilarious. You'll never guess what I just did!'

'What?'

'I finally stood up to Maeve like you've been telling me to!' she announced proudly. 'She wanted to meet me this afternoon and when I told her I had an appointment, she asked me to change it, but I refused.'

She heard him clapping in the background. 'About time, I've only been telling you for weeks that you needed to do that, but well done, I'm proud of you.'

'So what time are you picking me up at?'

'I'll be at your office around two. We don't want to be late. I can't wait to see our little bean again.'

'Well, according to my book, our bean is now a banana.'

'Hmm. "I can't wait to see our little banana" doesn't have quite the same effect.'

She laughed.

'I can't believe that today we'll know whether it's a boy or a girl.' She could already imagine Rob playing in the garden with their son or daughter, showing them creepy-crawlies hiding under a rock or soaking them in a water fight. He was going to be a brilliant father. 'I'm so excited.'

'Me too. I'll see you later. I love you, Em.'

* * *

As Emily hurried out of the office, people stopped to ask her questions; she answered them over her shoulder as she made her way to the lift. She wondered if they had noticed her rounded tummy yet. She had been hiding it with loose-fitting blouses and big scarves; she hadn't wanted to tell people in work until they had had the big scan out of the way. She would tell them first thing tomorrow, she decided as she ran out the door, full of excitement. And after she had told the team, she would need to pluck up the courage to tell Maeve too, her brain reminded her grimly.

She saw Rob's car parked outside the building and she hurried over to it.

He greeted her with a kiss as she climbed inside.

'Ready?' he asked.

'Here we go. So what do you think we're having?' she asked as he signalled and pulled out into the traffic.

'My money is on a girl. I just know I'm destined to live my life being bossed around by women.'

She laughed. 'You should be so lucky. I don't know... I have a feeling it's a boy.'

'I bet you a tenner I'm right.'

She laughed at his confidence. 'Well, we'll know soon enough.'

They continued along until they reached the hospital. Rob parked and then they headed inside the yellow brick building. She fished the letter with the appointment details from her bag to find where they were supposed to go.

'It's on the second floor,' she said.

They continued down the corridor towards the lift. She noticed a sign for the Early Pregnancy Unit where, just a few weeks ago, she had been so worried and convinced that their journey was over, but miraculously here they were now, back again and halfway there this time. What a relief it was to be here for a scheduled appointment and not be worrying about the baby. They went inside and pressed the button to take them up. The lift stopped at the next floor and another woman got in. She was heavily pregnant and despite the bitterly cold weather outside,

Emily noticed she was wearing flip-flops because her feet were swollen. This time, seeing other pregnant women didn't sting; in fact, it made her excited. Soon, she would be one of them with a basketball-sized bump sticking out beneath her clothing; maybe she would have puffy feet and ankles too. She hoped so; she wanted to experience it all – the good and the bad, the aches, pains and niggles.

They exited the lift, headed down the corridor leading to the waiting room and took a seat. As Emily looked around her at all the other expectant parents, she felt like she had finally gained membership to an exclusive club. A club she had waited a long time to get access to.

'Emily Kavanagh?' a voice called eventually and they both stood up quickly.

She felt like an excited child on Christmas Eve. She couldn't wait to see their baby again and also to finally find out the gender and see which one of them had guessed right.

'Hello, I'm Helen. I'm the sonographer who will be doing your scan today.' She shook their hands and led them into a room with an ultrasound unit. She lifted Emily's medical chart and flicked through it. 'So, I see you had a bleed earlier on but everything was okay. Any problems since?'

'No, I've been feeling well and growing rapidly.'

'That's what I want to hear. Lie up on the bed there and we'll get started.'

Helen spread the cold gel on her stomach and began running the probe over the gentle curve of her bump.

'Do you want to find out the sex today?' she asked as she began doing her measurements.

'Yes, please,' Emily said keenly.

'Okay, I'll get the things we need to do out of the way first and then we'll get to the fun stuff. Sometimes, babies can be lying in an awkward position which makes it difficult to determine the gender but hopefully he or she will cooperate. How does that sound?'

'Great.' Rob beamed.

Helen concentrated on the measurements she was taking while Emily tried to study the monitor. Soon, she saw the baby moving on the screen and she felt a surge of love. It looked like a proper baby now with arms waving and legs kicking. She couldn't help but smile. *You clever little bean, growing and developing just like you're supposed to*, she thought.

'It's definitely a girl,' Rob said as she watched the screen.

'How can you tell? Can you see something?' Emily peered at the screen, studying it intently, but she couldn't see anything that would indicate the sex.

'No, but I just have a feeling.'

Helen was still silent as she worked away. She seemed to be focusing on one area of their baby; she zoomed in, clicked buttons and dragged lines across to take measurements. Eventually, she turned back to them.

'So, who had money on a boy?' she asked.

'Not me,' Rob sighed.

'Well, then you won because you're having a little baby girl.'

A girl. Every cell within Emily pulsed with joy. A baby girl. She would have a daughter. A little best friend. In that moment, images of girly shopping trips and nail appointments flashed before her. She could see them clapping her on at her school plays or cheering for her from the sidelines at a football match. There would be late-night chats when she came home after a disco and Emily would offer her a shoulder to cry on whenever she had boy trouble. A whole glorious lifetime together, as mother and daughter, spun out before her.

Emily watched Rob's face break into the biggest grin. 'Oh my God, I can't believe I'm going to have a daughter.'

'But you kept saying you knew it was going to be a girl,' Emily laughed.

'Yeah, but hearing it for real... well, it's kind of terrifying,' he said in disbelief. 'Wow.'

'And everything looks okay?' Emily said anxiously to Helen.

'Everything looks perfect. Would you like some scan photos to take home?'

'Yes, please,' Emily cried. For so long, she had peered at their friends' scan pictures as they excitedly pointed out blurry shapes that they said were arms or legs. Finally, *finally* it was her turn to do the same. Rob reached for her hand and she knew he was thinking the same thing as her: how lucky they were.

14

On a snowy day in late January, Emily was in the office. She was sitting at her desk staring out beyond the glass of her office, mesmerised as fluffy white flakes tumbled down in suspenseful fall. The streets were illuminated under the fuzzy orange glow of the street lights. A delicate blanket of snow covered the Dublin rooftops like someone had gently sieved icing sugar along their tops. Everyone else had long gone home. She had come to enjoy the solitude of her office once everyone had left for the evening and she could finally get through her workload without being disturbed. As she neared her due date, instead of winding down like most pregnant women did, Emily had been working later and later into the night, trying to get everything wrapped up, but it felt like one of those whack-a-mole games; whenever she crossed something off her to-do list, something else always popped up elsewhere.

Rob had called her two hours ago wondering when she would be home.

'Come on, Emily, you should be winding down now; you're in

the last trimester. I've made carbonara for us – your favourite. Come home and have dinner with me,' he had begged.

'I just want to get this last thing done and I'll be straight home,' she lied. She knew there was more to be done after that but if she told Rob, he'd start harping on about her needing to be taking it easy. 'I'll heat it up when I get in.'

In the last few weeks, her bump had grown and dropped. She had finally worked herself up to tell Maeve several months back and instead of congratulating her like most people did when a pregnancy was announced, the woman had replied with, 'But you'll still be contactable, of course?' Emily was about to explain that Cliona was very capable and would be looking after everything in her absence, but Maeve had cut across her with questions about the pricing of prime-time slots for their new TV advert.

She circled her stiff neck, trying to ease out the knots, then stood up from her desk. She needed to use the loo; she was running to the bathroom every few minutes these days as her growing baby pressed on her bladder. She used the arms of her chair to lever herself up when she felt a small rush of dampness between her legs. She didn't think much of it; her pelvic floor was under pressure. She continued across the office to go the bathroom when she felt a gush and she knew then it was her waters. As the wetness began to seep down her trouser legs, she felt panicked and scared. She still had five weeks to go until her due date. She wasn't ready yet. She hadn't packed a hospital bag, thinking she'd do it when she finished up work. Her plan had been to take her maternity leave at thirty-eight weeks like most pregnant women did and then she would start to prepare, but she quickly realised that their baby had other ideas.

She lifted her phone on her desk and called Rob.

'Em? You okay?' he answered.

'I... I think my waters have just broken.'

'Oh my God, are you serious? How do you know it's your waters and not... you know... the other thing...'

'Trust me,' she said through gritted teeth as she felt pain seize her abdomen.

'Okay, I'm on my way.'

* * *

Just over twenty minutes later, the lift doors separated and spat out a breathless Rob, carrying a holdall.

'I got here as quick as I could,' he panted as he ran into her office.

Suddenly, she was gripped by a ferocious pain and she reached out to Rob to steady herself.

'Just breathe through it,' he coached, holding her by her shoulders as she bent over. When the pain had eased, Rob unzipped the holdall that he had brought. 'I packed a few things for you... I wasn't sure what to bring.'

She saw her pyjamas and a towel. She spotted a packet of thick maternity pads that she hadn't bought. There were things inside the bag that he couldn't have packed in a hurry. She noticed a tiny white Babygro and hat, there were mittens and tiny socks, infant nappies, and she felt a lump ball in her throat. When had he done this, she wondered. She realised he had clearly researched what to pack a while ago and had had it ready and waiting until the time arrived.

'How did you...?' She had to stop as once again another contraction assaulted her.

He gripped her in his arms until it passed. 'I wanted to be prepared just in case. Turns out I was right. I brought your chart too,' he said. 'I have it downstairs in the car.'

Despite the pain in her body, her heart surged with love for him. She was blessed to have him. He was kind and he took care of her. He was such a good husband and now she knew he would be the best father. 'Thank you,' she mumbled before taking the holdall into the bathroom with her to clean herself up before they headed to the hospital.

'You okay?' he asked, reaching for her hand across the gearstick when they had climbed into the car a short time later. She nodded and looked out the window. Seconds later, she sucked in sharply as she was assailed by another contraction.

'They're getting closer together,' Rob said anxiously. 'There were only three minutes between the last two.'

'I know...' Her knuckles were white as she gripped the dashboard waiting until it passed.

'Breathe through it,' he coached. 'Big inhale now.' She mirrored his breathing, inhaling when he did and exhaling too.

The journey seemed to take forever as Rob tried to guide the car through the snow-covered streets. The roads had been blanketed by white powder and he had to rely on the tracks left behind by other cars to stay on course. The pain was so ferocious and she clenched the dashboard as wave after wave seized her body. It felt as though her body was separating in two but, finally, they reached the hospital. Rob abandoned the car in the set-down area and assisted her inside the hospital. The porter directed them to the delivery ward where they met with a midwife called Margaret who took Emily's chart from Rob.

'You're very close, Emily,' Margaret said after she examined her.

'Can I – get – an epidural?' she managed.

'I'm afraid there's no time. Your baby wants to meet you.'

'But I thought first babies were meant to take their time arriving?' Rob asked in disbelief.

Margaret laughed. 'Usually, they do but I guess this one has other ideas. They like to keep us on our toes.' She turned back to

Emily. 'Now, love, in just a few pushes, she will be here with us,' she coached softly. Emily squeezed her eyes shut as the surges of the contractions overpowered her and, soon, the baby slid out in a warm and slippery mess between her legs. The cord was cut and immediately the baby was taken away by one of the midwives. She felt Rob's fingers entwine with hers.

'Well done,' he whispered. 'I'm so proud of you.' She saw tears glistening in his eyes. The room was deathly quiet and she could hear a soft mewling, not quite a cry but nonetheless joyous.

Eventually, her baby was brought to her.

'Would you like to meet your daughter, Emily?' the doctor said, coming over with their baby in his arms. They had wrapped her in a towelling blanket and placed a pink knitted hat over her head.

'Is she okay?' Rob asked.

'She's a little early but she's breathing well on her own and she's a good weight so we're very happy with her.'

He placed the bundle in Emily's arms and she felt a rush of pure joy as she took her in. Emily stared at their daughter, still disbelieving that she was actually here. Just a few hours ago, she had been sitting in a meeting, pitching to a client and now she was a mother. She couldn't wrap her head around it.

'I'll go get you some tea and toast, Emily. I think you've earned it.' Margaret grinned as she retreated out of the room.

Once they were alone together, Emily took time to study her daughter as if trying to commit every detail to memory. She looked at her perfectly formed body, ten fingers, ten toes, a heart-shaped mouth and tiny snub nose.

'She has the same toes as you,' Rob remarked as he unwrapped the blanket around her feet.

'She does,' Emily agreed.

'What do you think we should call her?' he asked.

Suddenly, Emily was filled with doubt. 'I had a list of names but now that she's here, I don't know if they suit her.'

'Well, how about the Irish name, Alannah,' he suggested. 'It comes from the Irish *a leanbh*, or "child".'

'Oh, Rob, that's perfect for her,' Emily whispered.

'Hello, baby, Alannah,' Rob cooed to their daughter. 'We are your mummy and daddy and we've been waiting for you.'

15

For the next couple of weeks, Rob and Emily existed in a bubble of bliss. They muddled through the fog which a newborn brings, doubting themselves, second-guessing everything but feeling so utterly content with their new way of life. *Do you think she has wind? Did we sterilise that soother? Do you think the temperature of the bathwater is too hot?* Emily had always said if she was lucky enough to get the chance to be a mother, she would try to breastfeed and although she hadn't factored in how demanding and exhausting it would be, it was working out well. She savoured the time she spent feeding Alannah, those moments when it was just her and her daughter alone together.

One time, Rob came in to find her standing over the crib just staring at Alannah as she slept.

'She's amazing, isn't she?' he said, coming over and joining her. She was so grateful that Rob had been in a position to take a month off, a combination of paternity leave and annual leave, to help them find their feet, and the three of them spent their days getting to know one another and figuring all this parenting stuff out.

Having Alannah made them wonder what they had done with their time before. Life was busy, one feed rolled into the next, there were endless nappy changes, winding and bathing. But despite the hard work involved, it was as if they had both been born for this role. Emily genuinely couldn't remember their life without Alannah in it; she tried to recall how they had spent their free time before she was born and found she couldn't. Alannah seemed to have squeezed her way in and taken over both of their hearts. They had waited a long time for this but it had been worth it. Emily loved it all.

One morning, they were sitting in the kitchen bathing in the warm spring sunlight that shone through the glass.

'God, I need this,' she sighed, taking a sip of the coffee Rob had just made for her.

'That was a night and a half,' he said, nodding towards the crib where Alannah was asleep. 'Look at her ladyship sound asleep now; meanwhile, we're going around like two zombies.'

They both peered in at their daughter and smiled.

'The book said babies often have a growth spurt at three weeks. Maybe that was why she was feeding so often?'

'Who knows?' He shrugged. 'Or maybe she's just evil.'

Emily laughed and just then her phone rang on the table beside her. She groaned when she saw Maeve's number flash up yet again and dread poured into the pit of her stomach.

'Who is it?' Rob asked.

'Maeve,' she sighed, bracing herself for his reaction.

'You mean the Wicked Witch of the West,' Rob quipped.

It seemed Maeve Murray could not accept that Emily was on maternity leave. She had called the day Emily had come home from the hospital and Emily had quickly told her that Cliona was covering her work in her absence but Maeve didn't care and continued on ranting about how her competitors were gaining market share and they needed their campaigns to be more visible. She had called her several times since then too. Even though Emily had reminded her on countless occasions that she was on maternity leave, she still insisted on phoning her and Emily had no choice but to answer.

'You're entitled to your maternity leave, Em,' Rob would say, losing patience. 'Just don't answer her calls.'

'But I can't. She'll walk and she's my biggest client. Now that I'm on maternity leave, I need the business more than ever.'

It was almost as if Alannah knew who was on the phone because she suddenly woke up and began to bawl. Emily was torn between answering the call and going to her daughter. She knew Rob could probably handle Alannah for a few minutes but she was due a feed and there was only so long he could keep her amused. She lifted her phone and went into the living room, closing the door behind her.

'Maeve,' Emily began, answering the call.

'I know you're on maternity leave but this is important.' Maeve started every call the same way. 'The sponsorship of Dublin Stadium is up for renewal and I want to pitch for it,' Maeve launched. 'I think it would be a good fit for the bank.'

Emily's heart sank. This was a huge job and something the team hadn't worked on before so she couldn't just delegate it to Cliona. She thought about her hard-working team, trying to hold the fort in her absence and fend off Maeve. She imagined the stress they must be under, especially without her there as a sounding board or to guide them. She had left the office so abruptly when her waters had broken and hadn't had time to do a proper handover. And now Maeve was going to land this on them as well. 'When is the deadline?' Emily asked.

'The tenders are due in next week.'

'Next *week*?' she repeated incredulously. This was the kind of project that they would normally spend months working on. She placed her fingers to her head and massaged her temples. This woman was impossible. 'That's not enough time, Maeve, I'm sorry.'

She heard Alannah's shrieks grow more frantic in the background and she couldn't concentrate on what the woman was saying. Rob started singing to her.

'I think she's hungry,' he mouthed, coming into the room, jiggling her carefully in his arms.

'I won't be long,' she mouthed back as Rob walked around the room with the baby on his shoulder.

'Emily, I've heard it on good authority that Future Bank are tendering for it, so we are too. If they get it ahead of us, my job will be gone and without putting too fine a point on it, so will yours.'

Emily clenched her fingers around the phone. 'Okay, Maeve, leave it with me.' She hung up and ran her hands down along her face.

'I need to go into work for a few hours tomorrow,' she said as she took the baby from Rob, pulled up her top and guided her to latch on. Alannah's crying stopped instantly as she sucked greedily.

Rob looked at her incredulously. 'Are you serious? You're on maternity leave, Em.'

She exhaled heavily. 'Maeve wants us to prepare a tender for the sponsorship of Dublin Stadium and the deadline is next week.'

'Can't Cliona do it?'

She shook her head. 'I need to go through it all with her. Cliona has never done anything like this before. It's not fair to throw her in at the deep end. It's a really big deal.'

'But it's too soon. Alannah is only three weeks old.'

The guilt laced itself around her. She knew he was right. How long had she waited for this? She felt split in two. Desperate to keep the bank as a client and doing her best to be a mother.

'I know but I have no choice if I want to hold on to Maeve Murray's business. I can't drop that on the team as well as everything else they have to contend with while I'm gone. Maeve basically said that if the bank doesn't win the tender then she's pulling the account!'

'That woman is a bully!'

'Look, it'll only be for a few hours, I promise.'

'It won't be though. Maeve will have some other demand. Don't you see? You have to stand up to her!'

Emily bristled. 'Yes, I know, but it's my company, the buck stops with me so I have to do it.'

'But you're on maternity leave!' he repeated, before shaking his head and throwing his hands up into the air. 'It's a legal entitlement!'

'Not when you own your own business!' she snapped. It was easy for him, she thought. He didn't have the same pressures or responsibilities that she had. He didn't have the worry of keeping enough clients coming through their doors to pay everyone their salaries at the end of the month.

'Look, Em, I'm just looking out for you. I don't want you stretching yourself too thinly. You need to recover,' Rob pleaded. 'Alannah is still tiny. We won't get this time back again. Can't you do it from home even?'

'These things are better done face to face. I need to meet with Cliona and go through everything. I want to get her feedback on where she feels we should pitch and come up with a plan. This is all new to me too.'

Rob shook his head in a way that said he was disappointed in her.

'Look, I promise,' she said, her tone softer now. 'Just let me get this tender sent off and then that will be the end of it. The team will be able to deal with the rest of it.'

'And how will I feed her while you're gone?'

'I'll pump extra today. Please, don't make me feel even worse about it all, Rob.'

He walked over and kissed her on top of her head. 'I'm sorry. I'm worried about you, Em. You can't do it all. You can't breastfeed a newborn, recover from birth and try to work too. That's too many plates in the air; you're not Superwoman.'

'I won't be long, just a couple of hours should do it and once I've done that, I promise, that'll be it...'

16

The drone of the milk pump felt like it was going through Emily's brain and she had to battle to stave off the tiredness. Rob had gone to bed early with Alannah, while Emily had stayed up late pumping so that he would have enough milk to feed her while she was gone into the office the following day. When she finally had an adequate amount pumped, she put it in the fridge, then climbed into bed beside Rob, who was snoring softly. It felt like she had only just closed her eyes when she heard Alannah cry beside her, looking for her feed. She sat up, turned on her bedside lamp and lifted her mewling daughter out of her Moses basket. Alannah latched on greedily. As Emily looked at her feeding under the lamplight, she guzzled contentedly, her eyes closed as her tiny fingers wrapped around Emily's index finger. Even though Emily was exhausted, these were the moments she treasured when it was just her and her daughter, the house was quiet, life was calm; this was their special time together. She placed a kiss on her delicate covering of silky hair.

She rose the next morning as Rob and Alannah slept on. She tiptoed around the room, trying to find something to wear. Something that would accommodate her still-swollen shape, but that looked respectable enough for work. None of her clothes fit, which she knew was normal at only three weeks post-partum, but the maternity trousers were now too big so she felt in limbo. She eventually settled on a loose-fitting jersey dress which she hoped looked somewhat decent. She didn't delay to have breakfast; she wanted to get into the office and home again as quickly as she could.

'Emily!' Paulina exclaimed when she appeared in reception. 'Back so soon?'

'Just for today,' she explained. 'I need to go through something with Cliona.'

She went into her office which was like a flashback to the evening she had gone into labour. A dirty keep cup still sat beside her computer and the untidy paperwork that littered her desk was exactly as she had left it.

'Emily!' Cliona cried when she saw her. 'I know you shouldn't be here but I don't think I've ever been so relieved to see you.' She sank down into the chair opposite her.

'I couldn't let you do it on your own.'

'Maeve is a complete tyrant. I'm starting to think that she isn't human. She just does not stop. I've told her countless times that you're on maternity leave but she doesn't seem to get it. She never stops working. I've done my best to get the tender prepared by myself but there's still so much to do. We've to supply accounts and plans and images of the proposed branding. We've to prepare a document to show what Irish Alliance Bank can offer the stadium and why they would be the best partnership over other brands. It's a blind tender too so we've no idea who the other bidders are or how much they're offering...' She tossed her hands up into the air in exasperation. 'Maeve keeps saying that she doesn't want to pay over the odds but she also is insisting that we have to win which is *very* helpful,' she quipped sardonically. 'I've had to pull the whole team off their other projects to concentrate on this.'

'Well, look, let's make a start on it. I promised Rob I wouldn't be long; feeding time rolls around very quickly.'

'I remember those days,' Cliona said with a laugh. 'Right,' she said, opening up her laptop, efficient as always. 'Here's what I've done so far. I've made a few calls and word on the street is that Future Bank have gone in high so we probably need to be at that level too if we want to win it.'

The two of them strategised and worked on the wording for the pitch that emphasised what a partnership with Irish Alliance Bank could provide for the stadium. They ordered lunch in and continued working through the pitch and it wasn't until Emily raised her head that she noticed the sky had changed to inky blue beyond her office glass and she realised she had been there all day. She checked her watch in a panic. 'Oh God, I didn't realise it was so late. I'd better get home. I need to feed Alannah.'

'You go,' Cliona encouraged. 'I can handle it from here.'

Emily had just closed down her laptop when her phone rang. She saw it was Rob. She answered it and held it between her shoulder and ear as she continued packing up her belongings. She could hear her daughter's angry screams in the background and she felt her breasts become uncomfortably full with milk in response.

'Will you be home soon?' Rob said, sounding stressed. 'She's roaring here. I've no milk left.'

'I'm on my way,' she said. 'I'm so sorry, I lost track of time. There's another bag in the freezer. You can defrost it in a jug of warm water.' She hated herself. She should have been there to feed her daughter herself. Well, tomorrow would be different, she told herself; she was confident that Cliona knew what she was doing now and she could stop worrying because the project was in safe hands. 'I got loads done, though.'

But Rob had hung up before she had even finished.

* * *

Emily arrived home to find the house cloaked in silence. On the drive home from the office, she had been mentally steeling herself for dealing with a fractious baby and possibly a grumpy Rob so it was a pleasant surprise to hear everything sounded relatively calm.

'Rob?' she called out gently as she came down the hall, but there was no reply.

She continued into the living room and found the pair of them. Rob had dozed off on the sofa with Alannah cradled in his arms. The beauty of the two of them stopped her in her tracks; her heart swelled looking at the two people she loved most in the world. These were the moments she had once dreamed about. She shrugged off her coat and kicked off her shoes, then she gingerly lifted Alannah from his grasp, doing her best not to wake the child. She immediately felt the milk prickle in her breasts as it rushed in furiously. She brought her upstairs and changed her nappy, then she latched her on, thankful at last to be relieving them. She breathed in her milky scent and let her nose nuzzle into the impossibly soft skin in the folds of her neck. Her precious daughter.

'I'll be a better mum, tomorrow, I promise,' she whispered before putting her to sleep in her crib beside her bed when she had finished feeding. She stood staring at her daughter asleep on her back with her two hands poised at either side of her head like a champion weightlifter.

She knew it wouldn't be long before she woke again so she decided to try and get a head start by having an early night. She changed into her pyjamas, thankful for their comfort and forgiving waistband. She returned downstairs to Rob. She tried to rouse him to tell him to come up to bed with her, but he didn't wake. She knew he was exhausted after the day. She felt bad for how she had been with him earlier; he was only looking out for her. She took one of the throws off the back of the sofa and covered him with it, then she climbed upstairs and sank into her mattress, her lids closing before she had even hit the pillow.

17

When Emily woke next, someone was shouting at her. They were shoving against her shoulder and roughly tugging on her arm. She tried shrugging them off but they were insistent.

'Emily! Emily, wake up. You have to wake up!' a frantic voice was demanding.

It felt as though she had only just gone to sleep and she knew it was probably time to feed Alannah again. The cycle of feeding came around so fast.

She peeled her eyes open and saw Rob standing over her. There was something strange about his face; she couldn't work it out. Was he angry? But no, it wasn't anger... she realised with sudden clarity that he looked terrified.

She sat up in the bed. 'What is it? What's wrong?' she asked, rubbing her bleary eyes, willing herself to wake up. Her brain was tired and slow and felt as though treacle had been poured between the cells; everything felt fudgy.

But he wasn't looking at her. He had Alannah in his arms and he was bent over her.

'Call an ambulance!' he roared at her in a tone she had never heard him use before. Suddenly, she came to and jumped out of bed and rushed over to him. A sickly feeling spread down along her body.

'What is it? What's wrong?' she asked, hearing the panic lacing her words.

She saw then that Rob's mouth was covering their daughter's tiny face.

'What are you doing?' she shouted. 'Why are you doing that?' She was trying to make sense of the scene before her but found she couldn't.

'I said call the ambulance, now, Emily!' he screamed, panic rising from him like a bad odour. 'Stop wasting time!'

It was only when he moved his head back from in front of their baby's face to shout at her that she could see that Alannah looked funny. The skin around her mouth had a blue tinge to it and she looked floppy, almost like a doll. Then she realised with a jolt that Rob was administering CPR. He was trying to push air from his body into her tiny lungs. Why would he be doing that? Her brain tried to understand what was going on but her thoughts felt congealed and mushy like she was wading through concrete. So many reasons and explanations swirled around her brain until finally it landed on the right one. 'Oh my God, Alannah isn't breathing.' Bile forced its way up along her throat, spilling its acidic taste into her mouth. She scrambled for her phone, her fingers clumsily trying to hit the right buttons. *Dear God, no*, she thought. *No. No. No.*

Was this real, she wondered as she watched him doing his best to breathe life into their daughter. Was this really happening? *No, her brain told her, this is just a dream, an awful, awful dream and you're going to wake up now any minute and everything is going to be okay. Your baby will be sleeping soundly in her crib and you'll sigh with relief, then turn over and go back to sleep.*

'Please, baby girl,' Rob begged, 'please wake up.'

Eventually, she heard an operator speaking on the other end. 'Emergency services, what is your emergency?' The room began to spin around her and it felt as though he was talking to her through cotton wool; his voice was soft and spongy and everything sounded muffled.

'It's my daughter – she's three weeks old – she's not breathing.' She heard herself choke on the words.

'Can you give me your Eircode, please, madam?'

Her mind had suddenly gone blank. Like a hard drive that had been wiped clean, everything she knew, the mundane facts she used to navigate her daily life, seemed to have vanished.

'I-I can't remember... it's Groveton Road.'

'43,' she heard Rob shout.

'43 Groveton Road,' she repeated before the phone fell from her hands.

Later, when Emily thought back on this time, she could remember blue lights strobing around in the darkness. She remembered opening the front door to the two paramedics, one male and one female, and pointing numbly towards the stairs. She recalled them running past her, hurrying up the steps, taking them two at a time, to find Rob and Alannah. She could remember following after them and shivering uncontrollably as she watched them on the periphery as they worked on her daughter. She remembered Rob standing beside her, holding her up. She recalled the paramedics trying different things and yet their daughter never made a sound. Time seemed to take on an ethereal quality and she didn't know how long they were working on her for. It felt like a lifetime and yet it wasn't long enough.

Eventually, she noticed them nod to one another, before they both stood up and turned to face them, gazes lowered. She watched the male paramedic swallow down a lump in his throat before speaking. He had a soft, round face and warm hazel eyes.

'I'm so sorry. She's gone.' His shoulders sagged down in defeat. 'We did everything we could, I promise you.'

Emily tried to pull air into her lungs in great, heaving gasps but it was like the oxygen had been sucked out of the room. It felt as though she was sinking into the floor. She could see these people and hear their awful words but it felt as though she was far away from them. She heard someone shriek and it took her a moment to realise that the sound was coming from her. Her voice sounded stretched, like an elastic band just before it snapped.

'No!' Rob cried, shaking his head. 'Try something else... You have to...' he begged. He sounded so far away from her; she wanted to reach out to touch him. She needed to feel him to know if this was real or if she was caught in the midst of some awful nightmare, but her hands wouldn't work.

'I'm so, so sorry,' the paramedic said and she noticed that he had tears in his eyes too. She guessed he was probably a father himself.

'You have to try something else!' Rob roared and the desperation in his voice broke her.

Emily turned to the female paramedic then. 'You have to do something!' she pleaded with her, woman to woman. '*Please*, just do something.'

'It's too late,' the woman explained softly. She guided Emily down onto the bed and placed a blanket over her while Rob kept pacing around their bedroom wailing 'No' over and over again before eventually collapsing onto the floor at the foot of the bed.

'Do something!' Emily shrieked then at the man who wasn't listening to her. 'Just do something!' She broke into breathless sobs.

But he didn't do anything; instead, he stood there, head bowed, and said, 'I'm so very sorry.'

18

Alannah was buried on a bitterly cold, blue-sky February morning. The low white winter sunlight blinded Emily and Rob as they gathered in the churchyard of St Francis'. They had deliberately kept the funeral small, restricting it to just their families and a few close friends, feeling unable to deal with a large crowd.

The hours after the paramedics had arrived were hazy and surreal. After they had given them time with their daughter, they had gently explained that Alannah needed to be brought to the hospital for a post-mortem. That it was standard procedure. Emily and Rob had been allowed to accompany their baby girl's tiny body in the ambulance and they had sat holding her in the back, both stunned and numb as they journeyed towards the hospital. When the time came for Alannah to be taken away, Emily had clutched her baby close, not wanting to let her go with these strangers to lie in a cold hospital morgue, but Rob had gently prised Alannah from her arms and said, 'You have to let her go, love. They need to find out what happened.'

Emily had softened her grip then and handed her baby over. 'Make sure you keep her warm, I don't want her getting cold...' she had warned them as they took her away. 'Make sure you put her blanket on her. And her hat! Don't forget her hat! I don't want her to get cold,' she repeated.

They had nodded sadly at her as Rob had put his arm around her and guided her back down onto a chair. A kindly nurse had given her medication to take to dry up her milk supply and some tablets for both of them to help them sleep and then they had gone home back to the house in Groveton Road. Emily had gone up the stairs, noticing mucky boot prints on the biscuit-coloured carpet that she guessed were left behind by the paramedics. She had returned to their bedroom, needing to see for herself; she needed the evidence that this had really happened. It felt as though they were suspended in some awful dream and she was going to wake up at any minute. She entered the room and it looked like it did every other morning. The bed was unmade, the duvet roughly pulled back. The Moses basket still stood at their bedside like they had only just gone downstairs for breakfast. She walked across to the crib, feeling hope hold her heart in a vice grip but it crushed her fully to see there was no baby inside.

The next few days went by in a blur as whispered words of disbelief filtered out to their families and friends about what had happened. People gathered in their house in nearly as much shock as they were that a baby could be taken away as quickly as it had arrived. People stood around uselessly in their kitchen or their living room, muttering condolences, making pots of tea, while others wrung their hands, at a loss for something to say. As they hugged her and told her how sorry they were, it still hadn't hit Emily yet; *she's in the hospital now, she'll be home when she's better*, her brain told her. She couldn't fathom any of it. Why were they all here? What had happened or why? It felt as though she had been put on board a bus and everyone else seemed to know the destination but she wasn't sure where she was going or even why she was on the bus. Rob wasn't faring much better. He moved around the house in a daze. Every now and then, she would catch him staring at Alannah's crib and shaking his head as if he couldn't understand what had happened. As they had been dressing earlier to come to the funeral, she had walked in to find him punching their bathroom wall.

They made their way up the steps to enter the church and Emily noticed that Rob was wearing black trousers with a navy jacket. She wondered if he realised that they didn't match. Perhaps he had, but just didn't care. Under normal circumstances, she would have pointed it out to him but there was nothing normal about burying your child.

As Rob hoisted the tiny white coffin onto his shoulder, Emily felt her knees buckle beneath her. She followed after him as they entered the church beneath a Gothic archway. She recognised the familiar chords of Bach's 'Air on the G String'; they had had a quartet play it at their wedding ceremony in this very same church. As the cello reached a crescendo, tears came hard and fast, streaming down her face as she thought about the happier times they had had here. The agony of it all smacked her again and again and again.

Rob placed the coffin down before the altar, then he guided her into a hard timber pew behind it as the priest began the Mass. Light filtered in through the stained-glass windows and was scattered around the church in a kaleidoscope of colours. Her mind drifted off as the priest spoke. She thought about all the sacraments they should be celebrating with Alannah in this church: a christening that would never happen, a communion and confirmation too and maybe even a wedding day if their daughter would have wanted that. A whole future that they would never get to discover.

She was startled back to the present when she heard her name being called. She looked up at the priest who was giving his sermon. 'Emily and Rob, on your darkest days, you might question our Lord and ask why He has taken her to His kingdom so soon. It says in Ecclesiastes that there is a time for everything: a time to be born and a time to die. For some people, that time is a long life, lived through many decades, and then for others like Alannah, that time seems too short. Baby Alannah has been called forth and I say to you, we must trust in our Saviour's plan. Our Lord has a purpose for Alannah and we should take comfort that she rests in the arms of Jesus.'

Emily wanted to scream at him. What kind of a God would give them a baby only for it to be taken away again just a few short weeks later? What purpose could that possibly serve?

It wasn't long before the Mass came to an end and the scent of incense overpowered her nostrils as it wafted from the swinging thurible. Then Rob lifted the coffin once again and they walked back down the aisle. They stepped outside under an azure-blue sky, zigzagged with vapour trails, and traversed the churchyard towards the adjacent cemetery. Birds hopped along at their feet, scouring the rock-hard earth for something to snack on. Crops of snowdrops bravely poked their heads through the frost-tipped earth. A solitary magpie mocked them from a nearby oak tree. Soon, they reached the plot where Alannah was to be laid to rest and the sight of the gaping hole in the ground took her breath away. As the tiny white coffin was lowered down into the soil, it occurred to her that instead of laying their daughter to sleep in a crib like most parents of newly born babies, they were laying her in the cold, hard ground instead.

They went home to the house on Groveton Road and every-thing seemed different. The navy-blue hue in their hallway felt darker, more oppressive. Emily shivered; the house felt cold even though the heating was on. They hadn't invited anyone back;

they just seemed to appear and her mother and Karen set to making tea and sandwiches for everyone. *When in crisis, make tea,* Emily thought bitterly. Karen's husband Dave found chairs for people and refilled their mugs when their tea had cooled. People tried to creep around her but she became irritated watching them opening the wrong cupboards for mugs and searching for teabags in her cutlery drawer. Emily longed for everyone to go home and leave them alone. She wanted to go to bed and never wake up.

'Emily.' Her aunt Brenda came over and pulled her into a hug. She was a tall, slim woman with high cheekbones and closely cropped grey hair. Brenda was her father's sister and they didn't see much of her since her father had left them. Usually, it was just at funerals. It was an unwritten rule that they never spoke about her dad. Emily had wondered if he ever asked Brenda about what they were doing in their lives. Did he know that her baby – his granddaughter – had died? 'I'm so sorry for your loss,' she began.

'Thank you for coming, Brenda,' she mumbled; it had become her stock response today.

'I know it's tough right now for you, love, but everything happens for a reason. Maybe it was for the best.'

Emily was bewildered. What silver lining could possibly be gleaned from this?

'Well, perhaps there was something wrong with her... It was better the Lord took her now. Imagine if this had happened a year down the line; how would it be then? It would be much worse if she'd lived for longer and then you had to say goodbye.'

Emily stared at her blankly. 'I-I loved her. My daughter existed. The short time that she was with us for mattered. I didn't love her any less than a mother who gets longer with their child.'

Brenda tilted her head to the side. 'Oh, Emily, love, don't take me up wrong, that wasn't what I meant, but it would have been so much harder to lose her later in life when you'd bonded with her and got a chance to know her personality.'

Emily blinked in disbelief. Was she really dismissing her love for her daughter so callously?

'You mightn't see it like this right now but when you have more children, you will understand,' Brenda continued knowingly. She reached for Emily's hand and squeezed it inside her own. Then she released her and continued over to talk to another relative.

Emily pinched her eyes shut, willing herself not to cry.

'How are you doing?' Her mother came up alongside her with tears brimming in her eyes. Emily knew this was tough on Patricia too. She had buried her first and long-awaited grandchild today. She should have been proudly pushing a pram down the main street or showing off her darling granddaughter to the ladies in the golf club. She should have been buying her adorable frilly dresses with matching knickers because she had seen them in a shop window and couldn't resist, or spoiling her with sweets when she got a bit older.

'It just doesn't seem real...'

'I still can't believe it either,' Patricia said, shaking her head as if trying to order her thoughts. Her eyes landed on two of Emily's cousins across the room who were getting stuck into a bottle of wine. Patricia raised her brows in their direction. 'Do you want me to get rid of everyone?'

Emily nodded. She didn't think she could stand up for much longer. 'I'm so tired, Mum...'

'Oh, lovey...' Emily heard the crack of emotion in her voice. 'A mother's love runs deep and until you're a mother, nobody can understand just how vast that chasm of love is. I wish I could do something or say something to take the pain away but I can't.' Patricia pulled her into a hug and Emily allowed herself to be held in her mother's arms like she was five years old again and her mother was comforting her because she had fallen off her bike and not because today was the day she had buried her infant daughter.

As Patricia and Karen began cleaning up around their guests, people finally seemed to get the hint and began to gather up their belongings to leave.

'You get some sleep now, okay?' Patricia ordered as soon as the last person had gone. 'I'll be over in the morning.' She hugged Emily once more.

'I love you, Em,' Karen said with tears brimming in her eyes as she squeezed her older sister before she, Dave and her mother made their way to the front door.

Emily sagged on the sofa with relief as soon as everyone had gone. She was exhausted, right down to the marrow of her bones. The effort it had taken to get through the day had taken every ounce of her fortitude. To watch her husband carrying that tiny white coffin into the church, to see sticky brown clay being heaped on top of it, were images she'd never be able to scrape off her mind. Then when they had got home, she had had to put on a brave face for all their relatives. Everyone had remarked on how strong she was and how well she was doing. They believed it was a compliment, almost looking relieved that she seemed to be holding it together and they were spared witnessing grief in its rawest and most brutal form, even though on the inside she was crumbling. Now that they were finally alone, she could fall apart if she wanted to.

Rob flopped down beside her. The blazer he had been wearing at the church earlier had been long discarded and his crumpled shirt had been unbuttoned at the neck.

'That was horrendous. How are you doing?' he asked.

'I keep waiting for you to wake me up and tell me it was a nightmare.' It was like the aftermath of a crash; they had been thrown around in the wreckage and both were still caught up in the shock, unsure of what had just happened.

'It doesn't feel real,' he agreed.

'My auntie Brenda actually said it was just as well we hadn't bonded because that would be harder. But I loved her, Rob,' she choked. 'I loved her so much.' She had had a whole future planned out for Alannah as soon as she had seen that second line on the test. She imagined Alannah gripping her hand on her first day of school; would she have sprinted confidently through the door to the classroom, keen for her parents to leave, or would she have hung back, clinging to Emily's hand for reassurance, perhaps taking a little longer to settle? Would Alannah have been sporty or maybe she would have preferred to dance? Would she have enjoyed putting on shows for her parents like Emily had done as a child or maybe she would have spent hours building Lego like Rob had? There were so many things about their daughter's future that she had been looking forward to discovering and now she would never get to find out.

Rob reached out and pulled her against him and she dissolved against the solidity of his chest. He held her close and rocked her. 'I know you did, love.'

'Why did this happen to us? I keep going over it all. What did we do wrong? I fed her that night, then I put her in her crib. She was definitely lying on her back. Her feet were at the end of the crib, the way we always put her. I don't think the room was too hot or cold... Do you think I didn't refrigerate the milk properly? Or maybe the bag got contaminated in the freezer somehow or it didn't defrost properly... Do you think it could be that?' She struggled to get the words out between her great, heaving sobs. 'I did everything that it said in my book. I swear.' But the one thing that kept haunting her was that she had gone to work. *If you had stayed at home that day, would this have happened?* a voice in her head asked. 'I'm sorry, Rob.' Her nose was dripping and she wiped it with the back of her hand. 'I knew it was too good to be true; I knew this happiness couldn't last.' She shook her head at the injustice of it all, feeling the weight of his desperation sitting so heavily on top of her own. It was pushing her down, suppressing her so heavily that she felt as though she was sinking through the floor.

'Hey,' he said sternly, holding her at arm's length and turning her towards him so she was forced to face him. 'I don't want your apology. This isn't your fault. Or my fault. I don't know why this has happened to us but we were just really, really unlucky.'

But it was her fault. She knew it was.

19

In the days that followed Alannah's funeral, it was like slowly coming to in the aftermath of a bomb explosion. Life as they had known it had been obliterated; a thick layer of debris had descended upon the house, piles of rubble obscured Emily's view of the outside word and everything seemed hazy and dark. Grief infiltrated every orifice and creeped beneath every door; it choked them both until they couldn't breathe. Alannah's loss affected every part of them.

Emily spent most of her time sleeping or, if she wasn't asleep, she would wander around the house in a daze. She would creep into the nursery with its timber sleigh cot, the soft grey elephant decals running along the wall, the rocking chair in the corner never sat on, all taunting her. Although Alannah hadn't slept in this room yet, it stung to know that she never would. She would pick up one of the teddies from the shelf or she would open the wardrobe of tiny outfits and lift out a corduroy dress or a sleepsuit and hold it close to her. She would sink down onto the woollen carpet, feeling grief break her over and over again.

She and Rob co-existed in the house like flatmates working

different shifts and schedules. They rarely spoke; it was as if there was nothing left to say to one another. They were each too broken. They avoided one another as best they could and whenever they did happen to meet on the way to the bathroom or in the kitchen when she came downstairs to make a mug of tea or maybe a slice of toast, they kept their heads down and avoided one another's gaze. Emily knew if she saw the raw pain in Rob's eyes, it would be her undoing, so instead they moved past each other like haunted shadows.

Just the day before, she had walked into the kitchen to find him standing there, looking out towards the garden. He had his back to her and he didn't hear her come in. As she got closer, she noticed that he had his head cupped in his hands and was holding the buttery-yellow fabric of one of Alannah's Babygros up to his face. His shoulders were heaving up and down and it had jolted her to realise that he was crying. The part of her that loved this man and cared for him so deeply knew she should reach out to comfort him but it was like she was cloaked in a fog. She just wasn't able to help him. Her own grief was too heavy and she couldn't bear to see his so raw and exposed so she had turned around and walked out of the room.

Her mother and Karen were doing their best to help her through it. They would call over to sit with her and try to talk to her but she had nothing to say to them. What could anyone say in the face of what they had been through? It was like the lights had been turned off, everything existed in shades of grey. She felt like an observer watching through a haze and she couldn't connect with the real world. She knew they were grieving too; her mother had lost her grandchild and Karen her niece, but they could never really understand the depths of her loss. She didn't answer the doorbell when it rang. She didn't answer her phone, she had diverted her work phone to the office and had no idea what was happening with the agency and found she didn't even care.

One morning, Emily was woken by a blaring noise. She opened her eyes, rolled over in bed and automatically reached for Rob like she had been doing every day for years. She found the space empty beside her and the sheets cool to the touch. Then she remembered what had happened with awful, crushing realisation as she did now whenever she opened her eyes. Morning after morning, the remembering broke her. She went to sleep praying she wouldn't wake up and yet reality always snuck up and slapped her across the face. She realised the noise was coming from her phone which was ringing on the bedside table beside her. On autopilot, she fumbled to answer it.

'Mrs Kavanagh? It's Dr Weston, I'm a paediatrician at the Dublin Children's Hospital.'

'Oh, hello,' Emily said blankly. The light had been sucked from their world and yet Emily was stunned to find that life around them continued on like nothing had happened. People made phone calls. They went to work. It seemed surreal.

'I am calling to let you know that we have the preliminary post-mortem results available for your daughter,' he began delicately. 'We were unable to ascertain a cause of death so in cases such as these, it will be recorded as Sudden Infant Death Syndrome.'

'Sorry?' Emily said, struggling to keep up.

'It's a term used for when a previously healthy baby with no underlying conditions less than a year old passes away suddenly and no cause of death can be found,' Doctor Weston explained carefully, measuring and saving his words, as if they were bullets he was trying to load into the correct cartridge. 'In the past, we referred to it as "cot death" but Sudden Infant Death Syndrome or SIDS for short can happen anywhere, not just in a cot, which is why the term is outdated. Although the incidences of SIDS have declined in recent years, it is still one of the leading causes of death in babies aged from four to twelve months.'

'Why did it happen to my baby?' Emily demanded. She wanted a reason. She wanted him to give her something to pin the blame on to. She needed something she could rage at and be angry about because the injustice of it was killing her. Why them? Why their baby? She didn't wish this pain on anyone but it was so hard; they had wanted a baby for so long and then, finally, their dreams had come true when the much-longed-for second line had appeared on the pregnancy test, and then this had happened. Everyone else seemed to produce healthy children with ease; what was wrong with her?

'We don't know exactly why SIDS happens but I can assure you that this isn't something you did or didn't do. Unfortunately, there is no way to predict or prevent these deaths.'

'I went to work,' Emily blurted. 'My baby was only three weeks old and I went to work.'

The doctor cleared his throat and Emily knew he was judging her. He blamed her, she knew he did.

'I can assure you that that isn't why this happened. I'm so sorry, Mrs Kavanagh. We should have the full post-mortem report available in a few months. Once again, on behalf of myself and all the staff here at Dublin Children's Hospital, please accept my sincere condolences to you and your husband.'

Emily got out of bed and passed the crib that sat there empty as if waiting on their baby to return. She crept downstairs. As she passed the open living room door, she could see him lying on the sofa under one of the throws. Lately, she was spending the day in bed, while he had taken up residence in the living room and, for the last few nights, he had been sleeping there too. The curtains were drawn and he was surrounded by dirty plates and mugs.

She continued on into the kitchen, flicked the switch on the kettle and waited as it grumbled to life. She noticed bouquets of flowers sent by well-meaning friends sat decaying in the cellophane wrappers they had arrived in. She hadn't bothered to find vases for them. A pile of condolence cards sat on the marble countertop beside the cooker, still unopened. She looked out at the frost-tipped grass and an image of Alannah shivering in the cold, hard earth assailed her. She had to shake her head to rid herself of it.

She heard steps following into the kitchen after her and she turned around to see Rob standing there behind her. He was dressed in the same grubby hoody and tracksuit bottoms that he been wearing for days now. His hair was wild and tousled and he needed to shave.

'Dr Weston called,' she began. 'The post-mortem found no cause of death so they're blaming it on SIDS.'

Rob looked at her blankly. Up close, she noticed his eyes were red-rimmed and puffy. 'Isn't that cot death?'

'They don't use that term any more.'

He sighed heavily and ran his hands down along his face. 'But I thought that didn't happen these days now that babies sleep on their backs.'

'Clearly not,' she barked.

'I see,' he said as he tried to process this information. 'I don't know whether I should feel relieved or not. Like at least it was nothing we did wrong... but then, why did it happen to us?' he said bitterly.

She ignored him and reached up to take a mug down from one of the overhead cupboards. She couldn't bear to be near him and see his raw pain up close; she had enough of her own to contend with.

'So how are you doing?' he mumbled after a moment.

She turned around and narrowed her eyes at him. 'How am I?'

she repeated sardonically. She hated herself for treating him this way but she couldn't help it. He took her anger on the chin without retaliating and she knew he didn't deserve it but in the days since the funeral, she had felt untamed fury creeping up inside her. She hadn't been prepared for the tidal wave of anger that had risen up unbidden, like a dancing cobra, ready to lunge and bite. She was furious with everyone and everything. The anger was growing unleashed and wild and threatened to consume her with its sheer force. Its ferocity frightened her.

'I was thinking, maybe we should go for a walk,' he continued ignoring her barbed retort. 'I don't know about you but I could use some fresh air... Maybe we could... eh... visit the grave.'

'How is a walk going to help?' she snapped. She loathed herself for how she was treating him but she wanted to hurt him; she wanted to lash out at him and open a fresh wound in him. She wanted to unleash some of the pain that was burning inside her and inflict it on to him. Any other man would have told her to get lost but not Rob.

'Why are you being like this, Em? This isn't my fault; I'm grieving too.'

She knew he was right; he was a good person and he was suffering just like she was.

He was feeling pain and grief too but every time she looked at him, the magnitude of their loss was cemented and it was unbearable. She pushed past him without making the tea and returned upstairs alone.

20

Emily was upstairs in her bedroom when she heard her mother call out her usual refrain as she let herself into the house. 'It's only me, love.'

Her mother called over most days armed with that evening's dinner. She had been dropping over meals ever since the funeral. It was usually a lasagne, or shepherd's pie was another favourite of hers. 'I'll just leave it in the fridge,' Patricia would say as she filled the kettle and made a pot of tea. It was beginning to annoy Emily because it was only Rob who was eating the food. Emily didn't feel hunger any more; it was another one of the feelings that seemed to have died with Alannah. Whenever her body did require sustenance, usually a piece of toast was all she could stomach. Her mother had the same routine every day whereby she would sit at her bedside with a mug of tea, trying to get her to talk. Sometimes, she brought some home-made goodies too, scones or flapjacks or brownies, but they would stay there on the plate untouched and Emily would just drink the tea for its warmth.

She found her fleecy dressing gown, wrapped it around herself and went downstairs. She shivered as she entered the kitchen.

Even though she had her dressing gown wrapped tightly around her, she was cold all the time now.

'Sorry, love, I hope I didn't wake you,' Patricia apologised when Emily appeared in the kitchen. 'I've left a pasta bake in the fridge for you.'

'Thanks,' Emily mumbled and slumped into a chair at the table.

'Mary Mannion gave me this card for you.' Patricia produced a white envelope from her handbag. 'I think it's a Mass card,' she continued. 'It's nice to know people are thinking of you and praying for you.'

Emily rolled her eyes. 'If you believe in all of that...'

'I'll put it with the rest of them.' She ignored Emily's prickly reply and placed it in the pile with the rest of the unopened condolence cards.

'We got the preliminary results of the post-mortem,' Emily said blankly. She was still trying to get her head around it all. She had thought that being given an explanation for why their daughter had died would have given her answers, a reason or something to blame, but instead it just threw up more questions: why did it happen to them? Why her baby?

Patricia's face crumpled. 'Oh, love... what did they say?'

'They're putting it down to SIDS – or cot death.'

Patricia was shocked. 'I haven't heard of that in years! I thought that stopped when babies began sleeping on their backs.'

'It still happens.'

'Oh, darling, I'm so sorry. It all seems so unfair, especially when you did everything right.'

Emily shook her head in protest. 'It's all my fault.'

'How on earth can it be your fault? It's one of those awful things; nobody knows why it happens but you're certainly not to blame, Emily!' Patricia was horrified by her daughter's reasoning.

'But if I hadn't gone to work that day, she might not have died.'

'Now, love, you listen to me,' Patricia said sternly. 'This isn't your fault. Sometimes, horrible things happen and there is no explanation or reasoning.' Patricia paused. 'I went to the grave earlier,' she continued, her tone softening. 'I brought up some flowers. You should go, Emily; it helps.'

Emily shook her head. Her eyes fell on the pram that hadn't moved since the day before Alannah died.

Patricia followed her gaze. 'I can give you a hand if you want, y'know... to clear out the baby clothes and all the equipment...' she offered. 'It must be so hard looking at it all day, every day. Karen and I could do it together; you wouldn't have to do anything...'

Sometimes, Emily would go and sit in the feeding chair and let it gently rock her. She would look around the nursery feeling a sharp sting as she thought back to how excited and presumptuous they had once been when they had been decorating this room. Her and Rob with brushes in hand as they painted the wall a soft grey, laughing because her large bump kept getting in the way as they worked and smudging the paint. She would remember how Alannah would lie on her changing table looking up at the mobile that hung above, her eyes just starting to focus on its colours as she pumped her little legs. It was Alannah's room. She felt close to her there.

'I don't want anyone to touch anything!'

'Okay, love, there's no rush,' Patricia soothed. 'Whenever you're ready.'

Despite everything, Emily knew this was hard on her mother too; she was doing her best to be strong for Emily but there was no masking the pain in her eyes.

They both fell quiet for a few moments, each ruminating over their own thoughts, before Patricia spoke again. 'I've been meaning to tell you...' Patricia began tentatively, 'a letter arrived at the house. It was addressed to me so I opened it but inside it was a condolence card for you.' Patricia took the envelope from her bag and slid the envelope across the table.

Emily took it wordlessly and pushed it towards the pile of unopened envelopes that was steadily building.

'Aren't you going to open it?' Patricia asked, her fingers worrying at the gold crucifix she always wore.

Emily shook her head. 'They all say the same thing.'

'It's from your dad,' Patricia added.

Emily blinked rapidly. The words sounded alien to her ears. Her dad. Her mother never spoke of him and she had had no contact with him since he left them when she was a child.

'He must have heard about Alannah,' Patricia continued. 'I guess Brenda probably told him...'

The lottery of parenthood stung more now than ever. Her father's abandonment of them juxtaposed with the loss of her daughter. The injustice of her father having walked out on his two daughters, discarded like old bits and bobs that he no longer had a use for, and yet her beautiful and much-wanted daughter had been taken away from her after just a few weeks. How was that fair? The anger whirled like a vortex in her stomach. 'After all these years, he thinks *now* is a good time to make contact?' Emily said in disbelief. She picked the letter up off the pile and walked over to the bin with it.

'Don't you want to know what he says?' Patricia asked.

Emily shook her head. 'It's too late; he can't ghost us for over twenty-five years and then suddenly decide to drop me a line!'

'Well, he did send cards, you know...' Patricia confessed.

'What do you mean?'

'Well, every year he'd send a card with money on your birthday or at Christmastime...' Patricia trailed off.

Emily couldn't believe what she was hearing. 'Our father made contact with us and you never told us?' She was struggling to process this monumental admission.

'I was afraid you'd get upset.' Patricia's hands fluttered to her neck as she fingered her necklace once more. 'I thought it was for the best at the time, love.'

It was a seismic shift in how she viewed her father. 'For years, I believed that he wiped us out of his life without a second thought! Do you know how much that hurt, Mum? I grew up watching everyone else have their dad around and thinking that there must be something wrong with me because my dad left us.'

'I'm sorry.' Patricia's voice swelled with emotion. 'I was afraid that he'd do it to you again, that he'd get in touch for a few months and then disappear. It took a long time for you girls to stop crying yourselves to sleep every night and you finally seemed to be doing well when he made contact out of the blue. I was worried he'd set you backwards and I wanted to protect you both. Maybe I got it wrong...'

'You did!' Emily blazed. 'Have you told Karen?'

Patricia shook her head. 'This is the first time I've mentioned it. I thought with everything that has happened... it might be a good time to do it but maybe I was wrong. I still have all the letters; I was keeping them for you. I did intend to give them to you... I was waiting for the right time and then as the years went by and you both seemed to be doing so well, I guess I didn't want to uproot all that old pain again...'

'I can't believe this! You really picked your time!' Emily glared angrily at her chastened mother, who looked shrunken as she sat in her chair. 'I've just buried my daughter and you think it's a good time to break it to me that my father did actually try to stay in contact but you just didn't tell us!'

'Oh love, I'm sorry. I don't know what to do or say...' Patricia dissolved into tears.

It was unsettling to watch – Emily rarely saw her mum cry – but she wasn't capable of comforting her or telling her that although she didn't agree with keeping it a secret for all these years, she understood her actions. It was too much to take.

'I can't deal with this on top of everything else. Please go, Mum,' she said.

Patricia nodded and stood up from the table, her eyes filled with tears. 'I'm so sorry, Emily.'

21

Emily lay on the bed and massaged her temples. It felt like everything was closing in around her. The four walls of her bedroom were inching ever closer towards her so it was just her and her grief caught in the middle in a duel and she couldn't escape or avoid it. It was going to wrestle her to the death and swallow her whole. Between the loss of her daughter and her mother's revelation, Emily felt as though the bottom had fallen out of her world. It was like someone had removed a stopper from a plughole, leaving her life as she had known it to drain away.

She reached beneath her pillow for Alannah's comforter. It was a plush marshmallow-pink rabbit with a long, fabric tail. She had been keeping it there since she had come home from the hospital. She brought it up close to her face and breathed in her daughter's smell: a delicate mixture of newborn baby and antiseptic. The scent had grown increasingly faint since her death and the thought of it disappearing altogether terrified her.

As the days went on, her mother had called over, trying to apologise and get Emily to understand her reasons for doing what she did, but Emily found she wasn't able to deal with Patricia's remorse on top of everything else. Rob also tried to get Emily to talk but she shut him down at every attempt. If she heard him in the kitchen, she avoided going downstairs and waited until she heard the noise of the TV streaming up from the living room before she would emerge from the bedroom. She slept a lot. Most times fitfully but sometimes she fell into a deep sleep where she had dreams that Alannah was alive and healthy. She was in her crib beside the bed and was crying in great, fractious, hungry shrieks. She would bolt upright in bed and a wash of relief and gratitude that it was all just a horrible dream would flood through her. She'd stretch out her arms to lift her daughter up and bring her close to her chest to feed her but there was just startling emptiness where her crib should be and then she would remember all over again. She loved when her daughter came to her in her dreams but the visions were as cruel as they were beautiful as the painful reality of waking up slammed into her all over again. How were they supposed to live without their daughter? To continue on, even though the landscape of their life had been completely altered?

One day, she heard the hum of the shower in the main bathroom punctuating the silence that had cloaked the house over the last while. The sound seemed alien to her; neither of them had used the shower for days. After a while, she heard the slam of the front door and the thrum of Rob's engine reversing out of their driveway. It was such a shock to hear those ordinary, everyday noises that at one time she wouldn't have paid any heed to. A reminder of an older version of their life. She couldn't help wondering where he was going.

She must have dozed off because she was woken a short time later by the heavy set of Rob's footsteps on the stairs. He appeared in her room and she noticed he had changed out of the dirty hoody and tracksuit bottoms that he had been living in lately.

'I went to the shop,' he offered by way of explanation. 'I got us some fresh milk and bread and a few other bits. That sliced pan in the press had gone mouldy.'

Emily nodded wordlessly. She had been using it to make toast and hadn't even noticed.

He sat down on the side of the bed and, like a wounded animal, she instinctively moved away from him. He took a deep breath. 'I just wanted to let you know that I've decided to go back to work tomorrow.'

She felt winded, as though he had punched her with his words. How was he able to do that? She couldn't even imagine getting dressed, let alone functioning in her job. He was moving on. He was forgetting about Alannah and she hated him for it.

'How can you do that?' she said, choking back tears and holding the comforter close. 'You can't just forget about her.'

'Oh, Em, I'm not,' he replied softly, reaching for her hand across the bed, but she pulled it away quickly before he could touch her. 'Just because I'm going back to work doesn't mean I'm forgetting her, Emily – I'll never forget about her but no matter what we've been through, the world still goes on. There comes a time when we have to get back to normal whether we like it or not. Even though it feels like the world has ended, the bills are still coming through the door, the mortgage has to be paid. Besides, I think it will be a good distraction to have some routine back in our lives again.'

She blinked. 'You think I should go back too?' It seemed unfathomable, the very thought impossible. He was moving on but she was stuck. He was like a train slowly pulling out of the station while she was left stranded on the platform.

'Well, I wasn't sure if I should tell you but I've had a few calls from your team... They... erm... they didn't want to disturb you with everything going on but I think they're struggling without you... Apparently, Maeve is causing all sorts of trouble for them.

They mentioned something about the tender and that she is threatening to pull the account.'

Maeve. The name was like a reminder to a past life: a chasm opening up to the person she used to be. Something stirred up inside her as she remembered. How once she used to dance to this woman's tune; how this woman's whims could dictate her whole day. She felt unbridled fury as she thought of how she had spent her last day of Alannah's life trying to satisfy this woman's demands, not knowing how precious those hours were and how she would spend her whole life regretting it.

She was pretty sure that her team would have explained what was going on, so why couldn't Maeve give her the space to grieve or have the compassion to know that her marketing budget wasn't a priority for Emily right now? She knew it wasn't fair for her team to be left to handle Maeve on their own – Emily had always found her dealings with the woman difficult at the best of times – and that guilt sat heavily on top of all the other guilt like a layer of oil on top of a murky puddle.

'I've told them that you'll be back when you're ready but I just thought you'd want to know.' He stood up from the bed and headed towards the door.

She began balling the duvet with her fist. 'That's typical of you; you just move on,' she called after him. 'You're heading back to work without a second thought.'

'Woah, Emily, that's not fair. It isn't easy for me either. I'm struggling too but it helps though... if you keep yourself busy, it's a good distraction, and the day is a little bit easier to get through.'

'Well, good for you. I'm thrilled you're finding it so easy to move on,' she retorted sarcastically. Whereas he was emerging from beneath the blanket of grief, she was still fumbling around beneath its weight and it was smothering her.

'That's not fair,' he snapped. 'Everyone is concerned about you.

I know your mum told you about your dad getting in touch and I get that maybe the timing wasn't the best with everything else you're going through but she didn't intentionally try to hurt you. She's out of her mind with worry. Karen is too. Look, why don't you talk to someone? The hospital recommended a bereavement counsellor; I can call them for you.'

'What could they possibly say to make this better? What words could help me to make sense of any of this?'

'Nobody can fix it for us, Em,' he said, exasperated, 'but it might help you to talk to someone.'

Emily scoffed. 'It's easier for you. You weren't the one who was pregnant. You didn't carry her and feel her kick and tumble and hiccup. You didn't give birth to her or breastfeed her. You didn't have the same bond that I did!' Even when she was saying them, she knew her words were cruel, but she wanted them to puncture him; she wanted to release some of the pain that was swallowing her and inflict it on to him.

He shook his head at her in disgust and she saw the hurt in his eyes. She couldn't look at him so she turned her head away.

'You know, Emily, she was my baby too and I loved her just as much as you did,' he replied before walking out of the room.

22

The kettle began to rumble as it signalled it was boiled. Emily reached up and took down a mug and a jar of instant coffee. Her days were punctuated with the ritual of making coffee. These days, caffeine and the odd slice of dry toast were the only things sustaining her. Her bedside table was littered with dirty mugs and, eventually, only when there was no space for another one would she gather them all up, bring them downstairs and load them into the dishwasher.

She heard a key in the front door as Rob let himself into the house. He came into the kitchen dressed in his work clothes: a shirt and trousers and polished, pointy-toed shoes. It looked as though he had stepped out of another world, a world that was once familiar to her but now seemed so far removed from her life. She immediately thought of her malodorous appearance as she stood before him in her unwashed pyjamas with her greasy hair piled up in a messy bun.

'Hey,' he said.

'Hi,' she replied coolly and continued past him, clutching her mug in her hands.

'I've just had Cliona on the phone,' he called after her.

She turned back around to face him.

'They won the tender.'

Emily stared at him blankly. Did he think this news would cheer her up? That she would suddenly awaken from her grief, motivated and ready to get back to work? She really didn't care about what was happening in the agency.

'Apparently, Maeve isn't happy,' he continued.

There's a surprise, Emily thought to herself bitterly, that woman would never be happy. If only she had realised this sooner, would her daughter still be alive today?

'The tender E Creative submitted was over three times greater than the next bid and Maeve is getting it in the neck from the board because they've overpaid. She's out for blood and she's blaming E Creative for getting the pitch wrong. She's pulled the business from the agency. Cliona is distraught; she thought her sources who informed her about the level at which Future Bank were bidding were reliable but clearly not,' he continued. 'Not only that but Maeve has accused the whole team of incompetence and said she'd be warning other companies to steer clear of E Creative. Three other clients have also walked and Cliona knows it's because Maeve has ruined their reputation in the industry. Cliona's really worried, Em.'

Emily could hear what he was telling her but it was as though the words couldn't penetrate her brain. She knew she should react somehow but she just felt numb. It was like he was talking in a different language, a language that once had been her mother tongue but she had since lost the ability to speak. It was as if there was an impenetrable glass wall between them; she could see him, she could hear him, but she couldn't reach him.

'They're in trouble, Em. Maeve Murray is a powerful woman and it seems she is out to destroy them. They need you to go back and sort it all out before the agency goes down the tubes,' he pleaded.

She thought about the team panicking because they had just lost their biggest client and the worry they now had about the reputational damage that would ensue. Even though she knew this situation was serious, she wasn't able to process it from beneath the thick fog that she was blanketed under. All those people were depending on her but instead of this news jolting her awake, she felt herself sinking deeper under its weight. She shook her head. The very idea seemed impossible to her.

'I know it's difficult to even contemplate but you've got to go back in there and sort it out,' Rob implored. 'You founded that company, you worked your arse off to get it to the level it's at now; don't throw it all away. This isn't you, Em. That business was your life before all of this.'

An image of them all dressed up at the awards ceremony just over two years ago flitted into her head. She hadn't realised it at the time but it had been a watershed moment in her life; it seemed as though everything had gone wrong from that moment on. Back then, E Creative had been at the pinnacle of success. Other companies had looked to see what they were doing, trying to emulate it. Fees were booming. In fact, their services had been in such demand that they had had to turn clients away. It all seemed so trite now. All the things that had once been important to her were a façade.

'I can't,' she whispered.

He ran his hands down along his face. 'I feel as though I'm losing you, Em. What is it going to take to get through to you? You've shut me out and I can't find my way back to you. The old you is gone and you seem oblivious to all the things you once cared about.'

'That's because I'm not that person any more. How can I ever be her again?' she snapped bitterly.

He moved towards her and took her in his arms. 'Come on, Em, come back to me. Talk to me, let me in. We've lost our little girl and all the hopes and dreams that we had for her; I don't want to lose you too. I'd never survive it.'

He pulled her closely against his chest but she stood limply in his arms, unable to accept his gesture of intimacy. She was broken and in pain like a wounded animal and nothing was going to help that. He released her and let his arms fall back by his side.

'I just don't understand you.' He shook his head in despair as he moved away from her. 'You need to talk to someone. You need to get help.'

23

Emily woke to hear noise floating up through the ceiling from downstairs. She opened her eyes and it took her a second to come to. She tried to work out what time it was. In the days since Alannah had died, time had taken on an other-worldly quality where the hours blurred together without her registering their passing. How long had she been here for? Hours? Days? *Maybe weeks?* The pale yellowy light streaming in from beyond the curtains told her it was daytime. She realised she must have slept straight through to the following day. She pulled back the duvet and put her feet on the floor. She noticed that the crib was missing. Rob must have taken it away somewhere. When had he done that, she wondered. Her tummy growled and it took her a moment to recognise the feeling was hunger. She tried to remember when she had last eaten and couldn't. Her senses had been numbed by the loss of their daughter.

Downstairs, she could hear voices chattering. She listened out for a moment and recognised her mother's voice and Karen's too. It seemed today she had brought Karen along too. *Strength in numbers*, she couldn't help thinking bitterly.

She made her way out of the bedroom and headed down the stairs. She saw Patricia and Karen standing in the hallway with their coats on. Her mother was armed with a tinfoil-wrapped dish as usual.

'Emily,' her mother said sheepishly as she reached the bottom step. 'I was just dropping over some food for you, love.'

Emily walked past them wordlessly and proceeded into the kitchen. She filled the kettle from the tap and flicked the switch to set it to boil. She made a pot of tea and placed it on the table along with three mugs. Then she pulled out a seat at the table and sat down. Patricia and Karen took this as their cue to sit as they took seats beside her.

'How are you?' Karen asked, tilting her head towards her shoulder in a sympathetic gesture that everyone seemed to be using with her lately.

Emily stayed silent. It was such a stupid question that it didn't merit a response. Emily knew that nobody really wanted to hear the truth about how she was so broken inside that she didn't think she could go on. That every night before she went to sleep, she prayed she wouldn't wake up again.

Karen's eyes darted over to Patricia before she continued. 'Look, Mum is very upset,' she began.

Immediately, Emily knew that Karen had been brought over as a peacemaker. 'So she told you about the letters then?' Emily retorted.

Karen nodded. 'She did. It was a shock, I'll admit but,' she paused before looking across at their mother once more, 'but I guess I can understand why she did it...'

'I promise, love, I never intended to deceive you.' It was Patricia's turn to talk now. 'I was just worried it would upset you both when you finally seemed to be moving on.'

Karen placed her hand on her mother's shoulder and patted it gently.

Emily clasped her mug tightly between her palms. She could tell Patricia was distraught and even though Emily was still furious at her, she knew deep down that it wasn't fair to keep blaming her mother when it was their father who had caused all the pain by walking out on them in the first place. She knew it hadn't been easy for Patricia raising them on her own and trying to do the right thing; she was bound to make mistakes. A voice deep within told her that maybe she ought to cut her some slack.

Emily exhaled heavily. 'Look, Mum, I can't even deal with all of that right now, to be honest...'

Patricia visibly sagged with relief. 'Thank you, love.'

'How's Rob doing since he went back to work?' Karen asked, changing the subject.

Emily shrugged. 'Seems to be managing okay. We don't really see one another,' she admitted.

'Don't you?' Her mother's tone was concerned.

'I go to bed early most days. I'm so tired all the time,' she said by way of explanation.

'Well, make sure you look after one another; it's difficult for him too. Don't let what's happened destroy your marriage as well,' Patricia counselled.

Emily rolled her eyes scornfully at the advice. 'He's still able to go to work every day. He goes to the gym. He meets his friends. I think he's doing okay, Mum.'

'Oh, Emily, everyone grieves differently. When your grandmother died, I couldn't bear to talk about her but you and Karen were only children and you talked about her constantly like she had just gone to the shops. You didn't understand the finality of it and I found it so hard.'

'But Rob's not a child!' Emily protested.

'Look, all Mum is saying is not to lose sight of each other in all of this.' Karen took up the lead. 'You're still young enough to try again.'

Emily turned to Karen, her eyes ablaze. 'You just don't get it, do you? I can't replace Alannah with another baby!'

Karen sighed heavily. 'Oh, Emily, I promise I'm not deliberately trying to upset you.'

'It's hard to know what to say...' Patricia tried. 'It's difficult for everyone. I hate seeing you like this, lovey. You going around in your pyjamas all day long, not showering or looking after yourself, not leaving the house... it's not you.' She reached out and rubbed her arm. 'You're skin and bone, love. I want the old Emily back.'

'The old Emily is gone, Mum,' she snapped. 'I just buried my baby girl! I'll never be that person again. Losing Alannah has changed me forever!'

'Please let me take you to the doctor. I'll make the appointment and drive you over there myself. You don't need to do anything; just get in the car and I'll do everything else,' Patricia pleaded.

Her mother had been saying the same thing for a while now about visiting a doctor but she didn't understand that there was no cure for what she was feeling. Emily shook her head stubbornly. 'How can a doctor make this better? There is no medicine for what I'm going through. If there was, I'd be taking it, believe me!'

'I never seem to be able to do or say the right thing...' Patricia said forlornly.

'Look, Em, Mum is right,' Karen interjected. 'We're all worried about you and poor Rob doesn't know what to say or do. Dave was talking to him yesterday and he's in a right state about it all. You need to speak to someone; it might help you...'

'What good is talking going to do? I can talk until I'm blue in the face but it won't bring her back!' she spat.

'No, love, it won't but I'm concerned about you.' Patricia shook her head in despair and her voice snagged. 'I think you need professional help.'

24

Emily sat staring stonily at the ceiling of her bedroom. There was a water stain that had obviously been there a while but which she had only noticed recently. She spent most of her days like this, not doing anything, but yet the time crept past without her noticing. There had been a time in her life where she was always so busy – she had once seen her busyness as a badge of honour, rushing here and there, fitting in early-morning workouts, fuelling her body with takeaway coffees and eating lunch at her desk because she didn't have time to sit down in a café. There was a schedule of appointments, and a never-ending to-do list whirred through her mind constantly. Now her mind was emptied of everything except her pain.

She heard footsteps on the stairs and, suddenly, the door to her bedroom was pushed open. Rob marched into the room and moved straight to the window.

'I've just had a call from Cliona...' he said, sounding breathless. He pulled apart the curtains and then slid up the bottom sash, letting fresh air mingle with the stale bedroom air. Birdsong infiltrated the silence and, beyond the window, she could see wisps of cloud dancing on a gentle breeze. He turned back to face her and ran his hands down along his face. 'It's gone... A liquidator has been appointed,' he continued. 'The company has been wound up. Cliona said they're all devastated.' He held her gaze, waiting for a reaction.

She knew that he was deliberately firing the words at her like bullets, hoping to arouse her concern, but they couldn't penetrate. Her brain tried to process what he was telling her. Her business was gone. It was all over. She had known this could happen given the precarious way it had been operating over the last few weeks. Rob had tried to warn her but, somehow, his words had never seemed to land. They were like rubber ping-pong balls bouncing off her head; nothing seemed to get through. Instead of feeling sadness or shock like she once would have expected to feel hearing news like this, it was something else... something akin to relief. That part of her life was closed now. She was aware of something else swirling in her stomach. Guilt maybe? She felt so numb to everything that she didn't recognise her own feelings any more. She pictured her team being told that their jobs were gone, packing up their belongings, turning out the lights for the last time, leaving the office worrying about how they would get another job. 'Tell them I'm sorry,' she managed.

'That's it? That's all you've got to say? Twenty-two people have lost their jobs today. Some of them have families! They have mortgages and rent to pay. They have bills coming in...' he said in disbelief. 'You could have prevented it from happening. I know it might have been too late but you could have at least *tried* to stop the company from going under. Now all those people have to try and get new jobs. The ripples spread far wider than just you,' he cried out bitterly.

'Don't you see? None of it matters to me any more.' Nothing could make her happy or sad any more and when she tried to think of what their future might be like, she could only see nothing. Emptiness filled her body like lead. She was stuck down the darkest hole and she couldn't see how she'd ever climb out; she didn't even want to climb out.

'You've made a huge mistake letting it get to this. You're sabotaging yourself with grief but sooner or later, you will have to start living again.'

'Well, maybe I don't want to live!' she snapped. 'Every night, I go to sleep and hope I won't wake up in the morning, that I can be taken too and that my pain will be over.'

'I know it's tough but enough is enough. You're going to have to get it together; yes, we lost our daughter and it's a really shitty thing to go through but you can't let it ruin your whole life. You have to move on at some point.'

'So what? You want me just to forget about her like you're doing?'

'No, I'm not forgetting about her. I'll never forget her but moping around in your bedroom all day isn't going to help.'

There was something different in his eyes today. Yes, she could still see the sadness but now there was something darker lurking there too. Was it frustration? Resentment? And that was when she realised that they had moved on to different pages on their journey through this nightmare.

'Look at you, Em,' he continued. 'You think you're the only one hurting here. You've completely shut me out. Going through something like this should have brought us closer together because we're the only ones who know how awful it is, but you keep pushing me away right at the one time I need you. I try to reach out to you and you move away. I could really have done with your support over the last few weeks but you've just been so wrapped up in yourself that you haven't even asked how I'm doing or noticed that I might be struggling too. It's all about you. It's always been about you. Emily with the big job, too busy to talk on the phone, cancelling plans at the last minute because your job always came first. It's always been *you, you, you*.' He shook his head despondently. 'I don't know why I'm surprised; you've always been selfish. Why did I think you'd ever be different?'

She blinked rapidly, frightened by the vitriol in his words. Rob never spoke to her like this. He was being so aggressive; it was like he hated her. 'Wh-what are you saying?' she said, goading him. Like a hangnail you couldn't help picking at even though you knew it would be painful, she wanted to see his reaction.

He ran his hands backwards through his hair before continuing. 'You even went back to work when she was just three weeks old. Three weeks old!' he repeated for maximum effect. He pointed his index finger at her accusingly. 'You went back to work and then our baby died.'

The words hung, momentarily suspended on the air between them like a grenade that had just been thrown and hadn't yet reached the target. Suddenly, his accusation assailed her and she felt blown away by the impact. He was blaming her. The worst part was that she knew he was right; it was all her fault. She blamed herself too. She had racked her brain for a reason, for something else, anything at all that might explain why this had happened to them but she kept arriving at the same conclusion: the only thing that had changed in Alannah's routine that day was that Emily had left her newborn baby and gone back to work.

She marched forward and before she realised she was doing it, her hand had shot out and slapped him across the face. The sting spread instantly across her palm as Rob raised his hand up to touch his cheek in shock. He glared at her, full of fury, but it was worse than that, she could see hatred there too, and that was the moment she knew. She knew that that was it for them. There was no way back from here; they had reached the end of the road.

25

THREE MONTHS LATER

To: robk24@gmail.com
From: Emmyxx12@gmail.com

Dear Rob,

I've started this email so many times over the last few months but never know quite what to say or how to explain myself so I've just decided to throw it all down here and see what comes out, so please understand if it doesn't sound right. Firstly, I hope you're doing okay. I wanted to let you know that I'm sorry for leaving without saying goodbye and that it has taken me this long to get in touch. The truth is that I'm only able to send this now; I just wasn't up to it before. I hope you haven't been worried about me but I felt it was the only way. I know Mum and Karen were probably up the walls but I've sent them a message too, trying to explain everything and to let them know that I'm all right.

I've gone to New Zealand but I won't tell you exactly whereabouts I am because I need space and time to heal so please don't try to find me here. I wanted to get as far away as possible and I guess this is literally the furthest place I could go. I wanted to go somewhere nobody knew me. It feels like I'm at the very bottom edge of the world here, like I could walk off the underside of the globe. I don't know how long I'll stay for yet but I like it here. The countryside is quite like Ireland: lots of green, lots of rain – I never thought I'd find the rain comforting but when I feel the cool droplets on my skin, it reminds me of home.

When I first arrived here, I was a mess – I still have my bad days and I've a long way to go, but slowly, over the last few weeks, it's as though a chink of light is opening up again and life doesn't seem as hopeless as it did a while ago. With some time and space to think, I've come to realise that you were right; I was completely selfish in my grief. I know you were hurting too but I couldn't deal with your pain on top of my own or it would have drowned me and pulled us both under. I'm sorry I lashed out at you like that; I'll never forgive myself for slapping you. I let my anger cloud everything but I just couldn't see a way out. Every time I looked at you, it was like looking in a mirror; I could see my pain reflected in your eyes and it hurt too much. I'll always regret not supporting you through it and being a better wife. I'm sorry we've ended up like this; I'm sad about what became of us. We had so many good times together, didn't we? Never in a million years could I have imagined our life would go down the path it did. I thought we could take on anything together, we were a force to be reckoned with so I never thought that something so awful could happen that we wouldn't be able to get out of it together. It makes me angry whenever I think about how unfair it all is but I've learnt over the last few weeks that anger will destroy you if you let it, so I'm working on that.

I also keep thinking about how badly I let the team down

too. I don't think I'll ever be able to forgive myself for how I treated everyone and let the business go under without putting up a fight but I was in a dark place and just couldn't see a way out of it. If you see Cliona or any of the rest of them, please tell them I said sorry and I hope they've all found new jobs by now.

Despite everything we've been through, we made a beautiful daughter together and I will always be grateful for the short time we had together as a family. Those three weeks we got to spend with her are some of the happiest days of my life and I will always cherish those memories.

I hope in time you might be able to forgive me for how I've treated you. You are a good man, Rob, and you deserve better than me. Please visit Alannah's grave often, bring her flowers from me and tell her that I love her. I hope you'll find happiness again; you deserve only the best in life.

I'll never stop loving you both,

Em x

PART III

26

PRESENT DAY

Emily opened the door to her childhood home filled with a sense of dread. She hated entering the house knowing that her mother wouldn't be inside there waiting for her. Whispers of their late-night chats over a cup of tea when the girls came home from a night out still rang between the walls. Echoes of their laughter lingered behind the doors. So many memories had been made in this home. Of course there had been sad times too but, on the whole, so many good times had taken place under this roof. But it was as if the essence of the family had died with her mother and now it felt like stepping over the threshold of someone else's house; it no longer felt like home.

She climbed the stairs, seeing all their old school photos, increasing in age with every step. There were pictures of herself and Karen as neatly plaited junior infants all the way up to thick-fringed, sixth-class schoolgirls. Although their mother hadn't had much money as she raised them alone, she had always kept a wonderful home. She had been extraordinarily house-proud and had cleaned and polished daily so that the place always shone. She hung photos everywhere, put fresh flowers in vases: daffodils in the spring and bluebells in May, little touches that didn't cost the earth but gave their house a welcoming air. She baked her own soda bread and scones and the hearty smell would greet you as soon as you stepped inside. Emily missed it all.

She went into her old bedroom and slumped down onto the bed. She realised with a pang of regret that there was nothing left here for her any more. There was no reason for her to stay now that her mother was gone and Karen clearly found her intolerable. She didn't belong here now; it was time for her to go back to New Zealand. It would be a relief to get back on the plane again. It seemed that memories lay in wait around every corner, ready to trip her up and knock her off balance. Over the years, she had become very adept at compartmentalising her life and she knew once she was back in New Zealand, she could shut the door on her past once more.

She took out her phone and saw she had a text from Jonny asking how she was doing. He had texted her every day since she had come home to say he was thinking of her or that he missed her. She replied to say that she was doing okay and would be booking her return flight back to Auckland. He had replied instantly with a celebratory emoji and said that he couldn't wait to see her. Being away from Jonny had given her space to think about what she wanted and she had come to the realisation over the last few days that they didn't have a future together. She knew she needed to tell him as soon as she went back; it wasn't fair to keep stringing him along in the hope that, eventually, her feelings for him might change.

She went onto Skyscanner.com and searched for flights departing from Dublin to Auckland. She soon saw from the results that any of the flights with available seats in the coming days were extortionately priced so she checked prices for the following week. She managed to get a seat on a flight departing in nine days' time. It was still ridiculously expensive and she knew her credit card would almost be maxed out but she didn't have another option if she wanted to get back to Auckland sooner rather than later. Emily knew that Karen would probably be furious that she didn't stay long enough to help sort through their mother's belongings but, in the long run, Karen was better off without her. Karen would realise that eventually. Emily guessed that their mother, wanting to be fair to both girls, had most likely left the house to the two of them in her will, but Emily didn't care what Karen did with it; let her rent it out, put it up for sale, whatever she wanted. She didn't want her share of the proceeds. Quite frankly, she didn't deserve it.

She heard the doorbell go and, assuming it was another neighbour dropping off a Mass card or a casserole, she picked herself up off the bed and headed downstairs to answer it. She was surprised to pull back the door to find Karen standing there, looking glum.

'Come in,' Emily invited and then regretted her choice of words; Karen would probably have a go at her now for inviting her into their mother's home.

But if that was what her sister was thinking, she bit her lip and remained mute as she headed straight to the kitchen with Emily trailing after her.

'It's not the same without her,' Karen said sadly as she looked around the small kitchen. She ducked her head beneath the strap of her crossbody bag and hung it over the back of a chair before sitting down at the pine table. Emily realised this was probably Karen's first time in the house since their mother had died and she knew it would be difficult for her.

'I know,' Emily agreed.

Silence cloaked the air between them. 'Look, about earlier on...' She paused. 'I just wanted to say that I'm sorry. I shouldn't have brought all of that stuff up... I didn't mean it... well... not really,' she admitted. 'I don't want to fight with you. We only have each other now. Mum would be turning in her grave if she heard me.'

'It's okay, I get it.'

'Can you forgive me?'

'Of course I can. Grief does that to you. Makes you say things you wouldn't ordinarily say,' Emily said, helping her out. She remembered that seething anger after Alannah had died; how she had wanted to lash out at the world. She had wanted to physically hurt people. To see them squirm and feel pain like she felt in her heart. It was as though her tongue had been a weapon.

'I miss her so much...' Karen's voice wavered on tears. 'She did everything with us. She'd call over to eat dinner with us in the evenings or we'd go for coffee together and have a look around the shops on my day off. She'd help out with the kids whenever the childminder was sick. She came on holidays with us.' Her voice snagged. 'She was actually my best friend.'

Emily moved across to her sister and pulled her into a hug, savouring this mixture of sisterhood and family that she had missed so much. 'Me too. She was lucky to have you,' Emily soothed. 'I know she loved having you and the kids close by. She was always talking about what you were up to and telling me funny things that the kids said or did.'

'Well, for what it's worth, none of it matters because you were always her favourite,' Karen retorted.

'Me?' Emily asked in disbelief. In her head, it most definitely was the other way around. She was certain that Karen had been their mother's favourite. Her younger sister was good and compliant, she obeyed the rules and generally didn't cause their mother a moment's worry. She was a clear favourite because she had made being her mother so easy.

Karen shook her head. 'You could do no wrong growing up. You were her firstborn and you were so smart and sensible. When I came into their class two years after they had taught you, the teachers would shake their heads in despair and tut: "Why can't you be like your older sister?" Or another favourite was: "Your sister would have known the answer to that question, Karen," or, "Your sister had no bother learning her times tables when she was your age – you're just lazy, you know". It didn't come easily to me; you had the brains, whereas no matter how hard I worked, I'd still never get the same results as you. Keeva has recently been diagnosed with dyslexia and I see a lot of similarities between the two of us so I think I probably have it too but was just never diagnosed.'

'I'm sorry,' Emily said, feeling guilty that her perception of it had been different. 'I never realised school was so hard for you.'

Karen shrugged. 'Look, things have worked out okay for me since so it's water under the bridge.' She didn't need to add that Emily's life had gone down the tubes since then but Emily knew that's what she was thinking. 'Then you went and set up the agency and bought the big house on Groveton Road,' Karen continued. 'Mum was so proud of you. She loved telling everyone she met about you. After all those years struggling on her own to make ends meet, you were her great success story. I was proud of you too: my big sister, the go-getter. Remember we used to walk home from school down that road and we'd make up scenarios about the people who lived in all the fancy houses and what their jobs were?'

A carefree memory of them coming home from school, heavy school bags digging into their shoulders, flooded back to her. 'I'd forgotten about that...'

'We'd say that lady in number six looks like she works in a bank but by night, she has a boyfriend called Ringo; he comes over on that motorbike parked in the driveway. He's crazy about her but she won't marry him because she's afraid he's only after her money.'

Emily exploded with laugher at this chapter of her childhood that she had completely forgotten about. 'How do you remember this stuff? I loved that game.'

'So then when you and Rob bought an actual house on Groveton Road, it was kind of a big deal. You really had it all. Never in a million years could I have afforded a house there on my measly salary but my big sister had gone and done it. It was like giving Dad the two fingers for all the tough years Mum had struggled to put food on the table and keep a roof over our heads all by herself.'

'And then I went and threw it all away...' Emily exhaled heavily.

'Look, Emily,' Karen said after a beat. 'I can't even begin to imagine the pain you went through back then. Now that I'm a mother myself... well... it's every parent's worst nightmare.' She shook her head.

'Except it was my reality,' Emily said sadly. They both fell quiet for a moment as they thought back to those awful days. 'I booked my flight home, by the way,' she said eventually.

Karen straightened in her chair. 'Oh, so you're going back then?'

Emily nodded.

'I just thought you might... well, now that you've come home, you might realise that this is where you belong,' Karen said.

'My job, my flat, everything is over there now...'

'Well, you know, you could stay,' Karen tried. 'This place is free now and you could get another job here. Every business in the country has a sign up in the window crying out for staff. And I'd love my kids to get to know their Auntie Em a bit better.'

Emily smiled sadly. 'It's easier over there.'

'You don't have to keep running, Em,' Karen said softly,

stretching her hand across the table and placing it over her older sister's. 'Don't be too proud. This will always be your home.'

Emily shook her head. 'I can't...'

A shared moment of understanding passed between them. So much hurt and pain. The fierce love between sisters that had at times almost bordered on hatred, but blood was always thicker than water and no matter what life threw at them, they would always have one another's backs.

'Who knows, maybe in the future...' she said to appease her sister.

'Well, look,' Karen said, shaking her head and looking down at the table. 'Obviously it's your choice...'

27

The next few days blurred together as Emily waited for her flight home. Now that she was back on Irish soil, there had been something on her mind that she knew she had to do. Over the last few days, she had felt a pull to visit Alannah's grave but she was terrified of all the old pain that would be uprooted. She hadn't been to visit her daughter since the day of her funeral and the guilt she felt for abandoning her in the cold, hard earth cut her open like a knife so she knew that if she returned to New Zealand without going to visit her, she would never forgive herself. The time had come to finally face up to it.

She took the Luas towards the city centre and got off at Ranelagh. She walked down the familiar streets that she had once called home. She noticed so many new cafés and restaurants had opened in the area since she was last here. It wasn't long before she saw the spire of St Francis' church looming in the distance and instantly she felt her breath come in short and shallow pants. She continued on, telling herself with each step that she had to do this; she couldn't avoid it any longer. She traversed the churchyard and, soon, she had reached cemetery gate. She pushed it open and went inside. As she treaded over the lichen-blotched path, it all came rushing back to her. The pain bursting from their hearts, the shock and disbelief that this was really happening. That it had happened. The violent anger. She inhaled deeply to still her breathing. Crows screeched and cawed above her as if gossiping with one another: *Well, would you look who's finally arrived?*

She noticed the burial plots had expanded into an adjacent field since she was last there. She stopped walking along the winding path, suddenly unsure where to go. The place seemed different to how she remembered it. Then she noticed the oak tree. She remembered how that brazen magpie had sat in its branches, eyeballing her on that cold February morning all those years ago. She continued along the meandering path towards it and, eventually, she stopped before a simple granite headstone. Her breath caught in her throat as she saw her daughter's name etched on the marble.

In Loving Memory of Baby Alannah Kavanagh
Born January 27th 2014
Died February 20th 2014

It was like being hit by a truck as she was instantly shunted back to that time nine years ago. Her breathing turned ragged and the pain swelled inside her as the injustice of it all smacked her once again. Tears pressed forward and stung her eyelids. She noticed a bunch of fresh daisies had been placed on the grave and it was neatly tended with no weeds. Someone – Rob, she guessed, or perhaps it had been her mother – obviously visited regularly.

She knelt down onto the gravel, feeling the stones prick her skin through her leggings. She reached out and traced her fingers over the dates of her daughter's birth and death: a life cut staggeringly short. She felt tears roll down her cheeks.

'I'm sorry, baby girl,' she whispered. 'I'm so, so sorry.' She knew no matter what the post-mortem said or how many times people told her that it wasn't her fault, she would always blame herself. She would always wonder if Alannah's routine had been kept the same that day, would it have even happened? Why had she let Alannah dream feed instead of waking her? Because she had been selfishly hoping to get some sleep herself, that's why, a mocking voice chimed in her head. She was still tormented by so many questions. Would her daughter be alive today if she hadn't gone to work? If she hadn't been exhausted from her day in the office, would Emily have woken earlier and realised Alannah had missed a feed, instead of sleeping straight through? Her instincts might have told her that something was wrong if she had spent time with her daughter that day. She might have noticed there was something different about her, something off. Although Rob had assured her that Alannah had been fine and that there had been nothing out of the ordinary about their baby girl that day, Emily would always question herself. She would carry the blame around with her for life. She was tethered to it like a suitcase she was dragging alongside herself; it would always be with her and when she died too, she would be buried beneath the earth and they could use its weight to push her down. She wondered if Rob ever tortured himself in the same way. But motherhood was so much more complex.

Just then, she heard voices approaching from behind and when she turned around, she saw Rob and his daughter were coming towards her. Her heart stumbled at the sight of the little girl wrapped up in a powder-blue puffa coat with a purple bobble hat pulled down over her head. The child was clutching a bunch of yellow primroses clasped inside the chubby fist of her right hand. Emily quickly wiped her eyes and picked herself up from the ground, feeling vulnerable and exposed, as if he was getting a glimpse into her innermost soul.

'Emily – I'm sorry.' He put his hand up. 'I didn't realise you were here... We can go...' He thumbed in the direction of the gate.

She shook her head. 'No, no,' she said quickly. 'I was finished anyway.' She tucked her chin down inside the roll-neck of her jumper, keeping her head buried.

'You remember Molly, don't you?' he prompted after a beat.

She nodded, the words she intended to say getting lost somewhere between her throat and mouth. She was transfixed by this little girl. The curve of her smile, the soft honey-blonde waves framing her heart-shaped face. The vision of all her hopes and dreams was standing here before her. She was everything that she had imagined his daughter to be and more. She was beautiful.

'So how are you doing?' he continued.

She nodded. 'I'm okay, I guess...'

'Look, I wanted to apologise about the funeral; I didn't mean to upset you. I know I was probably the last person you expected to see there but I was very fond of her.'

She shook her head. 'No, it's okay...'

They were interrupted by Molly saying, 'Daddy?'

He turned away from Emily and looked down at her. She was staring up at him intently, her eyes two pools of blue. 'Yes, love?'

'Is this the lady who you said was your friend a long time ago?' Molly asked.

'Yes, Molly, that's right.' He looked back at Emily. 'After we met at the funeral, Molly was asking me about you...' he muttered by way of explanation.

Their eyes locked upon one another and in a fleeting moment a world of shared pain flashed between them. Emily found herself looking down at the ground, digging at the concrete with the toe of her runner.

'She looks nice,' Molly continued.

'She does,' he said tightly and Emily noticed he was starting to blush.

'Why is she here, Daddy?' Molly pointed her pudgy index finger in Emily's direction.

'Now, love, you know it's rude to point,' he scolded gently.

'But, Daddy!' she protested, with her left hand splayed out. 'I want to know, why is she here?'

'She wanted to visit Alannah just like us,' Rob explained.

'Oh,' she said thoughtfully before looking up at Emily. 'Alannah is my big sister but I never metted her because she died when she was a teeny baby and I wasn't borned then.'

Emily was stunned that this beautiful child spoke of her daughter and it took her a moment to process it.

'I picked these flowers for her because Daddy said she'd like them,' Molly continued.

'They're really lovely,' Emily said, feeling her heart twist. Despite the sadness that floored her, it gave her such joy to see her daughter being called to life by this beautiful child; in her eyes, Alannah was a sister, someone who liked flowers. To Molly, Alannah was someone who was talked about and remembered.

'I'm sorry,' Rob said, stepping forward. 'She's a chatterbox. We'll go and leave you alone.'

Emily shook her head. 'Please, don't. You don't know how good it sounds to hear Molly talk about her like that,' she said, entranced by the child. Emily bent down onto her hunkers and faced the child. 'I knew Alannah too,' she began gently. Her voice was shaky and she did her best to keep it on an even keel, wishing nothing to upset the magic of this moment.

The child narrowed her eyes sceptically. 'How did you know her?'

Emily felt tears pool in her eyes as she whispered, 'I was her mummy.'

The child wrinkled her nose and pulled back from her. 'No, you're not. My mummy is her mummy.'

Rob sucked in sharply so that the breath whistled between his teeth. 'Emily, I'm sorry...' His eyes darted towards the child who was looking up at both of them, her innocent eyes two huge pools of confusion as she wondered what was going on between the grown-ups. He shook his head sadly. 'She's too young to understand...'

Emily nodded and stood up. She felt tears prick her eyes. Her head was woozy and her legs wobbled beneath her. 'Don't worry, I get it.' She turned back to Molly. 'I need to go now,' she explained to the child, 'but thank you for bringing Alannah flowers.'

She turned away from them and tried to make her way towards the entrance gate but it felt as though she was staggering down the path. Her legs felt like they were made from marshmallows. Her steps were awkward and clumsy and her body wasn't moving like it should.

'Emily, wait! I'm sorry...' Rob called after her as she hurried off down the path, her head in a spin by the encounter. She didn't turn around because she knew she couldn't hold it all in for much longer and she didn't want the child to witness her upset. In New Zealand, she had almost been able to compartmentalise that part of her life, pretend that she was a different person now, but it was so much more difficult here. Years of pain were erupting inside her and she couldn't run from her grief any longer.

28

Instead of taking the Luas home, Emily walked back to Ballyrath village in a trance. She couldn't remember anything of her journey; she must have done it on autopilot. She hadn't noticed signposts or traffic lights or pedestrian crossings. She had been too upset. She knew it wasn't Molly's fault; she could hardly expect the child to understand the complicated history between Emily and her father. Molly was too young for Rob to have explained that he had once been married before he had met her mother and that Alannah was the daughter he had had with his wife, but even though Emily knew the child had intended no malice, it still hurt. It was like her connection to her daughter had been forgotten about and Alannah had been neatly bundled up with Rob's new family. Tears pressed forward in her eyes as she walked. Even now, after all these years, the grief could still catch her and suck the air from her lungs. It might be if she passed a woman pushing a tiny infant in its pram or whenever she saw a pregnant woman in the restaurant, she longed to shout at her to do everything properly, don't make any little mistake like she had because if you did, you could be serving a life sentence. One time a few years back, she saw a little girl she guessed was the same age that Alannah would have been if she had lived, skipping down Queen Street with her hand slotted inside her mother's. The child was wearing a coat with a picture of Elsa from *Frozen* embroidered on to it and Emily had wondered if her daughter would have been a fan of the movie too? Grief lay in wait unsuspectingly; it lurked around every corner like an intruder, ready to attack you when you least expected.

She continued on until she found herself standing on Karen's doorstep on Seaview Road. She rang the bell and eventually, through the glass side pane, she saw her sister coming down the hallway towards her wearing a pair of sheepskin slippers and with a tea towel slung over her shoulder. Karen opened the door and Emily collapsed into her arms in a sobbing mess.

'Em? What's happened? Are you okay? Come in,' she ushered. 'Don't worry, Dave has taken the kids swimming so we've the place to ourselves.' Karen placed an arm around her shoulder and led Emily down to the kitchen. Karen guided her into a chair at the island. 'I'll make us a cuppa.' She set about filling the teapot with water from her Quooker tap and, after she had made two mugs of tea, took a seat adjacent to her. 'So, tell me what is it? What's the matter?' she began.

'I went to the graveyard,' Emily blurted as Karen poured a mug for each of them.

'To visit Mum's grave?' Karen guided gently as she took milk out of the fridge and offered some to Emily.

Emily shook her head. 'No, I went to St Francis'. I went to see Alannah.'

'Oh, Em,' Karen consoled, reaching out and covering her sister's hand with her own. 'That must have been so tough after all this time.'

Emily removed it from beneath her sister's to wipe her tears away. They just wouldn't stop coming. 'I met Rob there,' she continued. 'And Molly.'

Karen bit down on her lip. 'I see.'

'Molly asked me how I knew Alannah.' She sniffed. 'And I said I was her mummy but she said that I wasn't, because *her* mummy is Alannah's mummy.'

Karen brought her mug up to her mouth. 'Oh, Em, come on, she's a child. She didn't mean any harm; she wouldn't understand the history there and the relationship between you and Rob.'

'I know that but it was just a shock, you know... It caught me off guard. I guess it felt like Rob and his family had claimed her and lumped her in with their family. I know it sounds ridiculous when I say it out loud... but it felt like they had wiped me out of the picture.'

Karen nodded sympathetically. 'I'm sure they weren't being deliberately insensitive but I can see why it would upset you.' She reached across the marble countertop for the box of tissues. She pulled a few out and handed them to Emily. 'I know it's hard on you but they've had a rough time of it too.'

'How do you mean?' Emily asked, taking a tissue and dabbing at her eyes.

'Well, you know...' Karen raised her brows. 'After all they've been through...'

Emily looked at her blankly, not following her prompts.

Karen looked at her quizzically, her brows hiked. 'You don't know?'

'Don't know what?'

'Are you serious, Emily?' Karen asked, her eyes wide with disbelief as she placed her mug down on the island.

'What?' Emily demanded, growing impatient with the guessing game.

'Rob's partner, Steph, is dead, Em. She died almost two years ago.'

'Oh God,' Emily gasped, reeling from Karen's revelation. She felt a snag on that old wound.

'You honestly didn't know about Steph?' Karen was clearly stunned.

'No, I didn't even know he was in a new relationship. The first time I knew about it was when I saw him holding Molly's hand at Mum's funeral.'

'But surely Mum must have mentioned it to you over the years?'

Emily sucked in sharply. 'We never talked about him. I guess with everything that happened, it wasn't really a topic that either of us brought up...'

'Oh, Emily, you've missed out on so much. Steph was American. She was a lovely person, beautiful and warm and just so much fun to be around.'

Emily felt a sting of jealousy for this woman that had replaced her in Rob's life and immediately berated herself for it. 'It sounds like you knew her well.'

'Well, I did... we were friends, actually,' she admitted.

'But how?' Emily asked in bewilderment. Karen's words were spinning in a loop around her head but she couldn't make sense of them: Rob had found someone new and Karen had befriended her. It sounded like one big practical joke.

'I met her at a mother and baby group,' Karen explained. 'Cara and Molly were born within a couple of months of each another. One of the other mums was lecturing the group on the environmental benefits of cloth nappies and Steph leant over and whispered in my ear, "Could you be arsed, though?" And that was it; I knew this was a woman I could get on with. We clicked right away.' Karen laughed at the memory.

Emily was trying to picture this vibrant woman that had shared the same intimacy with her husband as she had. They had had a child together and the shared experience of that could only have added new depth to their relationship. So many questions stirred up inside her. Did they have their own sides of the bed and were they the same as her and Rob's? Had Steph warmed her cold feet up on his legs when she climbed between the sheets at night?

'But wasn't it awkward between the two of you, y'know after everything that had happened? Did she know that you were once Rob's sister-in-law?' Emily demanded. She was trying to process what Karen was telling her but the more Karen explained, the more questions flooded into her brain.

Karen shook her head. 'That was the thing. Neither of us realised it initially. It wasn't until I bumped into the three of them in the supermarket that we put it all together but, in fairness to Steph, she didn't make it awkward. I thought it might affect our friendship and that she might be cooler with me when we went back to the group the following week but she continued on like everything was normal. She was so easy-going...' Karen paused. 'Look, Em, I know it might sound strange to hear me talking about Rob's new partner like this but you have to understand that he was devastated after you left so it felt good to see him finally moving on. For months, he went around like a zombie; he couldn't comprehend why you had walked out on him like that. All we had was the letter you left on the kitchen table for him telling him that you were leaving; we had no idea where to even begin trying to track you down. We were so worried about you and your mental state. We went to the Gardaí and they told us there was nothing they could do because you had voluntarily chosen to disappear. Apparently, people do it all the time. Then a few months later, you sent that email to say you were in New Zealand. Rob wanted to go there and track you down but we managed to talk him out of it. We told him to give you space. We all thought you would only be away for a short time and that once you had some breathing room you'd be back, but then a whole year went by and then another one, and he finally accepted that you weren't coming back. Rob wasn't in a good place back then but a friend of his brought him hiking and he got really into it. That's where he met Steph. They were in the same club. She was from Colorado and really outdoorsy. I remember bumping into him in O'Malley's shortly after they met and it was like the lights had finally been turned back on for him; the old Rob seemed to be coming back. They fell pregnant with Molly very soon after. Then I met Steph at the mother and toddler group after she was born.'

Emily held her breath and asked the question that had been tormenting her ever since she had found out about Steph. 'So how did she die?'

'She had breast cancer. She was diagnosed when Molly was only six months old. It was a horrible time for her and Rob; she was going through chemo and looking after a small baby but she never complained because she knew she had to go through it if she wanted to be around for Molly growing up. She even did a sponsored head-shave in O'Malley's and raised over five thousand euro for charity. She was amazing. The day she found out that she had beaten it, she and Rob threw a big BBQ for everyone. It was so much fun; her hair was starting to grow back, Molly had just started walking and she and Cara were both wobbling around the patio together like two little drunks and we were running after them. She turned to me and said, "Karen, it feels so good to be normal, just the ordinary moments like this, I won't ever take them for granted again." I'll never forget it. She was looking forward to the future. Unfortunately though, her cancer came back again and she was told it had spread. It was a huge shock for her but she accepted that, once again, she had a fight on her hands and was prepared to do whatever it took to beat it, except this time, she didn't get a chance to fight. Her medical team said it was too advanced for treatment and there was nothing more that could be done for her. It was awful. Despite what the doctors were telling her, she was determined to be around for Molly and she fought so bravely right to the end, but sadly, it was so aggressive.' Tears filled Karen's eyes as she recounted the story for her sister.

'That's so sad,' Emily said as her eyes began to water too. This story was heartbreaking and she wasn't sure if she could handle any more sadness. 'Poor Rob. He's been through the wringer.'

Karen nodded. 'After she passed away, Steph was cremated and they scattered her ashes over Lugnaquilla because she had loved it there so much. Rob went into a really dark place. Molly was only three and didn't understand what was going on. We all rallied around him as best we could. Myself and some of their other friends made a rota; we'd bring food over, do laundry, take Molly off his hands for a couple of hours. We were all really worried about him. None of us knew how he was going to cope going through more grief on top of everything that he had already been through losing Alannah and then you too. He's been through more than most go through in a lifetime.'

Emily's heart ached for Rob and guilt curdled somewhere near her stomach for her role in it all. Despite everything that had happened between them, she still cared about him deeply. To lose two people in his life, both taken far too soon, was devastating. He had been through unimaginable grief once before but to experience such loss a second time was cruel. How had he survived it, she wondered. And yet he continued on...

'You know Mum always had a soft spot for Rob,' Karen went

on. 'After you left, they got close. You'd email her or ring her and she'd call over to tell him if she'd heard from you. Then when he met Steph, naturally she stopped doing that. She knew it wasn't appropriate to be calling around and giving him updates about you now that he had found somebody new and so they didn't see one another as often. Sometimes, they'd meet at the playschool, if Mum was helping me out with the school run or if it was one of the girls' birthday parties. But when Mum learnt that Steph wasn't well, she reached out to them. You remember what she was like; she was always the first one to help in a crisis.'

Emily smiled at the familiar memory. It was true. Her mother had always been one to rally whenever something went wrong for her friends or family.

Karen continued. 'With Rob's family down in Cork and Steph's family in the States, they didn't have much support around so Mum would mind Molly while they were at the hospital or she would bring dinners over for them. She got very close to Molly. Mum adored her and Molly loved her too...' She broke off momentarily before adding, 'She even called her Nanny Pat.'

Emily blinked in disbelief. 'Nanny Pat?' she echoed.

'I know it probably sounds mad to you,' Karen explained, 'but Molly was around in the house playing with my kids one day and Mum was there as well and they were all calling her Nanny Pat, so Molly did too and it just kind of stuck...'

Emily felt the ugly face of grief sting her once more; it should have been *her* daughter calling her mother Nanny Pat; it was yet another thing that she had been robbed of. It felt like Karen was talking about a stranger and not their mother. 'I can't believe I never knew any of this...' was all Emily could manage. All these people had banded together in her absence; they had a shared love of Rob's partner, Steph, and now it was she who felt like the outsider. It was like everyone she loved and cared about most had been at a party together and not only had she not been invited, she hadn't even known it was on. She had believed Rob was at the funeral in order to sympathise with her; she hadn't realised that he and Molly had had their own relationship with her mother.

'I'm sorry, Em,' Karen said. 'I know this is probably a lot for you to take in. So much has happened since you were away... I still can't believe you never knew about Steph... Didn't Rob ever ask for a divorce?'

Emily shook her head. 'He never asked for one, so I had no idea that he was in a new relationship.'

'But when it came to selling the house on Groveton Road, you must have had contact then?' Karen pressed.

Emily shook her head. 'It was all done through our solicitors. He wanted to sell it, his solicitor sent the paperwork to my solicitor, I signed the documents and that was the only contact I had with him about it.'

'I see,' Karen said, shaking her head, clearly in as much disbelief as Emily was about the whole situation.

'So that's why Rob and Molly were at Mum's funeral...' Emily said as the last piece of the puzzle finally slotted into place for her.

Karen nodded. 'It was little Molly who kept him going over the last few years; he knew he couldn't fall apart because he had to be there for her. It wasn't easy for him, but he got up every morning and kept the show on the road. He's doing a great job. He's a really good dad. His work has been very flexible so he's able to be there for Molly as much as he can. Him and that little girl have been through the mill so it's good to see them both doing well again.'

Of course he was a great dad. Emily had always known that; hadn't she seen it first-hand in their days with Alannah? He would race her to the crib to pick their daughter up when she cried and he would hold her tiny form in the crook of his arms, just staring lovingly at her, and she would look back at him, her eyes two pools of bottomless blue, so deep, you could get lost in their depths. But it hurt her to think that it wasn't her daughter he was being a father to now. That another child had replaced her daughter in his heart.

29

Emily went home from Karen's house that day, her head swimming with thoughts. She was still in disbelief after everything she had learnt about Rob and the path his life had taken in the aftermath of her departure. Then when he had found love again, he had had to endure the tragedy of losing it for a second time. How had he survived it? It had also stung to discover that her mother had deliberately concealed his story from her. It was yet another thing that Patricia had kept hidden from her and although she could understand why her mother hadn't told her about Steph and Molly, it still stung. It was like everyone in her life was privy to this great secret and she was the last to know.

She went upstairs and pushed open the door to her mother's bedroom. She closed her eyes and breathed in the scent of the woman she had loved so much. Notes of her perfume with its hints of lavender and bergamot still lingered on the air. She padded across the carpet and sat down on the edge of the bed. She lifted a framed photo of Karen's children from her mother's bedside table. It had been taken at the beach; the two girls were wearing matching seersucker dresses and baby Seán, who only looked to have been a few weeks old, was wearing a striped romper suit. There was another photograph of Emily and Karen standing on either side of their mother that Emily remembered being taken at Patricia's sixtieth birthday. She had looked beautiful that night. She lifted the Patricia Scanlan novel that her mother had been reading and idly flicked through the pages before replacing it down on the table again.

Lately, she had been thinking about what her mother had said about having kept all the cards that their father had sent over the years because she had intended giving them to her daughters eventually. Emily picked herself up from the side of the bed and walked across to her mother's wardrobe. She opened the doors and was immediately greeted by her mother's clothing; there were coats and dresses hanging in there that Emily vividly remembered her wearing. The outfit she had worn at Emily's wedding hung in a dry-cleaning bag and her heart snagged at the memory of how radiant her mother had looked that day as she had walked her down the aisle and handed her over to Rob. It had been a proud moment for both of them. She reached up to the shelf above the hanging rail where her mother kept her jewellery and other possessions. There were various boxes and Emily began to open them. One was a box containing old photographs of the girls when they were younger. She lifted out a few, smiling at the old-fashioned hairstyles and clothing. Another box contained birth certs and other important documents. She made a mental note to let Karen know about it; she might need it when it came to sorting out Patricia's will.

Finally, she came upon an old black shoebox that had been pushed towards the back of the wardrobe. She pulled it towards her and lifted the lid. Inside, she saw a pile of cards and she knew it was what she was looking for. They were all still in their original envelopes but the paper had since yellowed. She picked up the top one and saw the ink of a UK postmark over the stamp of Queen Elizabeth II. Her breathing stilled and her heart rate quickened. She noticed that the gummed seal had been opened. She lifted the flap of the envelope and gingerly took out the card. She turned it around to see an old-fashioned sugar-pink design that read, *Happy Birthday Daughter*.

She opened the card and inside found a ten-pound sterling bank note. The card read:

To Emily,
Happy 8th birthday,
Love from Dad

Emily replaced the card in the envelope, feeling tears pulse in her eyes. She continued to the next one and, once again, there was a ten-pound note inside. It read:

To Karen,
Happy 7th birthday,
Love Dad
P.S. I hope you buy yourself something nice with this

The next one was a Christmas card with a Victorian scene of carol singers gathered in front of a snow-capped church. It said:

Happy Christmas to my daughters,
I hope Santa Claus is good to you,
Love Dad

Emily continued down through them. The cards looked dated now compared with modern designs. They all said a version of the same thing: curt birthday messages without any real feeling, emotion or even interest shown about what they were up to in life. The cards all had either a ten- or twenty-pound sterling note enclosed and Emily wondered, had this been her father's way of trying to make up for abandoning them? Had sending the cards just been a box-ticking exercise for him? A way of easing his guilty conscience? Even though money had been tight for her mother, raising them on her own, it shocked Emily that Patricia hadn't removed any of the money from inside the cards. Patricia had been a woman of principle and maybe she felt it wasn't her money to spend or perhaps she was too proud to take a penny from her ex-husband. They would never know for sure what her reasons were but she had to admire her. Emily noticed that there was no return address inside any of the cards or even written on the back of the envelopes. Had her dad been afraid that they'd track him down and land on his doorstep if he had included it, she couldn't help wonder bitterly.

Emily continued down through them and the letters seemed to stop when the girls were teenagers. Maybe their father had grown despondent because he never received a reply from them or perhaps it was because they were no longer young children and he didn't feel obliged to send a card for their birthdays or Christmas any more. Or maybe he just couldn't be bothered, Emily thought angrily.

She replaced the cards in the box and put it back up on the shelf, feeling fury warm her veins. She slid down onto the carpet, letting her back rest against the wardrobe. Suddenly, she could see things from her mother's perspective. Her father had had two daughters that he had chosen to walk out on. He had turned his back on them, seemingly because a better offer came along. It was a privilege to have a child and if you were so blessed as to have one then you should thank your lucky stars every day for the rest of your life. He had taken the gift of parenthood for granted and it incensed her because she of all people knew just how fleeting it could be. He didn't deserve any sympathy. Sending a few measly cards with hastily written words wasn't enough to repair the damage he had done. She now felt so guilty for how she had reacted when her mother had first told her about the existence of the cards. She could now understand why Patricia had kept his letters a secret; she knew that she had only been trying to protect them. How she wished her mother was still alive; Emily would hug her tightly and tell her that she forgave her.

Just then, she heard the doorbell go downstairs. She picked herself up from the floor and headed down the steps. Through the frosted glass, she could make out the outline of a man. She opened it and her stomach lurched when she realised it was Rob. Her heart rate quickened and she hated how it still reacted to him. She inhaled deeply to calm her body.

'Come in,' she invited. 'Where's Molly?' she asked as he followed her into the house. It was strange seeing him without his daughter. Up until now she had only seen Rob with the child in tow, it was like the pair of them were a package; you never saw one without the other.

'She's playing at a friend's house. I just wanted to make sure you were okay,' he began, 'y'know, after earlier. I hope you weren't upset...'

She put a hand up to stop him, not wishing to prolong the awkwardness for either of them. 'She's a child; she didn't understand what she was saying. I'm sorry for how I reacted... I guess it just caught me off guard...'

He nodded. 'Kids are lethal. I never know what she's going to come out with.'

'I was about to make a cuppa; would you like one?' she offered. It was a lie but she felt she needed to talk to him properly after everything she had learnt today.

'Sure.'

They went into the kitchen and he sat down at the small, circular pine table while she made a pot of tea for them.

'I didn't know about Steph,' she said eventually as she sat down opposite him. 'Karen told me everything. I'm so sorry.' She filled his mug from the pot in an amber arc.

He looked at her in shock. 'Really? You never knew? Nobody ever told you?'

She shook her head. His eyes were so scalded with pain that she was forced to look down at the tiles.

'I figured you already knew...' he said. 'It's been a rough few years.' He exhaled deeply.

'I didn't know you had met someone else. You never asked for a divorce...'

'I know,' he said sheepishly. 'I did plan on asking you for one; I just never got around to it. Steph fell pregnant with Molly pretty soon after we met, so we were focusing on that and then after Molly was born, she discovered she had cancer so it all got put on the back-burner.' He sighed. 'I guess we had bigger problems to deal with...'

Emily nodded in understanding. 'I didn't realise that you and Mum had grown close after everything...' she continued.

'Your mum was a great woman, you know that we always got on well, but when you left... that's when I really got to know her. She helped me through a very tough time. She was the only one I could talk to about it all. Then when I got back on my feet again, I met Steph and I didn't see so much of your mum any more. It was around that time that Steph and I bought a house in Ballyrath so, sometimes, we'd bump into her in the supermarket or if we were out for a walk along the promenade. Then we had Molly and it was so strange when she and Karen hit it off – neither of them made the connection to me at first but when they figured it out, they never let it stand in the way of their friend-ship. As you know, Molly and Cara grew up to be best friends and I guess our lives became intertwined. When Steph got sick, your mum was a great support to us. She was almost like a grand-mother to Molly...' He broke off, clearly thinking about that diffi-cult time in his life. 'After Steph passed away, Patricia was very good to Molly; Molly even called her Nanny Pat! They had a really close bond.'

And yet her mother had never mentioned it to her. Had she really known her at all, she wondered. Maybe she had been afraid of how Emily might react to the news that she was friendly with Rob and his new partner and that, in particular, she was very attached to their little girl.

'Didn't she ever tell you?' Rob asked as though reading her mind.

Emily shook her head. 'I feel like I didn't know her at all in the years since I moved away...' she said forlornly.

'Oh, Em, I didn't mean to upset you... She was the same woman that you knew and loved; nothing changed there. I guess she was just trying to protect you by not mentioning how involved she was in our life.'

Emily nodded. 'Maybe she was afraid of how I'd react,' she suggested with a wry smile. When she thought about it, she could understand her mother's reluctance not to share this with her. She knew it wasn't in Patricia's nature to intentionally hurt her by concealing a secret; she guessed she was probably trying to shield her from any more pain. 'To be honest, she was probably right. I would have lost my shit if she'd told me something like that over the phone but now, since I've come home and got to know your story, and got to know Molly and see how wonderful she is, I can understand how my mother would have become taken with her.'

'I guess she may have felt caught in the middle,' Rob agreed.

'She was a great woman. I'll always be indebted to her. Myself and Molly really miss her.'

Despite the shock of hearing how her mother had been involved in Rob's life and had even helped out with his daughter, it felt good to listen to him speaking about her so fondly. Of course, Emily had known that her mother was a generous woman and always the first to offer help in a crisis, but to hear it validated by someone else made Emily so proud of her.

'You've been through so much. It can't be easy doing it all on your own,' Emily said after a beat.

'I won't lie, it has been tough, but we have a lot of support. When something like that happens, you really see who has your back. Molly is a real live wire but she has been amazing; she makes me get up every morning and doesn't give me a minute to mope around, feeling sorry for myself.'

Emily noticed how his face lit up as he spoke about his daughter and, yet again, she felt that familiar crush in her heart that it wasn't her daughter that he was speaking about so lovingly.

'She makes it all worthwhile,' he continued. 'Well, for the most part... except when she gives out to me for not being able to plait her hair.' He laughed and she caught a glimpse of the old Rob, the Rob with a cheeky smile and a glint in his cool-blue eyes that she had once fallen madly in love with. 'Anyway, enough about me; what have you been up to in Auckland? Your mum said you were working in a restaurant?'

'Yeah, it's a good spot; it's known mainly for its seafood but it does a mix of everything. I rent a flat nearby and that's pretty much it.'

'Did you ever meet anyone else?' he probed.

She shook her head and lowered her eyes to the floor. For some reason, she found herself holding back on telling him about Jonny. 'It feels like I've missed out on a lot while I was away,' she said sadly. 'I'm doing so much catching up. It's difficult being in this house without Mum here.'

'I can imagine.'

They both fell silent, ruminating over everything that had led them here.

'Rob, I want to say that I'm sorry,' she began after a beat.

He cut across her. 'You don't have to—'

'For everything,' she continued, unperturbed. 'For walking out on you like that. I wasn't in a good place. I can't even remember deciding to go, isn't that crazy? I definitely didn't have a plan. I think I just threw some stuff into a bag and went to the airport. I'm also sorry for only seeing my own pain and not recognising that you were grieving too. You deserved better than that. I'm not trying to excuse my behaviour but I wasn't thinking straight... I just wanted to get away from everyone and I thought you were all better off without me. I was selfishly thinking about myself but it's only now since I came back that I can see how much my actions hurt everyone. You, my mum, Karen, I don't know how I walked out on you like that but I don't even recognise that person any more.'

'When you sent that email to say you were in New Zealand, I wanted to go over there to find you but I didn't even know whereabouts to start. I was worried sick about you but everyone told me to leave you alone, that you needed some space. I knew your mental health wasn't good and I was terrified that I was going to get a call to say you'd done something stupid.'

'I thought about it, believe me,' she admitted.

'I replied to you, you know. I sent you so many emails but I never heard from you again.'

'I know. I'm sorry. It was just too hard. If we had kept up emailing one another, I wouldn't have been able to move on.'

'I honestly thought that you just needed a short break from it all. Everyone said that you'd be back again after a few weeks and we'd be able to get through it together. I waited for you for almost three years, hoping you'd arrive back at the house again. I never expected you to stay away permanently. Eventually, I had to accept that you weren't coming back.' A film of tears hazed his eyes, and she hated herself for how she had treated him.

'I never intended to stay away for all this time. I guess the longer I was away, the more difficult it became to come home. I really wish I had come back to see my mum; I'll always regret that.'

'She understood, Em,' he said softly. 'She knew it was difficult for you.'

'I loved when Molly called Alannah her sister, by the way; it felt so good to hear her remembered by someone else.'

He nodded. 'We talk about her all the time. Molly tells everyone she meets that she has a big sister who died; it can totally kill a conversation.'

Emily laughed. 'I can imagine. She's a great kid; she's so sparky and confident. You're doing a great job with her.'

He blushed and they both fell quiet once more.

'I wish things had turned out differently for us...' she said after a moment. Tears welled in her eyes. The tide of emotions from riding the crest of the wave of the high of welcoming her first baby to plumbing the depths of having to say goodbye to her all within the space of a few weeks still caught her sometimes.

He moved his chair closer to hers and put his arm around her. 'Hey,' he soothed.

She allowed herself to be comforted by his embrace. God, it felt so good. So right. These arms had always been her refuge until she had been so blinded by grief that she hadn't been able to seek shelter there any more. How long had it been since she had been physically comforted by someone? In New Zealand, she didn't let anyone close to her; Jonny was the closest she had allowed anyone to get but she would hardly call that a solid relationship. Although she had friends, they were really only acquaintances, people she worked with or the girls renting the flat next door that she sometimes hung out with and watched TV. She realised with a shock that she hadn't let anyone get close to her since Alannah died. She kept everyone at arm's length.

Then it hit her; he wasn't her Rob any more. She didn't belong in these arms any longer. He was Steph and Molly's Rob and he wasn't the same man that she had once loved. She stiffened in his arms and pulled back. She quickly wiped her eyes.

Rob sensed the change in atmosphere and he moved away from her. 'Sorry,' he mumbled, standing up quickly. 'I should probably head on. It's nearly time for me to get Molly anyway.'

30

Sunlight streamed in through the glass sliders in Karen's kitchen, bathing them all in its warmth. Ever since Emily had found the cards their father had sent, she had wanted to talk to her sister about it all. It was eating away at her; she had thought she would be able to cast it aside and forget about their dad but she found it was playing on her mind and she wanted to get her sister's perspective on it. Karen was the only other person in the world who would understand and, once again, Emily was grateful that she had a sister. Sisters knew you better than anybody else. Having a sister was a little bit of childhood that could never be lost – no matter how old you got. Since their mum had died, Emily was keenly aware that Karen was her last remaining tether to her family.

Karen unloaded the dishwasher while her nieces were kneeling on chairs, hunched over colouring books at the table, and a dribbly Seán crawled around at their feet. As she looked over at Keeva and Cara passing markers to one another, she thought how lucky they were to have one another and get to share that sisterly bond too.

Just then, Cara placed down her marker. 'Auntie Emily, do you want to play a game with us?' she asked.

'Of course. How do I play?'

'We draw something and you have to guess what it is, okay?' Keeva explained as she climbed down from the chair and came over beside Emily. Cara brought over a sheet of paper and some markers and followed her sister.

'Sure,' Emily replied.

Keeva lifted the marker and proceeded to draw something; Emily guessed it was an animal of sorts but she couldn't be sure.

'Is it a cat?' she asked, studying the misshapen drawing for clues.

'No,' both girls chorused, shaking their heads in unison.

'A dog?' Emily tried.

'Nooooo.'

'A hamster?'

'No. You're not very good at this game, Auntie Emily.' Cara shook her head in disappointment.

Emily threw her hands up into the air. 'I give up; you're too good.'

'It's a capybara!' Keeva announced as if it was the most obvious thing in the world and she and Cara gave one another a high five.

Emily laughed. She had never even heard of a capybara, let alone tried to recognise one in a drawing.

'How did you not get that?' Karen teased as the girls skipped off, delighted with themselves at having got one over on a grown-up. Emily was enjoying spending this time with her nieces and nephew. All her previous interactions with them had been done over FaceTime but, inevitably, they would get bored and wander away from the screen, so it was good to get to know them properly.

'It's Cara's birthday at the weekend,' Karen groaned.

'Gosh, yes, she'll be five.'

'Usually, I'd have everything organised by now but with Mum gone, I can't seem to summon the energy to do anything... Mum was great whenever it was one of the kids' birthdays, she'd make the cake and give me a hand with the food... I don't know how I'll do it without her.' Her voice wavered. 'To be honest, a party is the last thing on my mind after everything that's happened lately but Cara will be expecting a fuss.'

'Well, it's not every day you turn five, after all,' Emily agreed.

'I know,' she conceded with a heavy sigh. 'I called all of the play centres and of course they're already booked up. I've left it too late to book somewhere which means I'll probably have to have the party here. I break out in hives at the thought.'

'Well, I can help you,' Emily offered. She wasn't going home for another few days yet and she'd enjoy being around for the party.

'Oh, would you?' Karen's shoulders sagged with relief. 'That would be amazing.'

'I'd love to. A few Rice Krispie buns, a bit of pass the parcel and some cake; how hard can it be?'

Karen looked at her, wide-eyed. 'When was the last time you were at a kids' birthday party?'

'Probably not since the eighties,' she admitted.

Karen laughed. 'Well, you're in for a surprise. These days, we have to invite the whole class because we don't want anyone to be left out so that's twenty-seven little girls running around here.' She circled around the room with her index finger. 'And because they're so young, most of the parents will probably stay so we need to cater for them too. We have to be careful of allergies because one girl in the class has a nut allergy.'

'Wow, parties have come a long way since my day.'

Karen's expression grew serious and Emily knew there was something more she wanted to say. 'Y'know, Cara will want to invite Molly,' she began tentatively. 'But I totally understand if you'd rather we didn't? I could explain it to Rob and we could work something out between us; he'd understand... Cara would never have to know.'

Emily shook her head. 'It's her party, of course she wants her bestie there. I'll be fine.'

Karen tilted her head to the side. 'Are you sure?'

Emily nodded.

Karen grinned and clasped her hands together pleadingly. 'So can I put you on face-painting duty?'

Emily groaned. 'Go on then.'

She fell silent for a minute before bringing up the reason for her visit.

'I've been meaning to tell you...' Emily traced her finger over the grain in the table. 'I went through some of Mum's stuff yesterday...'

'Oh yeah?' Karen asked, giving her sister her full attention.

'I found a box with insurance policies and lots of other official docs which you'll probably need when it comes to sorting out her will. It's on the shelf in her wardrobe.'

'That's good to know, thank you.'

'I... eh... I also found the cards...' she added tentatively.

'What cards?' Karen asked.

'The ones Dad sent to us. Mum kept them all in a box.'

'I see...' Karen said, falling silent.

'There were birthday cards and Christmas cards but they didn't say much. They all had money inside them. Mum obviously left it there for us.'

'Oh, God, poor Mum,' Karen choked. 'That must have been hard on her getting those cards and not knowing what to do about them...'

Emily nodded. 'I know. I was angry when she told us about them initially but I understand it now. She did the right thing.'

Karen fell silent. 'Do you ever think about...' She jiggled her shoulders, not wanting to say the words. 'Y'know...?'

'What do you mean? Making contact with him?'

Karen nodded and pinched her eyes shut. 'God, I feel like I'm betraying Mum by even mentioning it.'

'I guess over the years, I did. I imagined we'd have this big, tearful reunion where he'd explain his side of the story and I'd forgive him because it was all just a giant misunderstanding. But then I read the cards yesterday and I can't explain it... I felt... nothing for him. There was no remorse or even emotion in them, he didn't even give a return address, so I guess he didn't want us to contact him... It's too late now for me. But if you wanted to try and contact him, I'd understand. I'm sure Auntie Brenda would give you his address?'

Karen shook her head. 'No way. I'm definitely not ready right now. I can't say how I'll feel in the future but at the moment, I couldn't go there. As Mum always said, "Us Gallagher girls have to stick together." We've managed okay without him for all these years; I think we'll be all right.' She smiled at her sister.

Emily reached for her hand across the table, grateful she had this special person in her life.

31

The following weekend, Emily sidestepped out of the way and lifted the birthday cake up high just in time to avoid a child colliding with it. 'Woah there,' she cried, but the little girl continued running, making no effort to slow down, oblivious to the near disaster that had almost ensued. She continued down the hallway and into the kitchen where her sister and brother-in-law were both puff-cheeked as they blew up balloons. Emily set the cake down on the island. She had made a two-tiered, white-chocolate Kinder Surprise cake because Karen had told her that Cara loved Kinder Eggs. Apparently, she spent hours watching other children opening them online, which baffled Emily.

'What a cake!' Karen cried as she tied the balloon she had just been inflating. 'I'd forgotten how good you were at those. Cara is going to love it!'

Baking the cake for family celebrations had always been Emily's thing. She had a knack for plying fondant and perfecting delicate decorations that nobody else seemed to have patience for. The concentration it took allowed her mind to switch off and be quiet which had been rare in those days. People had always told her that she should set up her own baking business but it had been a hobby; she was pretty sure if it had been a job, the enjoyment might have worn off very quickly.

Soon the rest of the children had arrived and they zigzagged through the house in every direction. Emily noticed that none of them walked; they all ran wherever it was that they wanted to go. Just looking at their boundless energy was enough to exhaust her.

Dave came up alongside her as if reading her mind. 'Welcome to the jungle,' he hissed. 'It's going to be a long two hours.'

She set up her face-painting stall in a corner in the kitchen; soon the first child sat down on the stool before her and she got to work.

'Why are you here?' Molly asked, pointing her index finger at her as she entered the kitchen and ran over. 'Everywhere we go, you're there too.'

'Because I'm Cara's aunt. I like your sparkly dress,' Emily said as she worked on the child sitting on the stool.

Molly whipped it up above her waist. 'I put shorts under it in case I want to play football.'

'Clever,' Emily replied. She finished the child in front of her and then Molly, who was next in line, took a seat on the stool. 'What would you like me to paint for you?'

'I want to be a bat.'

'Oh, like Batman?'

'No, just a bat.'

'Really? Okay.'

'Hey there,' Rob said, coming up alongside her.

Her heart stalled and she hated how it betrayed her so easily after all this time. She could never have imagined how entwined Rob's life and her sister's life had become and she knew she was just going to have put her own feelings aside and forget about it. Today was about Cara.

'I see Karen roped you in to help,' he continued.

'I don't mind.' She concentrated on painting Molly's face, relieved that she had an excuse not to look at him. 'It's nice to be here for Cara's birthday.'

Emily noticed a sizeable queue had started building behind Molly so she worked faster. Soon the child was unrecognisable as her porcelain skin was covered in menacing black face paint, drawn in the shape of bat wings.

'What do you say, Molly?' Rob prompted when she had finished.

'Thank you, Emily,' she sang as she ran off towards Cara.

'You might be a few days trying to wash that off,' Emily apologised.

'I'd better let you get on with it.' He raised his brows in the direction of the line of children waiting for her services. 'You have some very impatient-looking customers.'

Emily laughed as the next child took a seat in front of her.

The party went by in a blur. The children had kept coming and Emily barely had time to raise her head. She saw Karen across the kitchen juggling trays of sausage rolls and chicken nuggets as she attempted to slot them into the oven and Dave was kept busy pouring copious cups of orange squash.

It was a relief when she finally heard Karen announce that it was time for cake. All the guests gathered around Cara in the kitchen and the child beamed as her friends sang 'Happy Birthday' to her. After Cara had blown out her candles, Karen cut the cake while Dave handed slices out on paper plates. Then eventually, when Emily felt ready to collapse, people began to leave.

When all the children had gone home, Rob entered the kitchen with his palms raised in mock surrender. 'Karen, I'm sorry. I can't get Molly to come home. They keep ganging up on me whenever I try get her to leave.'

Karen laughed. 'Molly has you wrapped around her little finger, Rob. Those two are as thick as thieves. Leave them play for a bit. I think the grown-ups deserve a little party of their own now.' She produced a bottle of wine with a flourish. 'We've earned this, what do you reckon?'

'Now, this is my kind of party,' Dave said, rubbing his hands together.

'I won't say no,' Rob sighed.

Karen uncorked the bottle of wine and poured four glasses. She handed one to her husband, one to Rob and then finally one to Emily. Emily raised the glass to her lips and breathed in its heady aroma.

'Well, that was a success.' Karen raised her glass in a toast. 'Thank you all for helping out.' Then she turned to her older sister. 'And you, Emily, were a lifesaver making the cake and doing the face painting today too. I couldn't have done it without you. The children all loved it. Thank you so much.'

'I'm glad I was here for it.' It was the truth; she had enjoyed herself. It was good to spend time with her nieces and nephew and see them having fun with their friends. She felt like she knew them a little better and she couldn't help wonder now how many similar days she had missed out on over the last few years.

They clinked their glasses together and Emily felt her shoulders start to unwind as she drank her wine. Although she hadn't been under as much pressure as her sister, she had barely had time to look up as child after child waited in line for her to paint their face. Some of them had requested simple designs like a princess but a few requests had thrown her, like the little girl who wanted to be an airplane, leaving Emily stumped.

They chatted and laughed and, as Emily started to relax, she found she was enjoying herself. Karen opened another bottle and refilled their glasses.

'I really enjoyed myself today. It's good to have you back, Emily. It's like the good old days,' Dave said, raising the glass to his lips. 'Before the kids came along and ruined everything.' He laughed.

Karen shot a look in her husband's direction. 'Dave!' she hissed, hiking up her brows.

He soon realised his faux pas. 'Oh shit, guys.' He looked desperately from Emily to Rob and back again. 'Sorry,' he added. 'Talk about putting my foot in it... I just meant it felt good, I wasn't thinking about all the other stuff...' He broke off, realising he was digging a hole for himself.

'It's okay,' Emily said, feeling sorry for him. She knew what he meant because she felt it too. Today had reminded her of better days. She could hear the echoes of all those times they had spent in this house before kids had arrived. Sunny BBQs and dinner parties stretching late into the night, birthday celebrations, watching the All Ireland final with a few beers. So many happy days. It was hard to believe just how much the course of all their lives, but most especially her life and Rob's, had changed immeasurably in that time.

The atmosphere had turned and the carefree laughter that they shared just minutes ago had evaporated. Just then, Molly and Cara appeared in the kitchen dressed in princess dresses.

Rob cleared his throat and stood up. 'I'd better seize my opportunity,' he announced, standing up off the stool and glancing at his watch. 'It's nearly Molly's bedtime.'

'I'd better go too and let you get the kids to bed,' Emily said. She leant in and gave Karen a kiss on the cheek. 'Thanks for a lovely party.'

Karen hugged her back warmly. 'No, thank you for everything. It was good to have you here today, Em.'

32

Rob, Emily and Molly left Karen's house and walked down Seaview Road together. With the help of a party bag stuffed with sweets, Rob had finally managed to bribe Molly to leave Cara's side. The curve of Dublin Bay spread out below them where the sunlight played with the light-dappled water. From up here, at the foothill of the Dublin Mountains, the view stretched from furze-covered Bray Head, right down to the candy-striped Poolbeg chimneys like a scene from a pop-up picture book. Woodsmoke from nearby chimneys was belched out in cumulous puffs and it scented the cool evening air.

'So when do you go back to New Zealand?' Rob asked as his breath fogged the air between them. Molly skipped along in front of them, happily munching on her jellies.

'In three more days.'

Molly swung around and interrupted them as she bit the head off a jelly baby. 'Daddy?'

'Yes, sweetheart?'

'Did Alannah like jelly babies like me?'

'I don't know. She was too small to eat them.'

'Oh yeah, I forgotted that babies don't have any teeth.' She fished another sweet from the bag and popped it into her mouth and went back to her skipping.

Rob rolled his eyes pleadingly at Emily in a manner that said, *See? Do you see what I have to put up with?* and Emily couldn't help but laugh.

'You're probably looking forward to getting back to your life over there,' he continued as Molly went ahead of them.

She shrugged. 'I guess so... my boss in the restaurant has been very good. He's given me as much time off as I need but I have to get back to work eventually.'

Soon they came to a stop outside her mother's house. Molly swung around and looked at her father, her small face alight. 'Are we going to Nanny Pat's house?' she asked hopefully.

'No, sweetie.' He shot an anxious look in Emily's direction. 'Nanny Pat died, remember?' he explained carefully.

'Oh yeah, she's in heaven with my mummy.'

'That's right.'

He looked back at Emily and mouthed, *Sorry about that.*

She waved her hand. 'Don't worry about it.'

Silence cloaked the air between them until, eventually, Emily gestured towards the house. 'I... eh... I'd better go.'

Rob shifted awkwardly on his feet. 'Goodnight, Emily. If I... eh... don't see you before you head back... safe travels...' He dropped his gaze to the ground. 'I wish you all the best. I hope life will be good to you...'

Her heart twisted for all they had once shared. There was so much water under the bridge between them, and although they carried the scars of their invisible wounds, they had also shared something bigger that would always connect them: a love for their child. 'Thanks, Rob, you too.' She could hear the wobble in her voice. 'Take care of yourselves.'

Suddenly, she found herself leaning in to hug him; she felt the brush of his stubble against her cheek. She inhaled the familiar scent of his aftershave, the same musky scent that he had worn since she had met him. She breathed him in for the last time. Then she turned away and began walking up the cobble-locked driveway.

'Hey, Emily?' she heard Molly's lisp calling after her.

Emily turned around to see the child pointing her finger accusingly at her.

'Why are *you* going into Nanny Pat's house? She's not there because she died-ed.'

She noticed Rob wincing beside her. 'Molly!' he chastised, but he knew he was wasting his time; he was no match for this wilful little girl.

'Because this used to be my house when I was a little girl,' Emily explained. 'I'm staying here until I go back to New Zealand.'

'Did you know Nanny Pat too?'

'I did; she was my mother.'

'Wow...' Molly said as the cogs in her head started to work it out. Suddenly, her face lit up. 'So then your mummy died like my mummy!' She looked pleased by the fact that they had this in common.

Emily could see Rob looked mortified. *Sorry*, he mouthed over her head. Emily smiled back at him. You couldn't help but laugh at the child's lack of tact. Molly's attitude to death was refreshing. Emily knew that the little girl was too young to understand the full implications of loss. Nature was clever how it could protect a child's fragile mind from the awful, enduring reality of death; she wished it worked the same way for adults, but Emily loved how Molly said whatever it was that she was thinking. She never skirted around the subject or feared mentioning a loved one's name for fear of upsetting the person like most adults did. In fact, she talked about Alannah and her mother like they had just popped out for a bit and that they'd be back again soon. Emily found it soothing.

'Can we go into Nanny Pat's house too?' she asked Emily.

'No,' Rob said firmly, cutting in before Emily had a chance to speak. 'We need to get you home to bed.'

'Pleeease, Daddy!' she begged. 'I want to see if my dappodils growed up yet.'

'You mean daffodils,' Rob corrected. 'What daffodils?' he asked in bewilderment.

'Me and Nanny Pat planted them and we were going to watch them grow.'

Emily was shocked. 'You planted daffodils with Nanny Pat?' It felt strange referring to her mother like this but she didn't want to confuse the child by calling her something else.

Molly nodded her head enthusiastically. 'She said I was a great gardenerer.'

'I guess they must have done it together one of the times Molly was over here when your mum was looking after her for me,' Rob offered by way of explanation.

'Look, why don't you both come in for a few minutes,' Emily said to appease the child, 'and let's see if we can find those daffodils.'

Molly began sprinting up the drive.

'Are you sure?' Rob said uncertainly. 'You don't have to, you know...'

'Of course I am. Come on.' She circled her arm in the direction of the house.

Emily put the key in the lock and let them all into the house, trying not to think about how strange this was. Here she was, inviting her ex and his daughter in and yet, strangely, she found she enjoyed being in their company. Being in Molly's presence was hypnotic and she couldn't help but fall under her spell as she spent time with her. It was like having a possible version of her daughter brought to life. As she had chatted to her earlier while she was painting her face, she had found herself wondering if this was what Alannah would have looked like. Would she have had the same porcelain skin and soft honey-blonde curls like this child? Would she have been as talkative, her curiosity as insatiable? Asking question after question until she was weary thinking up answers?

Emily brought them through to the kitchen, then she opened the French doors that led outside. Molly immediately ran towards a tall, thick-barked chestnut tree that stood proudly at the end of the garden. She and Karen used to climb high up into its sturdy boughs at kids. On sunny days, they would sit up there happily perched, reading their books. They had even carved their names somewhere in its bark.

'Look, there they are!' Molly cried, pointing to the base of the tree where a crop of sunny-yellow daffodils had recently poked their heads above the soil. 'They're the ones we planted.'

Emily felt a wave of emotion overcome her. It must have been one of the last things her mother had got to do and now she would never get to see the fruits of her labour. She could imagine how their cheery crowns would have put a smile on her face.

'You did a great job; they're beautiful,' Emily said. 'I think Nanny Pat would have loved them. And now every time I see them, I'll think about her.'

Rob looked at her sympathetically. 'Right then, Miss Molly, now that we've seen the daffodils, we need to be heading on.'

The three of them made their way up the garden path and back into the house.

Molly came to a stop in the kitchen and pointed at one of the pictures that was displayed on the fridge. It was of a painting of a smiling Santa face with a cotton wool beard. 'That's my painting!' she cried. 'I maded it for Nanny Pat at Chrissamas time.'

'Wow, it's very good,' Emily said.

'Can I have a biscuit because I didded a good picture?' Molly asked, pointing towards one of the kitchen cupboards.

Emily laughed at how clever the child was. 'How did you know Nanny Pat kept the biscuits up there?' She smiled. Her mother had kept all the sweet treats in this same press since she and Karen had been children.

'Because she always gave me lots of treats.'

'I bet she did.'

It was comforting to see Molly's affection for her mother; they had clearly had a close relationship.

'Come on now, Molly, you've enough treats in your party bag,' Rob said. 'We need to get going. You've a big day tomorrow.'

'Oh yeah?' Emily asked.

'I've got my first ballet 'cital,' Molly announced proudly. 'Nanny Pat was s'posed to come to watch me but she can't now because she's dead-ed.'

'Molly!' Rob held his head in his hands.

'What?' Molly protested.

Rob turned to Emily. 'I'm sorry,' he explained. 'Your mum sometimes took Molly to her ballet class if I got stuck late in work and she had said she'd come along to the recital tomorrow. Molly was really looking forward to having her there.'

'I had a special surprise for her,' Molly said, turning down her bottom lip wistfully.

'You did?' Rob asked. 'I didn't know anything about that. What was it?'

'I can't tell you, Daddy.'

'Well, maybe I could come see it instead, if you wanted?' Emily offered because she hated seeing the child looking so glum. But no sooner had she said it than she regretted it. Would Rob think she was overstepping the mark? She wished she could pick the words up off the air and shove them back into her mouth once more.

She watched as Molly's face lit up. 'Yes, please,' she sang.

'Are you sure?' Rob asked, turning to face her. 'I know you're probably busy getting packed up and everything...'

'Of course... I'd love to... I'm very intrigued by this surprise,' she added weakly. 'Where is it on?'

'It's in St Mary's parish hall at five.'

'Great, I'll be there.'

'Thanks, Emily,' he said and she noticed a flicker of gratitude in his eyes. He paused as though there was something else that he wanted to say before he changed his mind. 'Right, Miss Molly.' He placed his palm on her head and steered her in the direction of the door. 'Now this time, we are definitely going.'

'Aww,' she groaned. 'Goodnight, Emily.'

'Goodnight, Molly. I'm really excited for the recital tomorrow.'

33

Early spring sunlight lingered on the evening air as Emily made her way towards the parish hall the following day. She could hear her mother say, 'There's a grand stretch in evenings now,' and she instantly felt that familiar sting of sorrow that she wouldn't get to hear her say those words this year. The predictability of her mother's sayings had sometimes driven her mad, but now she would do anything to hear that refrain again. How was it that the things that once irritated her no end were now the things she missed most?

'Emily!' Rob cried, pulling her out of her thoughts. 'Over here.' He waved. She saw the two of them standing outside the building, waiting for her. Emily guessed from the low, flat-roofed design and the pebble-dashed walls that the hall had been built sometime in the fifties. Molly was standing beside her father wearing a marshmallow-pink tutu that fanned out around her tiny waist. She was grinning with those perfect baby teeth of hers and her eyes peeped out from beneath a fan of dark lashes. She looked as sweet as spun sugar and Emily felt her heart stumble once more. She waited for a gap in the traffic before hurrying across the street to meet them.

'Sorry, I hope I'm not late,' she said, slightly out of breath when she got there.

'Not at all. Molly wanted to wait for you so that the three of us would all go in together.' Rob smiled at her and she felt her stomach flip. Even after all this time, he still had this effect on her.

They went inside the building and instantly the dank, musty smell took her back to her childhood. It was the same hall where Emily had performed her own school concerts and spent many long days at Irish dancing feiseanna but it seemed smaller than she remembered now. Once inside, parents and ballerinas bustled about them. They followed the other parents down to a room where the children were gathered with their teacher.

'There's Ms Cecile, Mol,' Rob said to Molly. 'You go over and line up with the other girls.'

But instead of running over to her friends like they would have expected, Molly clung tighter to Rob's hand.

'Are you okay?' Rob asked.

Emily noticed she looked a little pale and withdrawn. She wasn't her usual self, springing around with bounce and energy.

'My tummy feels all icky, Daddy.' She placed her palm on her stomach for emphasis.

'You're probably just nervous,' Rob explained. 'Sometimes, our tummies can feel funny when we're a little scared but I know you'll be great.'

Molly looked around at the other dancers. 'I don't look as good as everybody else,' she said, anxiously scanning the row of girls as they lined up.

'Of course you do,' Rob said.

'But my hair isn't like their hair.' She pushed back a stray curl that had fallen in front of her eyes. Emily glanced at the other children with their hair pulled tightly off their faces and swept back into neat buns. Each stray hair carefully matted down with clips and gels and sprays. She looked at the bun that Rob had attempted to do; he had done his best but it sagged at the nape of Molly's neck and loose coils of hair sprung out from it. Years of experience of female hair told her that Molly's tangle of hair would be tricky to manage at the best of times.

'Do you want me to try and fix it up a little?' Emily offered.

Molly's eyes shone up at her. 'Yes please, Emily.'

Emily gently untied the child's hair, remembering how much she had hated getting her own hair done as a child. She used her hands to guide the curls into place and then smoothed it all down. She twisted it into a coil and then used the hair elastic that Rob had originally used to secure it in place.

'There,' she announced when she had finished.

'That's so much better than my effort,' Rob conceded.

Emily bent down on her hunkers and held the child at arm's length. 'You look so beautiful.'

'Are you sure you're feeling okay?' Rob asked.

She nodded solemnly. 'I know my mummy is watching me. She said she'd be with me every time I was scared or nervous.'

Emily pushed down a lump in her throat as Rob said, 'You're right, she is here, watching you, and I know she's very proud of you.'

'Do you think Alannah is here too?' she asked.

He nodded. 'Oh, I think so.'

'And I'm pretty sure Nanny Pat is here to see the show as well,' Emily added. 'I know she wouldn't want to miss the surprise.' She heard her voice crack with emotion. This poor little mite had been through crushing grief that no child should ever experience.

Just then, they heard Ms Cecile clap her hands together. '*On y va*, girls,' she announced in her French-hybrid English.

'You'd better go,' Rob said to Molly. He planted a kiss on the top of her head as she walked slowly towards the group. Suddenly, she spun around and ran back to them. She threw her arms around Emily, catching her completely by surprise. 'Thanks for doing my hair, Emily,' she said before running back over to her friends.

Emily watched as the children all lined up like Ms Cecile instructed, then she and Rob headed out to the hall to take their seats in the audience. She tried to switch off the part of her brain that told her that this was crazy. What the hell was she doing here with her ex watching his daughter perform at a ballet recital? How had she allowed herself to get entwined in their life? She knew she shouldn't be allowing this to happen and yet she couldn't stop herself; the child enthralled her. It was like they had tied her to the end of a string and lured her into their world. Just being in the presence of Rob and his little girl had stirred up feelings that Emily hadn't experienced in years. She knew she was being pulled in to a dangerous place where the waters could swirl and eddy and yet she found she didn't want to leave.

Soon the curtains parted and Emily forgot about her worries and instead watched the tiny ballerinas with their fluffy tutus as they filed onto the stage on tiptoe with their arms arched above their heads. Ms Cecile stood before them and guided them through their performance. Then she moved to the side and they were both stunned when Molly stepped forward on her tiptoes into the centre of the stage, as the other girls stood in a semicircle behind her. She began to dance a solo part, twirling in a circle and sweeping her arms gracefully to the right, then to the left. Emily's heart leaped into her mouth as she watched her perform. She suddenly felt a rush of fierce protectiveness towards this child after everything that she had been through. She thought about the nervous little girl who had stood clinging to her father's hand backstage and how she had now mastered those nerves to dance alone on the stage with all the eyes of the audience fixed upon her. She imagined that this must be what it was like to be a parent and feel a primal instinct to protect your child from all the world's pain even though you knew that you never could, because that was the frailty of the human condition. She didn't know how Rob was faring but a quick glance to the side told her he was feeling emotional too. Emily noticed a film of tears wetting his eyes as he held up his phone to film her.

When she had finished, they both stood up out of their seats and clapped for her.

'She was amazing,' Emily gushed. 'You should be so proud.'

'I don't think there has ever been a prouder father. When I think of all she's been through...' His voice choked.

After the dancers had left the stage, they went backstage and Ms Cecile brought the children out to meet their parents.

Molly giggled and ran over to them when she saw them.

Rob lifted her up and swung her around. 'You were amazing. You never told me you had a solo part!' Rob gushed.

She crinkled her nose. 'That was the surprise, Daddy!'

'Well, it was a big surprise. I'm so proud of you.'

They left the hall on a high and walked home together. They reached Rob's house first. Emily saw that he had bought one of the ex-corporation houses towards the end of Seaview Road. It wasn't too far from where her mother and Karen lived. Like most of the neighbours, he had modernised it with anthracite-grey windows and a navy front door. After the house on Groveton Road had been sold, the mortgage paid off and all the professional fees paid, they had each received a small sum of the proceeds. She guessed he must have used that money as a deposit for this place.

'Can Emily come in to our house, Daddy?' Molly asked as they stood on the path outside.

Rob turned to Emily, shifting from foot to foot. 'Do you... eh... want to come in?' he offered.

'Sure,' she found herself saying, even though her head

screamed at her to say no. What the hell was she doing? But she had enjoyed the evening so much, and the thoughts of going back to her mother's empty house all alone filled her with despair. So, even though it went against all her better judgement, she followed them inside the house.

Rob led her into their living room which had been painted a vibrant, sunny yellow colour. In an age where most people chose to decorate their interiors in muted, neutral tones, this room was a brave colour choice but it worked. She looked around at the quirky furniture and guessed these had been Steph's touches. Immediately, Emily got a sense that Steph had been a fun and vivacious woman. At the end of the room, she saw a gallery wall of family photos. She moved closer and saw a picture of Rob, Steph and Molly taken at a birthday party. Another was of the three of them, screaming open-mouthed on a rollercoaster. Her heart twisted at the image of the smiling, sun-kissed woman that looked back at her from the photos.

'She was beautiful,' she said to Rob as he came up alongside her.

'She was,' he agreed sadly.

Then her eyes landed on a photo of Alannah taken when she was just two weeks old, sitting propped up against the back of the sofa. She was wearing a mint-green dress with matching tights, a set that Emily remembered buying. She had adored the outfit on her. It was a photo that Rob must have taken because she didn't have that one. Her heart snagged at the image of her beautiful daughter. She moved closer to the photo and traced her finger over the glass. She hadn't expected to see a photo of Alannah hanging on his wall but she was so glad that he had included her in his family photos. She hadn't put up any photographs in her flat in New Zealand. She told herself it was because the landlord didn't allow her to hang anything on the walls but she knew really it was because she was afraid that having a constant reminder of her loss displayed in her flat would break her. She was surprised to find that seeing Alannah's photo here actually felt good. Maybe when she went back to Auckland, she'd put some photos of her around the place, she thought. She felt ready now.

Molly yawned loudly. 'Me tired, Daddy.'

'Come on, love, I'll bring you up to bed,' Rob said. 'You've had a long day.'

'Can Emily tuck me in tonight, Daddy?'

'Well, I don't think...'

'Pleeeeese, Daddy?' she begged.

Rob shot a nervous look in Emily's direction.

'I don't mind,' she offered.

'Are you sure?'

'I'd love to.'

Before she could change her mind, Molly grabbed her by the hand and led her towards the stairs. They climbed the steps together and then Emily followed her down the landing to a bedroom painted in a delicate calamine-pink shade. A canopy draped down over the bed and had colourful butterflies dotted all over it. She followed Molly over to a little reading nook with a beanbag and bookshelves.

'Your room is lovely, Molly.' It was a room for a little girl without being too sugary. It was the type of bedroom she had once envisaged for her daughter and again she felt that familiar pang of regret that she would never get to experience that.

'My mummy did it. She was a ninterior designer.'

'She had good taste.'

Molly began kicking off her trainers. Then she took off the leggings and sweatshirt that Rob had changed her into before they left St Mary's hall. She pulled a tiny blue nightdress over her head and headed into the bathroom to brush her teeth.

'Can you squeeze this for me, Emily?' Molly called out. Emily joined her in the bathroom and used her thumbs to push some of the paste onto the bristles of the toothbrush. Emily waited while the child brushed her teeth and tried to hum a song at the same time. Then when she had finished, she ran back into her room, dived onto the bed and wormed her way beneath the duvet.

Emily sat down on the edge of her bed and saw a framed photograph of Molly and her mother. The woman had auburn-coloured curly hair but shared many features with her daughter.

'That's a lovely photo of you and your mummy,' Emily said. 'What was she like, your mummy?'

'Well she had really, *really* curly hair like me but it was a different colour. She had orange hair and mine is blonde. She liked baking and we always maded cupcakes together with loads of sprinkles. She was really pretty like you.'

Emily pulled the duvet up around Molly's shoulders so that she was covered right up to her chin. She stroked the smooth skin of her forehead. Molly's eyelids grew heavier and soon began to close as Emily traced delicate patterns with her fingertips. She sighed and snuggled deeper into the pillows. 'Me tired, Emily.'

'Well, you get some rest; you've had a busy day today.' She brushed the child's hair back off her face and Molly closed her eyes. She stroked the smooth skin of her forehead where a network of tiny blue veins ran along just underneath the surface. It felt like silk beneath her fingertips. Emily watched as the child's breathing began to slow as her body relaxed. Was this how it felt to stroke your daughter's skin ever so gently in feather-light, tracing move-ments until they finally gave into sleep, she wondered. Or to watch the shallow rise and fall of your child's chest as they drew breath into those ever so tiny lungs? All these intimate moments of parenthood that had been too quickly robbed from her.

Emily closed her own eyes and allowed herself to imagine

what it would be like if Molly was her child – just for a second – just to know how it would feel. Her period as a mother had been snatched away so quickly before she ever got to experience these things and now that she was in her mid-forties, she knew that the chance to have another child had most probably passed her by.

Suddenly, Molly let out a breathy sigh without opening her eyes. 'Emily?'

'Yes, sweetie?'

'Thank you for coming to my 'cital today. I liked having you there.'

Emily's heart constricted and a lump stuck like a clot in her throat. Dear God, this child. What was she doing to her? She was amazing and wonderful and she made her heart sing every time she was nearby. In getting to know Molly, she had entered a world where it was brighter and sunnier and now that she had experienced it, she didn't want to go back into the shade any more. But Emily knew that this was dangerous, like skating on a sheath of ice that was starting to thaw; the more she moved into the centre, the riskier it became. Emily knew she could fall, fall deeply if she wasn't careful, and if she did, she wouldn't survive.

Emily stayed sitting on the side of Molly's bed, watching the child with her mouth half open in a gentle O shape and her curls fanned around her head on the pillow as she finally gave up the battle and surrendered herself to sleep. Eventually, when she was sure she was in deep slumber, Emily picked herself up from the edge of the bed, taking care not to disturb the child, then she tiptoed across the carpet and crept out of the room before making her way downstairs again.

'Did she go off okay?' Rob asked when she came into the kitchen.

Emily nodded. 'She was out like a light.'

He moved to the wine fridge that was built into the island. 'I was going to open a bottle of wine; would you like a glass?'

She hesitated. It had been such a lovely day, she had enjoyed the time she had spent with Rob and Molly so much, but she knew she should probably go home.

'Just the one,' he encouraged, grinning at her in a way that was so familiar, it made her heart flip.

'Go on then,' she said as he uncorked the wine and poured a glass for each of them.

They sat down onto the teal-coloured sofa and sipped the chilled Pinot Grigio. This had once been a familiar routine for them: opening a bottle of wine on a Friday night after a long week in work. She picked up a pink paisley-patterned cushion from the sofa and hugged it against her. As she looked around the room at the furnishings, Steph's work as an interior designer showed. There were little touches of her personality everywhere. Her style was louder and more colourful than Emily's more understated tastes but, nonetheless, Steph had had a good eye for detail.

'Thanks for coming today,' Rob said as he took a sip from his glass.

'Thanks for inviting me. I enjoyed it.' They were both being polite. Guarded. There was so much shared experience between them – she had once known every inch of his body, she had almost been able to know what he was about to say before he said it – but now it was like sitting opposite a complete stranger. A lot had happened since they were last together.

'Molly loved having you there,' he went on. 'I think she likes having a female around, to be honest.' He used his thumb to make a path through the condensation that had built on the side of the wine glass.

'It must be hard on her without her mum.'

Rob nodded. 'I try my best but there are just some things that mums do better,' he said sadly. 'Like hair, for example.'

Emily laughed as the tension softened between them. 'Wait until you hit the teenage years. That's when the fun will really begin.'

He exhaled heavily. 'I'll have my work cut out for me.'

'You're doing a good job, Rob.'

'She adores you, you know. You're so good with her.'

'Well, she's a great kid.'

Silence fell heavily between them until Emily eventually asked the question she had wanted to ask ever since she had laid eyes on him in the graveyard that day. 'Do you still think about her?' she asked, holding her breath for his reply.

'You mean Alannah?' he asked, holding her gaze.

She nodded, feeling her breathing stop.

'All the time. Sometimes, it just gets me, you know? After all this time. I get caught up in what could have been. Especially when Molly does something new or comes out with something funny, I wonder would Alannah have done that too or would she have been the same?'

Emily nodded. They fell quiet and she guessed they were both thinking about Alannah and what might have been. All the unknowns that they never had a chance to discover.

'Did you... eh... ever think about having more children?' he ventured.

She shook her head, not trusting herself to speak. She felt all the old hurt rush up inside her, fizzing up like a soft drink that had been shaken too hard. The injustice engulfing her. Threatening to wash her away. All she had been robbed of. And then she thought about Molly sleeping soundly upstairs and how lovely it had been to tuck her up and watch her drift off to sleep. She'd never get to experience that now and it was like a second grief upending her once more. The air had changed between them. She needed to get out of here. 'I should probably go home...' She stood up to leave.

His face creased in confusion. 'Is everything okay?'

She bit down on her lip. 'It's just... well... this.' She gestured around the room.

Rob looked at her blankly.

'It's too hard, Rob. I keep thinking this is what it would have been like if things had gone right for us.' Her voice wavered on a knife-edge of tears. 'It feels like every minute I spend with you both, I'm torturing myself with what might have been.'

'Oh, Emily, I'm sorry. I never wanted to upset you. I should have known it would have been difficult for you...'

'It's not your fault and Molly's great... I love being around her but it's when I go home and think of everything I've lost... and all the experiences of being a mother that I've missed out on... that's what kills me. I worked so hard on getting myself back on an even keel again in New Zealand; I had some really dark days, Rob. Sometimes, when I got up in the morning, I honestly didn't know if I'd make it through until evening time. It took a long time for me to get myself back on my feet again. I'm in a good place now but I'm petrified that one little slip and it'll all unravel again and I can't go back there again. I'd never survive it a second time.'

'Hey.' He walked across the floor and took her in his arms. She breathed in his manly scent. So familiar and enticing, it was a balm to her wounded soul. She had tried to deny it but she knew that, lately, something had changed between them and she couldn't suppress it any longer. His face moved closer to hers until there was just millimetres between them. Suddenly, his lips found hers and she felt them press, warm and full, against her own. For a moment, she was stunned, as if she had forgotten what to do, but then her body remembered him and she felt herself soften as she kissed him back with all the same fervour. His hands moved up into her hair as he cupped her head closer to his. His touch was like a warm blanket. Safe and familiar. She wanted this just as badly as he did. Then her head caught up with her heart as reality hit her like a smack. What was she doing? How could she let herself come undone like this? She was playing a dangerous game and she knew she'd be left in the wreckage if she didn't end it now. She pulled back quickly, feeling the shock of cold air where his mouth had just been.

'I can't...' she said, pulling away from him before running out the door.

34

Back in her mother's house later that evening, Emily finally allowed the tears that had been threatening, to fall. She was furious with herself. What on earth had she been at, letting Rob kiss her like that? How could she allow herself to get drawn into their world so easily? She was playing with fire. Molly had already captured Emily's heart; she was completely enamoured by the little girl and the more time she spent with her, the more she was falling under her spell. And then there was Rob too: a decent and kind man, but there was too much shared pain to allow herself to go back there. She had spent so long building herself up, brick by brick; how had she let herself get torn down so easily like that? She knew she couldn't allow herself to be vulnerable so it was her own fault that she was paying the price for her stupidity now. Then she remembered Jonny; how would he feel about her kissing somebody else? Although their relationship was casual, she imagined he'd be hurt. When she had kissed Rob, she had felt herself come alive beneath his touch. It was like waking up again after being asleep for years; her whole body had responded in a way that she had never felt with Jonny.

It will all be fine once you get back to Auckland, she kept telling herself. *Just two more days and then you can forget about all of this,* she repeated. Life was easier over there when she didn't have to face these constant reminders of everything she once had. Once she was back in her familiar routine again, she wouldn't need to deal with these feelings any more. She could shut out her grief for Alannah and her mother's loss too. She could push Rob and little Molly out of her head and just get back to herself again. She could put them all into the same box and shut the lid down on it once more.

She got up the next day and began packing up her belongings. She unzipped the case that she had brought with her and began folding her clothes and putting them into it. She hadn't taken much. She had been reeling from the news that her mother was ill so she hadn't had the time to pack properly; she had just chucked a couple of sweatshirts, jeans, T-shirts and a few other bits into the bag. She was folding a pair of leggings when she heard the doorbell go. She stood up and went downstairs to answer it. She pulled it open and saw Rob and Molly were standing there. Her heart sped up and she felt the blood rush into her ears.

'You left your coat behind yesterday,' he began. 'I wanted to give it to you before you left.'

'Oh, thanks,' she mumbled, taking it off him. She hadn't even missed it. She had been in such a hurry to get home, her head in such a spin.

'Can I go see if the dappodils growed bigger today, Daddy?' Molly interrupted them.

'We're in a hurry, love, so maybe not today, okay?'

'Pleeeease, Daddy,' she begged.

'Well, only if Emily doesn't mind?' he relented.

'Of course you can,' Emily said, bending down to the little girl.

The child had enraptured her; it was impossible to say no to her. 'The side gate is open; run around the back there,' she instructed.

While Molly ran through the gate, they remained standing on the doorstep.

'Look, about last night...' Rob began when they were alone. 'I'm sorry.'

'You don't need to apologise.' She shook her head, wishing to spare both of them any more embarrassment.

'I think I just got caught up in everything. Yesterday was, well... we had a lovely day and I guess I didn't want it to end...' His gaze dropped to the ground.

Emily nodded. 'Don't worry about it.' How could she tell him that she had enjoyed it too? That as she had lain in bed the night before, she had replayed it in her head over and over again? Her body tingling all over as she relived it? It had felt the same as when they had first met. However, a lot of water had gone under the bridge since then and to have let it go any further would have been a disaster.

After a moment, Molly returned around to the front of the house with her arms stretched out on either side of her. 'They're this big now!' Her eyes were wide with wonder and Emily's heart twisted once again; this child was enchanting.

'That's amazing...' Rob said distractedly. 'Right, we'd better go now. I'm sure Emily has lots of packing to do.' He took the child by the hand as they went to leave. 'Well, I just wanted to wish you a safe flight back. Take care of yourself.' He paused as his eyes met her level. 'I wish you all the best.'

'Where are you going, Emily?' Molly asked, planting her feet on the driveway, refusing to budge another step.

Emily turned to the child. 'I'm afraid I'm going back to New Zealand.'

She watched as the child's face collapsed and she felt her heart fall too. 'Does that mean we'll never see you again?' Molly asked in a small voice, her bottom lip trembling.

'Well, I hope to come back to visit so perhaps next time I'm home, we can meet up,' she said to appease her but Emily knew it was a lie. She wouldn't be seeing them again.

Molly tugged on Rob's sleeve. 'We don't want you to go, tell her, Daddy! Tell her we want her to stay here!'

Rob bit down on his lip. 'Lovey, come on now, we have to let Emily finish packing.'

She pouted. 'It's not fair!'

'Molly!' Rob chastised her. His face flamed with embarrassment. He turned back to Emily. 'I, eh, I think she likes having you here... Normally, it's just me and her knocking around together but I think she's enjoying having a female around for a change,' he said sheepishly.

Despite the awkwardness of the situation, Emily couldn't help smiling at the child. She was so precocious and intelligent. She knew Rob would have his work cut out for him as her father but he would also be so rewarded to watch a child as spirited and full of life as she was grow up.

'We'd better head on. Goodbye, Emily.' His voice wavered.

'Goodbye, Rob.'

Then Emily bent down and hugged the little girl, breathing in her delicate scent for the last time. She felt the pressure of tears pulse forward in her eyes so she stood up and took a deep breath to steady herself.

'I'm really glad I met you, Molly. You're a great kid.' She heard her voice crack. She looked at Rob and their eyes locked on one another; in them, Emily saw so much history. The first time they had kissed. The night at the awards ceremony. Lazy Sunday mornings spent in bed lying wrapped in his arms. That second line appearing on the pregnancy test at long last. Alannah being handed to them by the midwives, swaddled in a white towelling blanket. That bitterly cold February day standing shattered and broken at the graveside in St Francis' cemetery in utter disbelief that this could have happened to them. She sucked in sharply. 'You and your daddy are going to be just fine.'

35

The smell of tarragon and thyme wafted on the air that evening as Karen removed a roast chicken from the oven. The scent transported Emily back to the mouth-watering Sunday roasts that their mother had cooked when they were children. Karen had invited her around for dinner. It was the night before Emily was leaving to head back to Auckland so it was to be a final farewell for them.

'Have you everything packed up for tomorrow?' Karen asked as she filled a fleur-de-lis-patterned dish with crispy roast potatoes and set it down in the centre of the table while Dave carved the chicken.

Emily nodded. 'I think so. I didn't have much with me anyway.'

'I don't want Auntie Emily to go,' Cara said, turning down her bottom lip.

'I don't want her to go either,' Karen sighed in agreement with her daughter, as she heaped potatoes and vegetables onto the children's plates.

'I'll be back to visit,' Emily assured her niece, wondering if that was really true or if she was just saying what they wanted to hear.

Karen handed Seán a carrot baton in his high chair. Emily watched, mesmerised, as the baby wrapped his chubby fist around it as he coordinated bringing it towards his mouth. They laughed as he grimaced initially, screwing up his whole face before deciding that he liked it and going back for another bite.

'I reckon we'd want to be leaving at around four at the latest; the traffic on the M50 can be manic at that hour,' Karen said as she cut into her chicken.

Emily nodded. She had offered to get a taxi but Karen insisted that she would drive her.

'Not to mention the nightmare security queues,' Dave said. 'I nearly missed my flight to that conference in Italy because of them.'

'I'm sorry I won't be around to help you clear out Mum's house and put it on the market,' Emily said.

Karen lowered her fork and waved her hand. 'Don't worry about any of that stuff. I'm not in any hurry and Dave will give me a hand when the time comes.' She turned to her husband. 'Won't you, love?'

Dave gave Karen a salute before rolling his eyes good-naturedly in Emily's direction. 'I just do as I'm told.'

'Thanks, darling.' Karen leant over and planted a kiss on his cheek as Emily's heart twisted. Karen and Dave were good for one another. They seemed so content with their lot. This picture of family togetherness was all Emily had ever wanted. It was how she had once pictured her own home – a loving family seated around the dinner table in Groveton Road, laughing and joking with one another – but sometimes, life had other plans for you. She had seen how fast your whole world could be flipped on its head and everything in it, all your hopes and dreams washed away.

'So... eh... did you say goodbye to Rob?' Karen enquired.

Emily lowered her gaze to the table. 'Yes, I saw them yesterday.'

'I see. Well, look... at least you and Rob have sorted things out between you.'

'I guess so...' she sighed in agreement.

'Are you okay?' Karen asked.

'I'm just tired,' she lied. The truth was that she was feeling all at sea. She had thought she was looking forward to getting back to Auckland but she had been filled with a sinking feeling ever since she had got up that morning. She realised that despite being home for the unthinkable reason of burying her mother, she had enjoyed spending time reconnecting with Karen and getting to know her nieces and nephew. She had loved helping out at the birthday party and going to see Molly's recital. It had felt good to belong. She hadn't realised just how small her life in Auckland was. Most days, she got up and went for a run, then she went to work and came home. She had a routine that was as familiar as it was safe. She kept herself busy and never had too much time to dwell on her thoughts. She had friends – well, acquaintances and work colleagues really – but nobody truly *knew* her. They didn't remember her birthday or invite her around for dinner or to see their child perform in their school concert. Her time in Dublin had seemed more vibrant – yes, it had been difficult, many old wounds had been reopened, but it had also been healing in its own way. She also kept picturing Molly's distraught face as she had said goodbye to them the day before. The child had got upset, begging her father to tell Emily to stay while Rob looked on powerless, knowing there was nothing he could say or do to stop her leaving. Emily knew that Molly had grown attached to her and the guilt for allowing that to happen was weighing heavily on her mind. She should have kept her distance from both of them and they wouldn't be in this situation now. Poor Molly was too young to understand how complicated life could be sometimes: how old feelings and hurts could linger like stale smoke, wrapping themselves around everything until they were tainted.

It would be easier in New Zealand, she told herself. She would go home to her flat, go back to work in the restaurant and get on with her life. And Rob and Molly would go back to their lives and forget all about her.

36

The next day, Emily waited in the living room with her suitcase standing by her feet. She checked the carriage clock on the mantle-piece again. She was sure Karen had said that she'd collect her at four to go to the airport but it was now ten past and there was no sign of her. It wasn't like her sister to be late. Perhaps she had picked her up wrong. She lifted her phone to see if there were any messages but the screen was blank. Perhaps she got delayed with one of the kids. Maybe Seán had had a dirty nappy or Keeva had needed help with something just as she had been running out the door.

Emily didn't want to stress her sister out by calling her, especially if she was running late, but when the hands on the clock changed to twenty past, she began to wonder if Karen had got the time wrong or even forgotten that she had offered to bring her to the airport.

She dialled her sister's number but there was no reply. All kinds of thoughts and worries flitted into her head. What if some-thing had happened? Or if one of the kids was sick? She tried Dave then but he didn't answer either. She knew they didn't have a land-

line so she couldn't call the house phone. She wondered if she
should walk over to their house – it was only a five-minute stroll
down the road from where she was – but what if she missed her in
the traffic? She tried ringing her sister once again but there was
still no answer.

Eventually, when she knew she was going to miss her flight if
she didn't leave soon, she decided to walk down to Karen's house
and see what was going on. She was just slipping her arms into the
sleeves of her coat when her phone rang.

'Oh, Em,' Karen cried, and Emily felt her blood run cold from
the panic in her sister's voice. 'I'm so sorry. Something's happened.'
The words came out choppy and staccato.

'What is it? What's wrong?'

'It's Molly,' she sobbed. 'We were at the play centre with the
kids earlier. We were all in the car park, ready to go home. Dave
was strapping Seán into his seat and Rob was parked across from
us, he was opening the door of his car for Molly to climb in, and
she must have remembered that she had forgotten to give Cara a
hug.' Karen's voice choked back tears as she recounted the story.
'Then before either of us could stop her, she began sprinting across
the car park towards our car...' Karen dissolved into sobs.

'What happened?' Emily asked, panicked, fearing where the
story was going.

'Oh, Em, it was awful. The car smacked into her; she was
thrown up into the air like a rag doll. It wasn't the driver's fault; she
came out of nowhere and he hadn't a hope of stopping in time.'

Emily felt a chill spread through her body as goosebumps
prickled along her skin. The fine hairs on her arms stood to attention. Everything stopped and an angry buzzing sounded in her
ears. She was transported back to nine years ago. To that same
feeling when Rob had woken her that morning to say that
Alannah wasn't breathing. The blood left her head and she felt her

legs go wobbly beneath her. She had to reach out to the wall to steady herself. She didn't think she could stand it but then she thought about Rob and his gorgeous child and knew that she needed to be strong here. This wasn't her time to fall apart.

She forced herself to stay calm. 'Is she okay, Karen? Will she be okay?'

'She-she's on her way to the Dublin Children's Hospital by ambulance,' Karen sobbed. 'Rob has gone with her.'

'But will she be okay?' she demanded impatiently. She needed certainty; she wanted Karen to tell her that everything was going to be fine.

'I don't know,' Karen wailed. 'I'm so sorry... I know you need to get your flight but I can't go anywhere... Dave and I need to take the kids home. They're all traumatised. They witnessed the whole thing. I'm sorry, I won't get to see you off properly...' she sobbed.

'Hey, don't worry about that.' Suddenly, getting to the airport was the last thing on her mind. Emily knew with every fibre of her being that there was only one place she was supposed to be. She swallowed hard. 'I'm not getting on that plane. I need to get to the hospital. I need to be with Rob.'

37

Emily scrambled in her bag for money to pay the taxi driver; she thanked him quickly before climbing out from the back seat and slamming the rear door shut behind her. She hurried over towards the building and ran into a segment of the revolving door that manned the entrance. Even though she knew it was futile trying to get it to speed up, she pushed on the glass with her palms anyway. Eventually, it spat her out and she ran over towards the reception desk. She swerved to avoid two nurses chatting about their holiday plans and an elderly woman clutching a teddy bear and a bunch of balloons as she worked out where to go.

'I'm looking for Rob Kavanagh,' she began breathlessly when she reached the desk.

'Is he a patient here?' the receptionist asked without looking up.

She shook her head. 'His daughter Molly is...' she panted. 'She was brought here by ambulance earlier on.'

'What did you say the surname was again?'

'Kavanagh,' Emily repeated.

'Just one moment now.' She began typing on her computer, her acrylic nails clacking off the keys as her fingers moved deftly over them. After a moment, she looked at Emily with narrowed eyes. 'Are you family?'

Emily nodded, feeling guilty for stretching the truth. Although technically, she was still Rob's wife as they had never got divorced.

'You should find him in the family room on the second floor. It's all the way down the end of the corridor, last door on the right.'

'Thank you,' she said gratefully as she raced towards the lift. She pressed the button to call it, willing it to hurry on but it seemed to be stuck on the fourth floor. She noticed a staircase across the way and decided it would probably be quicker. She raced up the steps, taking them two at a time. When she finally arrived at the second floor, she turned down the corridor and that was when she saw him pacing up and down. From a distance, his large frame seemed to have shrunk and he looked smaller somehow. His whole body was hunched over, his face deathly pale. Her heart ached at the sight of this broken version of him.

'Rob...' she began, hurrying over towards him, her runners squeaking over the vinyl, when suddenly she stopped dead in her tracks as she began to doubt herself. Was it really her place to be here with him? He might not want to see her, especially at a time like this. Given their history, it would be understandable if she was the last person entirely that he wanted to see right now.

'Emily?' he said in disbelief as he came to a stop in front of her.

'Karen told me what happened,' she blurted.

'I thought you were supposed to be going back to Auckland today?'

Emily shook her head. 'This is the only place I'm supposed to be right now.' Her mind ran to the hurried text she had sent Jonny while she was in the back of the taxi explaining that she wouldn't be on the flight. She hadn't even checked to see if he had replied yet. She knew he would be wondering what was going on but how could she even begin to explain everything that had happened since she had come home? Guilt swilled in her stomach and she knew she was going to have to set things straight between them whenever she went back to Auckland. Being back in Dublin had made her realise that she was sleepwalking through her life; she owed it to Jonny but most importantly to herself to be true to her feelings and if that meant ending things between them, then that's what she would have to do.

Despite the pain in Rob's eyes, she saw relief there too. 'I'm so glad you're here.'

'How is she?'

He shook his head. 'I've no idea. Nobody will tell me anything,' he spat bitterly. 'They've taken her in there.' He pointed towards a set of double doors at the end of the corridor. 'They told me to wait in the family room but nobody was coming near me to tell me what was going on so I thought I'd come out here and try and find out what is happening. I'm trying to catch someone going in or out but no one has gone through those doors since Molly was brought in there.'

'I'm so sorry you're going through this.'

'It's all my fault,' he blurted, clasping his hands behind his head and sucking in sharply.

'It's not your fault,' she assured him.

'I should have been watching her properly. If I had been holding her hand... If I had got to her quicker, I could have pulled her out of the way in time.'

'Stop now, Rob; you blaming yourself isn't going to change anything. In fact, it will just drive you mad and then you'll feel even worse.' She knew first-hand the damage guilt and self-recrimination could do. 'This isn't the time for that. Molly is going to need you to be strong now, okay?'

'I keep replaying it in my head – I tried to get to her, I ran as soon as I realised what was happening, but it was too late. I can't get it out of my mind – all the noises, my shouting, Karen's screams, the other kids screaming, the screech of the brakes, the bang of the car shunting into her, her tiny body flying through the air.' His shoulders heaved in great big sobs and she couldn't help pulling him in tightly against her chest. 'I won't survive if anything happens to her, Emily,' he said as he cried into her hair. 'I can't lose another person.' He shook his head as if trying to shake away this awful nightmare. 'I can't...'

She reached out for his hand and pressed it inside her own. 'She's going to be okay,' she soothed even though she didn't know if this was the truth. She usually hated when people said this when it was impossible to know what the outcome was going to be but, finally, she understood it. Right now, Rob needed to cling to something hopeful and that was the best she could come up with.

'But you didn't see it – you didn't see how hard it hit or how she was thrown so high up into the air.' He broke down into tears once more as he relived it again. 'Why won't anyone tell me how she is?' he blasted desperately as the other people walking past them in the corridor turned around to see what was going on.

'Hey, I'm sure someone will update you soon,' she soothed.

'They better. I'm going out of my mind here. I need to call my parents and Steph's family in Colorado but I can't face it yet.' He straightened up and wiped his eyes. 'Oh, God, I can't believe this is happening all over again...'

Her heart splintered for this man who had once been her whole world. She was furious at the injustice of it all. How could life be so cruel to him yet again? Why him? Why his child? He had already lost a daughter and then, when he had found love again, his new partner had been taken from him too. Hadn't he endured enough pain in his life? It seemed unfair how some people sailed by on an easy ticket while others got crushed through the wringer again and again and again.

38

Rob and Emily sat down onto a slatted wooden bench that ran along one side of the corridor. A nurse emerged eventually and Rob sprung up from his seat and launched himself upon her. She told them that Molly was still in theatre but, taking pity on them, she had brought them a mug of tea each and a blanket to share, which they had accepted gratefully, draping it around their shoulders to shelter them from the chilly evening air. As they sat there on the hard timber, it reminded Emily of the long nights they had spent together when Alannah was a newborn, both bleary-eyed with exhaustion and anxious about attending to her needs. 'Do you think she's hungry?' Rob would ask. 'Maybe she has wind?' she would suggest. They would circle around a list of what could possibly be ailing their newborn, trying to get to the bottom of it and, eventually, they would sag with relief when she would finally stop crying and settle back to sleep. They had been a good team, she thought sadly.

'It's all my fault,' Rob was saying. He had been saying a different version of these words since she had arrived at the hospital. 'I should never have let go of her hand. If I had just noticed her running off a split second earlier...'

'You can't blame yourself. Molly is lucky to have you as her dad.'

'Can't I?' he retorted bitterly. 'She wouldn't be in the mess she's in right now if I had been more vigilant.'

'Come on,' she coaxed, placing her hand over his. 'She's going to get through this. Stay strong.'

'I'm glad you came, Emily.' He squeezed her hand. 'It's good to have you here.'

A woman in green scrubs eventually approached them. Her dark hair was tied up in a loose bun and behind her thick-framed glasses, her eyes were red-rimmed with tiredness.

'Are you the parents of Molly Kavanagh?' she asked.

'Yes,' Rob said, jumping up. 'I mean – I am.' He shot an apologetic look in Emily's direction. 'I'm her dad.'

The doctor stuck out her hand to shake his. 'I'm Doctor Khalifa. The good news is that your daughter is out of surgery and is currently stable. The trauma she sustained has ruptured her spleen and, as a result, we have had to carry out a splenectomy. She also sustained a fracture to her left arm and her ribcage.'

'But will she be okay?' Rob pleaded.

'There are no guarantees, we still have a few more tests that we want to carry out in the coming days, but for now, we're happy with her progress. She's a very lucky lady today, all things considered. If the car had been travelling any faster, it could have been a very different scenario,' she added bleakly.

Emily watched Rob swallow down a ball in his throat. He had once again come face to face with the hand of death but this time, by some miracle, whether it was by grace or fate, it had glanced off him and he was getting a second chance with his daughter.

'She's sleeping now but I can take you to her,' Doctor Khalifa continued, breaking into a smile.

'Oh, yes, please,' Rob said gratefully.

Emily gestured towards the chairs they had just been sitting on. 'Do you want me to wait here...'

Rob shook his head. 'Come with me, Em.'

They followed the doctor through a maze of corridors until they finally entered a darkened room. Emily felt the breath being sucked from her lungs as soon as her eyes landed on Molly. She looked impossibly small lying in the huge bed surrounded by monitors and beeping machines. Her curls were spread out in a wild tangle on the pillow behind her. Wires trailed her tiny body. Gone was the lively, spirited little girl and in her place was this fragile, broken child. Her left arm was in a plaster cast, her beautiful face was grazed and a garish purple bruise marred her forehead.

'You can sit with her,' Doctor Khalifa instructed. 'She'll probably drift in and out of sleep. Her body has been through a lot and needs to rest.'

Rob took the seat closest to the bed and put his hand over his daughter's. 'I'm here, darling girl. Daddy is right here.'

Emily hovered at the foot of the bed. This was a hugely emotional time for him and she didn't want to intrude.

'Here, sit down.' He gestured to the chair beside him.

She did as he instructed and watched as he tenderly stroked his daughter's skin and brushed the curls back off her face.

'It brings me back, you know,' he said after a while. 'All those nights I spent sitting at Steph's bedside, shivering in the cool morning air, watching the sun come up outside the window, praying she'd get better but deep down, knowing that she wouldn't. I would try to bargain with God,' he laughed. 'So many I hours I wasted with promises like if you make her better again, I'll go to Mass every day, I'll quit my job and spend my days doing charity work. I would have given anything for her to stay.'

'That must have been a horrible time,' she consoled.

'When we lost Alannah, I didn't think I could ever bear pain like that again so when I found out that I was going to lose Steph too, I was so angry. I had done my time in hell, so why was I being put through more grief? I felt cheated by a God that I wasn't sure I even believed it. I was angry with the whole world but Steph was amazing. Even though she fought bloody hard to stay, when the time came and she finally had to accept her fate, she did it so serenely. I had to tell myself to cop on – she was the one suffering, she was the one who had to leave us, she was the one who wouldn't be around to see Molly grow up. I quickly had to realise that it wasn't about me and if I didn't get it together, I could ruin our final days together.'

'Anger is a dangerous emotion,' Emily agreed. Anger was one of the reasons she had lost everything. She now knew that it was like a tidal wave; it swallowed you up and you could either get spun around in its vortex and spat out or you could fight to float out on top and ride along its crest. The destination was the same; it was only the journey there that was different.

'For Steph's sake, I had to put my anger to one side and live our last days together as best I could. I'm so glad now that I was able to do that for her sake. We had some beautiful times together.'

'Tell me about Steph,' she said gently.

'Steph?' He was clearly taken off guard. 'Well... she had a great big smile and her laugh – you've never heard a more infectious laugh; when she laughed, you had to laugh too. She was always really social – she moved here knowing no one and after a few months had more friends than me.' He lit up as he spoke about her. 'She was colourful and full of life and great fun to be around. You never knew what she was going to do next. She'd call me up and say let's go for a sea swim after work even though it was February. Or she'd think nothing of hopping into the car to go down to Fota Wildlife park for the day. She'd say, "You Irish think a two-hour journey is so long; where I come from, you might have to travel two hours to get to the store." She was a force to be reckoned with. I think Molly takes after her in lots of ways. She definitely has her spirit and sense of fun. When she got sick, the cancer stole all of that from her; suddenly, she had no energy any more. Her laugh didn't have the same ring to it; her spark was gone.'

'Do you know something, Rob? I'm glad you found love again.' She meant it. When he spoke about Steph with such warmth and affection, she was surprised to find that she didn't feel any jealousy towards this woman who had brought solace to her husband: just sadness that he had lost this special person in his life.

He dropped his gaze to the floor. 'I never stopped loving you,' he admitted as he used the toe of his trainer to dig against the rubber.

She knew it was the same for her. Being back here had shown her that. She would always love him. What they had had been special; it was just a shame that they had let grief build a wall between them.

39

Purple morning light eventually pushed out the darkness as the sun rose on a new day. Emily and Rob had spent the whole night sitting at Molly's bedside, staring at her for a sign – or a signal – anything at all that might suggest she was about to wake up. Nurses appeared periodically to check her vital signs and when Rob would ask them anxiously if everything seemed to be okay with her, they would assure him that it was normal for her to take her time waking up. At some stage during the night, Emily had gone out to the corridor and found a machine to make two coffees that tasted awful, but they had clasped their palms around the cardboard cups for the warmth more than anything.

As dawn broke, they noticed Molly's eyelids began to flicker. They had both held their breath as eventually, they opened fully.

'Hey there, darling,' Rob said softly. 'It's Daddy.'

She blinked and looked around the room, taking in her surroundings. 'This isn't our house.' Her voice sounded so small and frail.

'No, love, you're in the hospital. You had a bit of an accident but the doctors and nurses are making you better,' he explained.

She wrinkled her nose and looked at Emily. 'Why are you here?'

'Emily came to see you,' Rob said.

'But I already saided goodbye to you,' she complained as if she was too busy to be doing things twice.

Rob laughed and looked at Emily. 'Well, at least we know her memory hasn't been affected!'

'I missed my flight,' Emily explained. 'When I heard you were in hospital, I wanted to see how you were.'

'Can you get on a different airplane?'

'We'll see... maybe... when you're better.'

They watched her small face break into a smile. 'I'm happy you came, Emily.' Then her lids closed down into sleep again.

* * *

For the next few hours, the little girl drifted in and out of sleep which they knew was normal as her body knitted itself back together. Monitors beeped periodically and they would both jerk upright to make sure everything was okay and then a nurse would come in and reassure them that everything was fine.

Emily stretched her neck and circled her shoulders to ease the stiffness that had crept in from the time spent sitting at Molly's bedside. Now that they knew Molly was out of danger, Rob had suggested to Emily that she should go home and get some sleep, but she had shaken her head and said no, she wanted to be there with him and he had smiled gratefully.

'Hey there,' they heard a familiar voice say from behind them as someone crept into the room.

They both turned their heads and were surprised to see Karen standing there. She raised her palms to face them. 'I know I probably shouldn't be here but I managed to persuade a very kind nurse to let me in for five minutes.'

'Come on in.' Rob gestured to the free chair beside him.

'So, how is she doing?' she asked as she sank into the chair. After Molly had woken up, Emily had called Karen to let her know the good news and she had sobbed with relief down the phone.

'She's doing well. They want to do some more tests today but everything looks good so far.'

'Thank God.' Karen exhaled heavily. 'It was such a relief to get the call last night to say she was awake. What a scare you must have got, Rob.'

He shook his head. 'It hasn't hit me yet.'

'You look wrecked,' she said.

He sighed. 'It's been a long night.'

She turned to Emily next. 'And you don't look much better. Why don't both of you go home for a few hours. Have a shower, freshen up and get something to eat. I can sit with Molly.'

'Thanks, Karen,' Rob said, shaking his head. 'But I'd better stay here. Just in case.'

'Look, Rob, she's asleep now so she won't even realise you're gone and I promise I'll call you if she wakes up,' Karen continued.

He glanced at Emily, feeling torn.

'Come on, Rob,' Emily coaxed. 'Karen is right. You're going to be spending a lot of time here over the next few days. You'll feel much better if you have a shower and you can come straight back in. Molly will be fine for a little bit.'

'Well, I do need to get some of her stuff...' he conceded. 'Some clothes, her books and things.'

'You two go and I promise I'll call you straight away if she wakes up. You can take my car,' Karen said, pressing her keys on him. 'Don't worry, my insurance policy covers anyone with a full licence.'

'Okay, thanks, Karen,' he said, standing up and stretching out his arms before taking the keys from her. 'I promise I won't be long.'

Emily hugged her sister goodbye and then she and Rob headed out into the car park and searched for Karen's MPV. They eventually located the Peugeot, haphazardly parked across two spaces. Rob unlocked it and Emily sat in the passenger seat. It was littered with children's clothing, water bottles and sweet wrappers: all the hallmarks of a busy family life.

'Do you want me to drop you home first?' he asked as they exited the car park.

She shook her head. 'Let's just go to your place,' she said. 'I know you're in a hurry to get back.'

'Thanks.' He nodded gratefully.

They drove along the suburban streets at a crawl, having hit rush-hour traffic. In the distance, the sea glimmered silver under the pale morning light. Eventually, they pulled up outside Rob's house. He parked in the driveway and silenced the engine. He let them inside and Emily found the house was chilly from being left empty for the last twenty-four hours.

'You go shower,' she instructed, 'and I'll make you something quick to eat.'

'You're a lifesaver,' he said gratefully as he trudged wearily up the stairs.

Emily entered the kitchen and began looking for ingredients to make a meal. She found some eggs in one of the cupboards and a packet of bacon in the fridge. She began scrambling the eggs in a bowl with some milk and after fumbling around with the unfamiliar hob, finally managed to get it on and heated the pan. She was just about to pour the eggs in when she heard Rob's phone ringing. She quickly turned off the hob and followed the tone out into the hallway. She found his phone lying on the console table that was just inside the door. Her heart picked up speed when she saw Karen's name flashing up on the screen. Fearing something had changed with Molly's condition, she hurried upstairs, fumbling for the answer button.

'Karen, it's me,' she began as she took the steps two at a time. 'I'll get Rob for you now; he's in the shower.' She hurried up the stairs. 'Rob?' she shouted when she reached the landing. 'Rob?'

'I'm in here,' he called back to her.

She followed his voice towards the bedroom. She entered the room and saw he had just come out of the shower. He was standing there with a fluffy white towel wrapped around him while water droplets glistened on his bare chest. His body had once been as familiar to her as her own. A moment of awkwardness passed between them until she remembered why she was there in his bedroom.

'It's Karen,' she said anxiously as she handed him the phone, doing her best to avert her eyes from his body.

He answered the phone quickly. 'Karen? Is everything okay?'

'Don't worry. Everything is fine,' Emily could hear Karen say. 'You're not going to believe this; she's just woken up and she asked me if she could go on my phone!' She laughed. 'I think it's safe to say she's all right.'

Emily saw Rob visibly sag with relief as he started laughing. 'I won't be long,' he said. She sat down onto the edge of the bed as her heart stopped racing.

'Take your time. She's in great form.'

He hung up and left the phone on his bedside table and filled Emily in. 'Can you believe it?' He shook his head and laughed.

'It's just amazing how quickly she has bounced back,' Emily said. 'She's a tough little thing.'

'Thank God,' he sighed with relief and sat down beside her. 'She's going to give me a heart attack one of these days.'

'She's a real handful. She certainly knows how to keep you on your toes,' Emily agreed.

He turned to her. 'I never got a chance to thank you for being there with me yesterday and last night. I'm so sorry you missed your flight back.'

She waved her hand to dismiss him. 'Don't be silly. There's nowhere else I would have been.'

'Will you be able to get another one in the next few days?'

'Of course I will.'

'It has been nice having you around the last while,' he admitted before his gaze fell to the floor as silence sat heavily on them. Eventually, he spoke again. 'Look, Em, you can tell me that I'm wrong or that I'm crossing a line here but if I don't say this now, I'll regret it forever. I know there's a lot of history between us and it's certainly not the most straightforward situation – a lot has happened since you left – but since you've come home, it's reminded me of the way we used to be. Before it all went wrong. Maybe I'm imagining it but there's still something between us, I don't know... a connection or whatever you want to call it... I can feel it... I don't know if you felt it too but it's there... It's still there...' He trailed off.

She had felt it too. No matter how much she pretended that she didn't, it was definitely still there. She had been drawn towards him. There was an undeniable connection between them; he had pulled her in like opposing charges on a magnet until the force was so strong that it was impossible not to give in to it. Suddenly, she longed to touch him. She wanted to relive that closeness that they had once had. His body was calling to her and she yearned to feel his skin against hers. The air felt charged and she knew it was now or never. Before she even realised she was doing it, she reached across and cupped his face in her hands. He ran his fingers through her hair and his mouth met hers with the same intensity.

They kissed deeply and, this time, there was no warning voice in her head, telling her that she was making a mistake. It felt so right. They moved backwards onto the bed and he pulled off her top while she fumbled to unwrap his towel. She found her body remembered him and responded in familiar ways.

40

Afterwards, they lay there together, their breathing ragged, their bodies spent. So close that it felt like they had never been separated. How had so much happened between them and yet despite everything, *something* – whether it was their undeniable connection or fate – had brought them back together.

She felt him still beside her and she knew there was something that he wanted to say to her.

'So what happens now?' he said eventually.

Her body stiffened beside him. 'How do you mean?'

He propped himself up on his elbow and turned to look at her. 'Well, doesn't this change things? Can't you stay? Can't we try again?' Rob begged. 'I know there are no guarantees that it would all work out but if you go back to New Zealand without giving it a chance then we'll never know what could have been.'

She hesitated. It was the same voice that had been growing louder in her mind over the last few days. Lately, the idea of going back to her life in New Zealand filled her with dread. She didn't want to leave Rob and little Molly. She had liked being a part of their world over the last few days. With a sense of dawning clarity, she realised that she enjoyed the togetherness the three of them had experienced, that feeling of being included, of being a part of something. She had found herself thinking of Rob and Molly and wondering, what if? What if she stayed? Could she allow herself to become a part of their world? But these thoughts were met with so many questions and doubts. Would Rob want her to stay? Was he even ready to love again so soon after losing Steph? Could she come back to her old life and try again? But then a louder one drowned it out. Everything had changed. The landscape had altered completely. In the years she had been away, Rob had found love again with Steph, he had had Molly and he was not the same man she had left behind on that bleak February morning all those years ago. Both of them were different people now, whether they liked it or not.

'You're not imagining it. I can feel it too,' she whispered, feeling as though she was being pulled onto dangerous ground. 'Whatever is between us is real.'

She watched his face light up but she continued on, knowing what she was about to say was important.

'But I'm terrified of letting you both down. My track record when the going gets tough isn't great. And it's not just you this time; I'd have to think of Molly too. She's already been through so much; what if I wasn't able to be the person she needed me to be?'

He nodded glumly. 'I get it. I have a lot of baggage.'

She looked at him as she realised that he thought she saw Molly as an obstacle. 'It's not that – Molly – well... she's... amazing. I love being around her. Sometimes, I let myself imagine what it would be like to be a part of her life and in those dreams, it's wonderful... but then I remember what happened before and who I really am, what I'm capable of... and I'd be so scared that I would do that again.'

'But it might not happen. What if it was different this time?'

She marvelled at his optimism. How was he able to do it? Life had beaten him down so many times and yet he still got up again and continued on. She knew his strength was deep but she didn't want him to have to carry her too – his load was heavy enough. 'How can you be so sure it would all work out?'

He shrugged. 'After everything I've been through, I know there are no guarantees in anything we do but if there's one thing I've learnt, it is that life is too short and we need to live each day to its fullest. If you go around too scared to take a risk or afraid of opening your heart, you're not really living. Life is brief and oh-so fleeting, so when you see a chance of happiness, you have to grab on to it. You have to snatch it with both hands and treasure it because it can disappear when you least expect it. Tomorrow isn't promised, so if you care about someone, tell them; if you love someone, show them. I can't promise you it will all work out and we'll all live happily ever after but it might just, if you were willing to take a chance on us.'

Ever since she had come home and had been spending time with Rob and Molly, it was like they had tempted her into a world where it was sunny and bright and she liked it there, basking in their warmth, but then she would remember that it wasn't her life. He was selling her a dream, luring her into a trap and she needed it to end. She wanted to cover her ears with her hands and scream at him to stop.

'I'm sorry.' She climbed up from the bed. She scrambled around the floor, picking up her discarded clothes and putting them back on.

'Please stay,' he pressed.

She shook her head and watched his whole face fall.

'Why can't you let yourself be happy?'

'I am happy.'

'Well, maybe you are, but I think you could be happier.' He

raised his voice in frustration. 'Come on, Em! You have had your finger on the self-destruct button for your whole life.'

'This was a mistake,' she said as she buttoned up her blouse. 'We should never have let it happen, Rob.'

'So that's it? You're honestly telling me you'll go back to Auckland and that this means nothing to you?'

She nodded and even though she hated herself for it, she knew it was for the best. He might not see it right now, but he would thank her in the long run. She stuffed her feet into her trainers. 'I have to go.' She turned away from him and hurried out of the room. She could hear his footsteps coming down the landing behind her.

'Yeah, you keep running away, Emily,' he shouted. 'You keep running like you always do! Some things never change!' he called angrily after her from the top of the stairs, but she didn't look back.

41

The following day, Emily was sitting at the island in Karen's kitchen. Spring sunlight filled the space, brightening up the room. Dust motes danced in the rays. Keeva and Cara were outside playing on the trampoline while Seán was upstairs having a nap. Karen was keeping an eye through the glass on the two girls as they played. She pulled back the slider and stuck her head out. 'I said no backflips, Cara!' she warned before returning her attention back to Emily. 'You'd think after seeing what happened to poor Molly, they'd be a bit more careful!' She tutted.

'How are they doing?' Emily asked, nodding towards the garden. She knew her nieces had been upset at witnessing Molly's accident.

'They're okay. Once they heard Molly was all right, it's business as usual as far as they're concerned. Kids.' She shrugged. 'They live in the moment. Were you talking to Rob today?'

Emily shifted in her seat. The fight with Rob the day before had been playing on her mind like a bad movie. After she had left his place, Emily had walked back to her mother's house, her head spinning with what he had said, while she guessed Rob had returned to the hospital to sit with Molly. She had spent the previous night staring at the shadows on the ceiling, wondering if Rob was right. Could she stay? Could she take a chance? But as she had lain awake, she knew it was just wishful thinking. She had got sucked into their world, but it was *their* world, not hers and she knew she had to let them both go and forget about them. She hadn't heard from him today and although she wanted to enquire about how Molly was doing, every time she began typing a message to him, she kept thinking about their time together and would delete it without sending it. She shook her head and immediately felt herself start to blush. She cursed her face for betraying her.

'What is it? What's wrong?' Karen asked, noticing her high colouring.

'I booked my flight back for tomorrow,' Emily announced in a bid to throw her off the scent.

Karen's face fell. She put down the cups she was taking out of the cupboard and folded her arms across her chest. 'So you're definitely going back then?'

'Of course, why?'

'Well, it's just after everything that happened... I thought you and Rob seemed to be getting on well...' She broke off. 'Maybe I'm wrong but when you went to the hospital to be with him, I thought that perhaps something was happening between you...'

Emily had to think quickly of what she could say to explain this but she had been caught off guard and her mind was blank.

'I'm right, aren't I?' Karen pushed. 'Something has happened between you.'

'We slept together,' Emily confessed, knowing Karen would see right through her if she tried to lie.

Her younger sister's mouth dropped open and her eyes were

wide with shock as she took in this news. 'Well I never...' Her face broke into a grin. 'When?'

'Yesterday, while you were in the hospital with Molly and we came back to his place to freshen up. One thing led to another... it wasn't planned... it just kind of happened...' Emily cringed, feeling like a teenager. Saying it out loud now in the cold light of day made her want to shrivel up in the corner.

'And how was it?' Karen asked, hanging on every word that left her sister's mouth.

Emily thought about how Rob had delicately kissed along her collarbone and up along the nape of her neck, his lips moving over her skin as delicate as butterfly wings. The time they had spent together had been magical, like it had been in the early days of their relationship. 'It was good. Really good.'

'So doesn't this change things?' Karen asked as she set to making the coffee.

'What do you mean?' How could she explain things to Karen when she didn't even understand what was happening herself?

'Oh come on, Emily, there's a lot of history between you both. You sleep together and think nothing of it? Technically, you're still married, for God's sake! You're just going to go back to New Zealand and pretend nothing has changed?' She tossed her hands up to the heavens in frustration.

'Pretty much. It shouldn't have happened.'

'But it wouldn't have unless you both still had feelings for one another after all this time,' she argued, passing Emily a mug.

Emily recalled how her body had yearned for his and she felt herself tingle. How her skin had come alive under the familiarity of his touch. Then she remembered his face contorted with anger, shouting after her as she had been leaving. He was better off without her. He would realise that eventually.

'Even if we did still have feelings for one another, I've got to go back to Auckland.'

'Do you? Haven't you been away for long enough? Maybe it's time for you to come home,' Karen said softly.

'Well, yes, I do... There's only so much leeway my boss will give me,' she said obstinately. 'And besides, I have residency there now.'

'But you could come back if you really wanted to. I know there would be a bit of work involved in getting your stuff shipped over and you'd need to get a new job here but you'd pick something up fairly easily. Mum's house is sitting there empty so you wouldn't have to worry about finding a place to live and I could give you a hand financially until you got back on your feet again. We'd love to have you home, Em,' she pleaded, clasping her hands together in prayer. 'Now that Mum is gone, we only have each other and I wish you were closer.'

Emily shook her head resolutely. 'I can't go there again.'

'What do you mean?'

'What if I get hurt again? I'd never survive it.'

'You have to take a risk, Em. If you keep your walls up, afraid of letting anyone in, how will you ever find happiness again? Rob clearly still has feelings for you. It isn't the most normal of situations, I'll give you that, but if you, Rob and Molly could be happy together then who cares what everyone else thinks? Sod the lot of them!'

Emily clasped her mug and stared glumly out at the garden. 'You make it sound so easy...'

'It can be easy if you want it to be. Just follow your heart; don't think about the other stuff: the complications or the logistics. If being with Rob and Molly feels right then it probably is.'

'Well, anyway, I don't know if Rob is even in the right head-space, y'know, after Steph and everything?'

'I don't think he would have been with you if he wasn't ready. He's not the type to mess someone around.'

Emily exhaled heavily. 'Even though he's still my husband on paper, Rob isn't mine any more, Karen. He belongs to Molly and to Steph too.'

'And once, he belonged to you. Life isn't black and white, Em; it's messy and complicated and there are so many shades of grey in between. Can't you take this chance at happiness and see where it leads?' Karen suggested.

Emily shook her head. She was terrified that she would be swept away by her emotions, carried along by the swell and, if it all went wrong, that she may never regain her footing in the world. 'I was a shell when I left for New Zealand the last time; I can't risk letting myself become that person again.'

42

The traffic stalled and started as they made their way across the M50 during rush hour. The wipers on Karen's car screeched across the glass, doing their best to keep up with the soft mizzle that was falling on the screen.

'This bloody traffic!' Karen's knuckles whitened as they clenched the steering wheel. 'It used to just be at rush hour but its permanently gridlocked these days.' She exhaled heavily. 'By the way, I had a message from Rob earlier. Molly was released from hospital this morning.'

Emily felt her heart shred at the mention of Molly's name. 'Thank goodness,' she sighed with relief. 'That's such great news.'

'It sure is. Rob has to be careful with her because her immune system will be low now that her spleen has been removed but she's doing well all things considered. The doctors are amazed at how quickly she has recovered. It really is a miracle. When I think of how it could have been... I don't think I'll ever get those images out of my head.' Karen shuddered. 'Steph must have been looking down on her.'

Emily nodded. 'I was going to call into the hospital yesterday and say goodbye to her myself but then I thought it might upset her.'

Karen smiled sadly. 'The poor kid was really taken with you. She's going to be sad when she realises you're gone.' Karen paused, her tone turning tentative. 'So, how... eh... was it when you had to say goodbye to Rob?'

Emily stayed silent and looked out the window where the drizzle ran down the glass in rivulets.

Karen looked across to the passenger seat, her left hand resting on the gearstick. 'You did say goodbye to him, didn't you?'

Emily shook her head. 'I thought it was better not to,' she admitted, dreading the lecture she was about to get from her sister.

Karen's voice climbed higher. 'I don't believe you, Emily!' She was incredulous. 'You're walking out on him for the second time!'

'It's not like that—'

'Well, I wonder if Rob will see it that way?' Karen retorted before turning around and looking out through the windscreen at the blur of red lights coming from the tailback as the traffic stalled again. 'Oh, come on!' She slammed her palm angrily against the steering wheel.

'Tell him that I'm sorry.' Once again, that image of him looking defeated and broken as she had left his house flitted into her brain and she hated herself. Being with Rob and Molly had opened a chasm in her heart that she would never have believed existed. They had pulled back a door and revealed a yearning inside her that she hadn't realised she possessed. Spending time with both of them had been magical but the price she now had to pay was the pain she was experiencing by letting them go. Now that she knew the possibilities of what she was missing out on, it was so much harder to say goodbye to them both and continue on but what choice did she have? She would go back to Auckland and get on with her life, Rob would stay here and get on with his and she just hoped that, in time, he might be able to forgive her for how she had treated him.

Karen shook her head. 'You should be the one doing that.'

'Please, Karen,' she begged.

Her sister sighed. 'Oh all right then...'

They eventually arrived at the airport and Karen pulled up in the set-down bay and turned off the engine.

'Well,' she sighed. 'Here we are.' She turned around and lifted a lunchbox off the back seat and handed it to her sister. 'I made you some flapjacks in case you get hungry along the way. You've a long journey ahead.' Emily was flying from Dublin to London, London to Shanghai and Shanghai to Auckland. There were more direct routes but they were very expensive so this seemed the least worst option and because she lost her money on the original flight that she had booked, she had had to take the cheapest one available.

Emily swallowed a lump that felt congealed in her throat. 'Thank you, Karen,' Emily said, touched as she took the lunchbox from her and put it into her backpack. These were the kind of things she missed out on by not having her family around her in New Zealand. 'You always think of everything. Despite the circumstances, the last few weeks here have been nice. I know it's not the same without Mum but I really enjoyed getting to know the kids and hanging out with all of you.'

'I love you, Em,' Karen blurted with tears welling in her eyes. 'God, look at me, getting all silly...' She brushed them away quickly. 'It's been good having you around; just don't leave it so long next time. The kids adore their Auntie Em; they've made me promise that you'll be back again soon.'

'I swear I will try to visit more often.'

'I mean it,' Karen warned, wagging her finger, 'I want to see more of you. We all do.'

Emily nodded.

'You'd better go and get checked in,' Karen said. 'The queues for security are probably crazy.' She pressed the button to pop the boot open and Emily climbed out of the car.

She went around to the back of the car and lifted out her case. Karen followed after her. 'You mind yourself, okay?' she said, pulling her into a tight hug.

'Thanks, Karen. For everything.' As Emily breathed in the scent of home for the last time, she felt the pressure of tears push forward in her eyes and she knew if she didn't go then, she never would. She released her sister and didn't look behind her as she headed inside the terminal.

43

Emily moved through the crowd on autopilot. Harried people pulling wheelie cases and saddled down by backpacks thronged the departures hall. Queues snaked from every check-in desk as she took a moment to get her bearings. She tried to focus on where she was supposed to check in but tears were clouding her eyes, making it difficult to see. She stopped dead in the middle of the floor as she looked around her, trying to figure out where she was going, causing a man to huff impatiently as he swerved to avoid her.

She finally spotted the familiar jade-green colour of the Aer Lingus check-in desk and, dragging her case behind her, she joined the line. *Come on, Emily,* she coached herself. *Just get back to New Zealand. You'll be fine once you're back there.* But no matter how many times she tried to convince herself, she knew it was a lie. Coming here had changed her. She wasn't returning to Auckland as the same person.

She shuffled forward as the queue moved along. She watched a family who were ahead of her in the line – a mother, father and a little girl roughly about the same age as Molly – and she felt her heart stumble as she thought about the little girl that had somehow become imprinted on her heart. She focused on a spot on the wall just above the lady who was working at the check-in desk in a bid to hold back the tears that threatened. She knew she was doing the right thing by leaving; she had become entangled in Rob's life and that could never have a good outcome for any of them. Going with her heart had led her wrong in the past; it was time to be sensible and let her head be in charge for a while.

Eventually, she reached the top of the line. She fished her passport from her bag so that she would be ready when she was called. It seemed as though she was waiting for an age until, finally, the person ahead of her was finished and she was just about to step forward towards the desk when she heard a voice shouting her name. She turned around in confusion and blinked with disbelief when she saw Molly coming towards her, her arm clad in a white plaster cast and Rob running after her, trying to keep up.

'Emily!' the little girl cried in her lispy voice as she slammed against her legs and flung her good arm around her.

'Woah there,' Rob said breathlessly as he caught up. 'Be careful, love, I don't want you to hurt yourself again.'

'Molly?' Emily blinked in bewilderment, sure that this couldn't be real. That her eyes must be playing tricks on her. She looked first at the little girl and then to Rob. 'Wh-what are you both doing here?'

'You didn't say goodbye to me!' the child cried angrily, her face covered in snot and tears.

'Oh sweetheart, I'm so sorry.' Emily used her thumbs to wipe the child's tears away. 'I thought it was for the best.'

'I'm sorry,' Rob panted as he tried to recover his breath.

Her brain was trying to work out what was happening but it couldn't compute the fact that Rob and Molly were standing before her. 'How did you know I was going now?'

'I was talking to Karen earlier and she mentioned she was leaving to bring you to the airport. I couldn't believe it when I heard you'd left without saying goodbye!' Rob went on. 'Although I don't know why, since running away seems to be your trick shot but after everything that happened... maybe I'm crazy... but I thought we meant more to you than that...'

'Oh, Rob...' she said as tears threatened to overwhelm her.

'Anyway, Molly overheard us talking and when she realised you were going home, she got really upset,' he explained. 'She insisted we come to the airport and try to find you to say a proper goodbye.'

Emily's heart lurched as she looked down at the child who was now gripping her father's hand. She hated herself for upsetting the little girl like this. 'I'm sorry,' she said, feeling abashed as she looked from Rob to Molly and back to Rob again. 'I thought it was better that way. I didn't want to make a fuss.'

'Well, look, we can say a proper goodbye now,' he said with an unmistakeable coolness in his tone, 'and then Molly will be happy, won't you?' he prompted.

The little girl shook her head defiantly. 'No, Daddy, it's not fair! Why does everyone always go away? Alannah went away before I was borned, my mummy is deaded, then Nanny Pat died-ded and now she's going too.' She pointed her index finger accusingly in Emily's direction.

Emily crouched down to the child's level. 'Oh, Molly.' Emily began feeling crushed by her words. 'Sometimes grown-ups have to do things that seem difficult for children to understand but perhaps when you're a little older, you might.' She gazed up at Rob while she was saying this part.

Molly narrowed her eyes sceptically in a look that said, *Don't palm me off with any of your patronising grown-up business.* 'But I don't want you to go. I like it when you're with us and Daddy does too, don't you, Daddy?' Molly continued.

'Molly, come on now,' Rob coaxed. 'Emily needs to get on her plane.'

'But I don't want her to go.' Her small face was filled with disappointment. 'I like it when you're with me and Daddy. Tell her, Daddy!' she implored a bewildered-looking Rob. 'Tell her to stay here. Tell her we want her to be in Ireland with us, tell her, Daddy!' She started to cry hard as the emotion overtook her.

Emily's heart ached for this precious child who somehow had woven her way into her heart. Molly was like a drug that you couldn't get enough of; she wanted more and more of her.

'Now, love, you know Emily has to go back to New Zealand,' Rob explained firmly. 'She has work and her friends are over there too.'

'But we're her friends!' she protested.

'Just say goodbye to Emily, Molly, and then we'll go,' Rob said, losing patience.

'I'm sorry, Rob...' Emily tried. The last thing she wanted to do was upset this child who had already been through too much in her short years. Emily's heart was torn and pulled until it felt twisted out of shape. Her head was in a spin. She wanted to stand there and cry with the child. The truth was that she didn't want to go either. Despite the sadness of the circumstances of her return to Dublin, the time she had spent with Rob and getting to know Molly over the last while had been an utter joy. When she had joined them to watch the recital, she had been a part of their unit and it had felt good to belong. In New Zealand, she belonged to no one or nowhere. Could she do it, she wondered. Could she really stay? She was being drawn into a world that she had thought had been closed to her a long time ago, except now another door had opened, a smaller side door that she hadn't known existed and she had to decide whether to continue through this door or turn away from it. Could she risk lowering her walls, allowing Rob and Molly to climb over the parapet, knowing they could easily wound her?

She bent down and whispered to the child. 'I'll tell you a secret, Molly: I don't want to go either.'

She saw Rob's face crease with confusion. 'You don't?' he echoed.

Emily felt a little seed of hope start to unfurl within her. Could she do it, she wondered. Could she really stay? Could she risk opening her heart to these two people? The danger was even greater now because it wasn't just her happiness or even Rob's that was at stake; Molly was part of the package now too and the pressure weighed heavily on her. Could she trust herself not to run out again? It was bad enough letting Rob down the first time, but this time around there was his daughter to think about too, a beautiful child that had already known too much sadness in her short life. She had to make the right decision here; she couldn't afford to get it wrong. If she did, she knew she could destroy these people and she didn't want to cause them any more pain. As well as worrying about their fate if things didn't work out, would *she* survive it? She knew if she went back to New Zealand, she would be firmly shutting the door on this chance of happiness. She needed to let her head rule this time. Her heart had always steered her wrong. There were so many reasons why she shouldn't stay, but then as she looked at Rob and Molly, the thought of leaving them was unbearable. 'I'm so torn,' she admitted, feeling her heart lurch inside her ribcage.

Molly's face lit up and she cocked her head to one side. 'So why don't you just stay?' she asked as if it was all so simple.

Emily turned back to the little girl. 'It might seem hard for you to understand but everything is over there: my flat, my job, all my things. There's a load of other reasons too.'

Molly folded her arms across her chest. 'They don't sound like good reasons to me.'

'To be honest, the thought of going back there and leaving both of you is making me miserable,' she admitted as a voice chimed in her head: *What are you saying? Why are you making yourself vulnerable like this?*

She watched Rob's whole face light up as he registered what she was saying. 'You mean you've thought about staying?' he asked, hardly daring to believe it himself.

She bit down on her lip and nodded her head.

'Then stay,' he begged. 'I know it's not a conventional situation but if there's a chance, even a tiny chance for us to be happy again, don't we owe it to ourselves to try? Please give us a chance.'

Could she do it? Could she stay like every fibre in her body yearned to do? Could she take this chance of having a family of her own, no matter how different it may be from the way she imagined her life working out? Was she brave enough to let go of past hurts and take a gamble on future happiness?

'But it's not just about us now...' she said, making eyes towards Molly. 'I don't want to let her down.'

Rob pulled her into a hug, his manly arms strong and safe around her, and she inhaled the familiar scent of his neck. 'Stay,' he whispered into her hair and her whole body started to come alive beneath his touch. There were no guarantees but if she didn't try, she knew she'd spend her whole life wondering, what if?

She pulled back and looked at him. 'Okay then.' She laughed nervously as excitement zinged through her veins. She felt like she was travelling in a car that had lost control but happiness surged through her body and she knew this was what she wanted. It was reckless and crazy but also so right.

'Are you really going to stay, Emily?' Molly was wide-eyed with hope.

'Yes, sweetie, it looks like I am,' she whispered nervously.

Molly jumped up into the air and squealed. Emily laughed because she could hardly believe it herself. She was really doing this. They were going to get a second chance to make it work.

'I've never stopped loving you,' Rob said, holding her at arm's length as if he couldn't believe this was happening.

'I've always loved you too,' she sobbed. 'I'm sorry it's taken me so long to realise it.'

'It doesn't matter now. We got there in the end.' He used his thumbs to wipe the tears off her face, then his mouth covered hers as they kissed.

Just then, they were interrupted by a voice and Emily was startled back to reality. 'Excuse me, madame, are you checking in or not?' They moved apart and she saw the lady working at the check-in desk looking at her impatiently. Suddenly, she became aware of the angry faces of the other people behind her in the queue, their expressions ranging from mild amusement to fury.

Emily giggled and looked up at Rob. He led her by the hand as they stepped out of the queue and the crowd melted away until the three of them were the only people left in the world. Rob pulled Molly in between them, sealing their unit, and they hugged and laughed and cried together, each of them having found happiness at last.

EPILOGUE
ONE YEAR LATER

The traffic stopped and started as they drove along Groveton Road. Horse chestnuts and sycamores spread their leafy branches in a canopy above them, their ancient, gnarled roots curling below the ground and digging up the pavement. Emily looked in admiration at the elegant red-bricked town houses fronting on to the street guarded with cast-iron railings. It seemed like a different lifetime ago when she had once called this street home too. The traffic inched forward again and her heart stalled as they came upon their old house, number forty-three. She noticed that the people living there now had changed the front door paint from glossy black to a vibrant emerald-green colour. It was a nice change, Emily thought. A Ford MPV was parked in the driveway and she saw a child's bike cast aside on the butter-coloured gravel. She wondered who lived there now. She guessed it was a family. She hoped they were happy and loved this house just as much as she once had. That house had seen some of her best days and also so many of her worst.

Rob glanced at her from the driver's seat and without needing to say anything, she knew he was thinking the same thoughts as her. He reached across the gearstick and put his hand over hers. The traffic stopped again and through the six-over-six Georgian panes of the living-room window, she could just about make out a little girl gazing out at the street. She looked to be a similar age to Molly. Emily waved to her and she smiled and waved back at them. Then she turned and ran off.

'Who's that?' Molly enquired from the back seat.

Emily turned around to Molly, who was clutching the gift-wrapped birthday present that she had chosen for Cara on her lap. It was Cara's sixth birthday today and they were on their way to the party which Karen had booked in a play centre in Dún Laoghaire. 'A long time ago, your daddy and I used to live there,' Emily explained, pointing towards the house.

Molly took a moment to process what Emily told her before asking, 'Was that when Alannah was borned?'

Emily nodded and smiled at this gorgeous child who had captured her heart so completely. How had she got so lucky? She still pinched herself daily that this really was her life. She shuddered every time she remembered how perilously close she had come to leaving it all behind. If Rob and Molly hadn't followed her to the airport that day, she would have got on the plane back to New Zealand without realising the happiness that awaited her.

Making the decision to stay in Dublin and to give her relationship with Rob another chance had been terrifying. It had felt as though her Achilles' heel had been exposed to the world. The fear of opening her heart not just to Rob, but to the little girl too, and of what could happen had been overwhelming. The fear of repeating past mistakes. But now she was so thankful that she had taken the risk. She had opened her heart to happiness that at one stage in her life she never would have believed was possible for her again after all she had been through. She and Rob had once travelled along the same life path together until life had beaten them and their trails had separated. Then, whether it was fate or serendipity, they had circled back to one another again, and by some miracle had emerged more united than ever before, except this time, their unit had grown and strengthened with the addition of little Molly. The three of them as a family was everything she had ever wanted. In fact, it was more than she could ever have imagined. It wasn't how she had ever pictured her future, but life had taught her that, sometimes, opportunities presented themselves in different wrapping paper and the challenge was being able to spot the gift that lay underneath. This was a different version of motherhood but it was nonetheless rewarding and joyous and oh-so precious.

Nobody knew what the future held, or what bumps or upheavals might lay ahead for them on their path, but Emily was grateful for her life right now. Right now, in this moment, it was perfect.

The traffic moved forward again and they continued on. She looked around the car at her little family, feeling a swell of gratitude plump out her heart. She had got a second chance at happiness and, this time, she was never going to let it go.

ACKNOWLEDGEMENTS

What a relief it is to finally be at this stage! No matter how many books I write, I often feel like I've completely forgotten how to write a novel and this story was one of those unruly beasts that tested me. Anyway, I got there in the end and need to say a special thank you to the people who have guided this book along the way.

Firstly, to my amazing agent Hannah Todd from the Madeleine Milburn Agency, always so supportive and approachable and on hand with the best advice. Thank you as always for your help with this book.

A huge thank you is also due to editors Caroline Ridding and Francesca Best for their guidance and affording me a little extra time. To Emily Reader for her superb copy-edit and Ross Dickinson for his thorough proofread, both of which have benefitted this book so greatly.

Thanks are also due to the wider team at Boldwood. You continue to get bigger and better, yet treat your authors with so much individual care and attention. I feel so grateful to be part of the team.

To all my friends, with a special mention to fellow author, the very talented Janelle Harris who is always there for a brainstorming walk/wine. I'm so lucky to have a friend who 'gets' it.

To all the booksellers, bloggers and libraries for their support.

I am so thankful every day that I get to do this for a living, so thank you to my readers, especially those people who leave reviews and contact me with lovely messages and kind words, you'll never know how much those messages mean.

To my family and friends for always cheering me on and lastly to my gang: my husband Simon and our four beautiful children, Lila, Tom, Bea and Charlie – how lucky am I! I may write a lot of my books in my car while you're training but I wouldn't change a thing. You each make me so proud with every day and I am so grateful for you all. Keep shining.

ABOUT THE AUTHOR

Caroline Finnerty is an Irish author of heart-wrenching family dramas and has compiled a non-fiction charity anthology. She has been shortlisted for several short-story awards and lives in County Kildare with her husband and four young children.

Sign up to Caroline Finnerty's mailing list for news, competitions and updates on future books.

Visit Caroline's website: www.carolinefinnerty.ie

Follow Caroline on social media here:

facebook.com/carolinefinnertywriter

x.com/cfinnertywriter

instagram.com/carolinefinnerty

bookbub.com/profile/caroline-finnerty

goodreads.com/carolinefinnerty

ALSO BY CAROLINE FINNERTY

The Last Days of Us

A Mother's Secret

A Sister's Promise

The Family Next Door

The Child I Long For

Boldwood